Puck Right Off

WESTON HEIGHTS WOLVERINES
BOOK ONE

JENNIFER ROSE

Puck Right Off

Copyright © 2024 by Jennifer Rose

All rights reserved.

Cover Designer: Coffin Print Designs

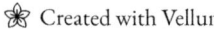 Created with Vellum

CHAPTER 1

Jordyn

read fills my heart as I stare at the two-story colonial house through my windshield. *You can do this. It won't be so bad.*

A long, tired sigh falls from my lips. Arguing with my overbearing stepfather, Robert Fowler, drained the remnants of my energy and ruined my summer. The only good thing about that jackass is he'd already paid my half of the rent on the apartment I shared with my best friend, Chelsea Brady, which allowed me to stay in New York.

But as summer ended, I had no choice but to face the stark reality—I couldn't afford Cornell University without his funding. After many tears and hugs, I left my best friend in my rearview mirror and drove four hours to Weston Heights University, home of the infamous Weston Heights Wolverines hockey team. The team my pain-in-the-ass stepbrother plays for.

With a long sigh, I stretch my arms overhead, then pull my cell phone from the pocket of my purse. My brows draw in as I read the text my stepbrother, Josh, sent me two hours ago.

Josh: Dad needs me, so I won't be there when you arrive. Tristan can help carry your stuff in.

I snort aloud. Typical. Daddy beckons and Josh goes running to do his bidding. He's such an ass-kisser. He's also lazy and probably broke out in hives at the thought of helping me carry my stuff into the house.

My gaze slides back to the front door. Everything is still, with no sign of life. Hockey God is probably inside, playing video games or whatever it is jocks do when they aren't skating around, chasing a little puck, and slamming one another into the boards.

I cringe at the thought of living with two hockey cretins for the next fifteen weeks. I give myself a pep talk, trying to find the positives in this situation. *It's temporary. A way to pursue your goals and save money.*

Dread fills my heart as I grab my phone and check the time. Great. I'm an hour early, *and I don't have Tristan's number to call or text him.*

I debate blowing the horn to see if I can summon the jock, but it's barely 8:00 am on a Saturday morning, and there are neighbors around us. I don't want to start off on the wrong foot.

Pushing the door open, I wearily drag myself from the car. Josh had given me the code for the front door, which has a keyless entry lock, and I put it in my Notes app on my phone.

My gaze returns once more to the front door. With a sigh, I head to the passenger side, grabbing my duffle bag and purse before trudging up the sidewalk. *I'll go inside and let Tristan know I'm here.*

After entering the code, I push the door open and step inside. The cool blast of central air hits my skin as I make my way across the foyer, surprised at how neat and clean the house is. I open my mouth to announce my presence when a grunt reaches my ears. Following the sound, I expect to see him with a controller in his hands, eyes glued to the TV, but that's not what I find.

I'm paralyzed by what is transpiring in front of me. My mouth hangs open in shock as I rapidly blink a few times, unable to believe what I see.

A brunette is on her knees in front of a muscular, blond-haired man, her mouth and tongue sucking his impressive cock. She works him like a pro, taking his long length and wide girth deep in her mouth. *She must not have a gag reflex.*

The guy is sprawled on the couch, his hands tangled in the brunette's hair, urging her on.

Oh hell. My new roommate is getting a blow job from a puck bunny. I need to get the hell out of here.

My feet betray me, remaining stubbornly rooted to the hardwood floor. I blink several times in disbelief, but the image doesn't change.

Say something so they know you're here.

But I don't. Instead, I stand there, watching them like a creepy voyeur.

The brunette pulls his dick from her mouth, allowing me a full view of his large member. Instead of putting her mouth back on him, she eagerly gets to her feet. He grabs the condom lying beside him on the couch, ripping it open, and sheathing himself, completely oblivious to me standing there. She climbs on the couch, her thighs straddling his. Grabbing the base of his dick, she lines it up with her entrance and slowly sinks down.

"You have such a nice big cock, Tristan," she rasps out as she begins moving.

His head falls back against the couch with a groan. He's so focused on the shapely brunette with big tits that he never glances my way.

As she rides him, a flush heats my skin. I should tiptoe to the door, praying they don't notice me, and head back to my car. That would certainly be better than standing here, watching, wondering if he'll make her come.

But I don't move.

I'm practically drooling as his hands move to her hips, guiding her up and down on his large cock, sexy moans falling from his lips. Although I've never been into jocks, Tristan is hot and buff as hell, with ridges and valleys of muscle on every inch of his body. I didn't even know it was possible for a man to look like that in real life.

His hands slide to her ass, squeezing it, while his gravelly voice grunts out, "Fuck yeah, baby. You're riding my cock so good."

Holy shit. I bite my lip as the arousal courses through me. *Why am I getting so wet from his words? Maybe it's the sexy way he bites his lip, his intense eyes focused solely on her.*

She moans in response, changing the rhythm and movement of her hips, bouncing up and down on him like a damn porn star. Envy surges through me as I take in her shiny, perfectly styled hair, lightly bronzed skin, and perky ass. Even naked, she exudes an aura that screams rich, popular, and gorgeous. The type of girl that has enough confidence for three people.

Tristan arches up, thrusting into her, emitting a moan that causes more moisture to soak my panties. I shift my weight, squeezing my thighs together, which ends up being a big mistake. The movement causes my duffle bag to swing wildly against my side. I grab it, but it slides through my sweaty fingers, hitting the floor with a loud thud.

Horrified, I stare at the offending duffle bag. My cheeks burn as I slowly die from the humiliation coursing through me.

4

CHAPTER 2

Tristan

"**F**uck," I yell, pushing the busty brunette from my lap as I scramble for my sweatpants on the floor. The brunette who was riding me screeches, whether from embarrassment or because I just shoved her off my dick, I have no idea.

"I'm so sorry," I splutter, my apologetic eyes lifting to find a gorgeous blonde staring at the floor like it's the most interesting thing in the world. Her cheeks are scarlet as she bites her lip. *Goddamn, she's stunning.*

Tearing the condom from my dick, I yank my sweatpants over my hips. "You must be Josh's stepsister, Jordyn." Running my non-condom-holding hand through my hair, I choke out words that sound like an accusation, although that's not my intention. "You're early."

"Mmm hmm." She crosses her arms over her chest, daring to peek at me beneath long black lashes. "Sorry about interrupting." She gestures between me and the brunette, who I'd forgotten about.

I open my mouth to reply, but the brunette appears at my side, her arms crossed over her naked chest. Her bottom lip

5

juts out in a pout as she stares at me, her expression pinched. "Aren't we going to finish?"

I gape at her like she's lost her damn mind. *What the fuck? Did she seriously ask me that?*

Releasing a sigh of impatience, I run my hand through my hair again. *Why the hell did I listen to Josh when he told me to fuck the pain away?*

The brunette sighs heavily. "We could go upstairs to your—"

"*No.* Hell no." The thought of her being in my bedroom is horrifying. That's *my* space, and there's no way I'm letting her in there.

She glares at me before opening her mouth, but I cut her off before she can speak.

"Get dressed," I snap, my eyes raking over her naked body. "It's time for you to leave."

"What?" she screeches like a bat, her eyes wide. "You're kicking me out."

I glare at her before turning my attention to the blonde frozen in the doorway, her eyes darting between me and the brunette. *I need to do some serious damage control.*

The problem is my brain isn't functioning the way it should be. Lack of sleep from the nightmares that plague me causes it to short circuit as I blankly stare at her shocked face. Or maybe the fact that she's so beautifully innocent has me tongue-tied.

While I stand there, mutely staring at her, she shifts her weight uncomfortably, biting her lip and fidgeting with the hem of her shirt like she'd rather be elsewhere. I can't say I blame her. I've never walked in on two strangers fucking on the couch.

"I've forgotten my manners in the...umm... chaos. I'm Tristan Harrington." Stepping closer to her, I hold out my hand, marveling at the golden-haired goddess in front of me.

She's far classier than the brunette angrily dressing behind me, muttered curses and huffs coming from her lips. I ignore her, mesmerized by the wide-eyed beauty in front of me, my heart sinking as she stares at me, blinking in disbelief.

Can things get any fucking worse?

Her gaze drops to my outstretched hand, and a giggle escapes her lips before she slaps a hand over her mouth. I look down at my outstretched hand, horrified by what I see. *Oh, hell. That's the hand with the condom in it.*

Fuck, I'm an idiot.

The blonde laughs harder, no longer bothering to hide it. I'm baffled, which is so unlike me.

Shoving the condom in the pocket of my sweatpants, I duck my head, peeking up at her. "Sorry about that. I forgot I was still holding it."

"I think I'll pass on the handshake." She flashes me a reassuring smile. "I'm Jordyn Reese. Nice to meet you, Tristan." Her musical voice swirls around me, captivating me in her spell. My heart pounds so fast that my limbs are weak.

"I don't blame you. I'm not in the habit of shaking hands with anyone holding a used condom. Maybe if it's unused and still in the wrapper..." I shrug one shoulder, a teasing smile on my face.

"Eww. Not even then." She glances over my shoulder at the brunette behind me, her smile faltering. I'd been so lost in the golden-haired goddess laughing at me that I'd forgotten about her.

I want her attention back on me in the worst way. "I've been tryin' to quit. It's a hard habit to break."

Her gaze moves back to my face, and a laugh bursts from her lips. "Good luck with that. I'll be sure to avoid shaking hands with anyone holding a condom so I don't become an addict." She pushes a lock of hair away from her face, and my eyes follow her movements like a stalker watching their obsession.

"Good idea." I wink at her, feeling more relaxed and in control than I have in weeks. I suck in a deep breath and hold it before exhaling, marveling at the sensation. *I can breathe again.* It feels so fucking glorious not to have a bolder crushing my chest, preventing my lungs from expanding with air.

I can't resist checking her out. She looks put together but not overdone in the red, sleeveless top and dark blue skinny jeans that hug every delectable curve. I grin at the Converse sneakers on her feet before my eyes trail back up her body, locking with her slightly dazed aqua eyes. The tension crackles in the air between us. I've never experienced anything like this before. *Fuck, what would it be like to touch her?*

She shifts her weight, unease in her rigid posture, and I scramble to find the words to make her relax again. "Can I help you with your luggage so you can get settled in your room?"

Jordyn's lip sinks into her teeth as her eyes move to something beside me. Unease travels through me as I take in the furious brunette beside me. Her long red talons dig into my skin as she curls her hand around my arm. Her expression transforms into sultry desire as she bats her lashes at me. "You don't want me to go, Tristan. Why don't we go upstairs and finish what we started?"

I lift a brow, not impressed with the show she's putting on. I've seen her type in the two years I've played hockey at Weston Heights. She's the devil, masquerading as a sultry angel. Once she gets her hooks in you, she'll bleed you dry.

My brows draw together from annoyance as I shrug away from her touch. "I need to help Jordyn unload her vehicle. Her stepbrother isn't here, and—"

"Oh, that's okay," Jordyn interrupts, her cheeks pink as

our attention shifts to her. Shifting her weight nervously from foot to foot, she shrugs. "I'll wait until Josh arrives."

Wrong answer, kitten. I'm helping you. My gaze narrows on hers, causing her to fidget with the ends of her golden locks. "I don't mind at all. Let's get your things."

"Oh, I really don't wanna interrupt..." Big aqua eyes shoot over to the brunette pouting at my side.

"See. She can wait." The brunette's whining voice is like nails dragging down a chalkboard.

What the hell is her name again? Her name is lost in the endless sea of puck bunnies trying to get my attention. I've ignored her until today when she caught me at my lowest point.

"I don't mean to be a bother." The way Jordyn's voice shakes, her eyes dropping to the floor, pisses me off. I narrow my eyes, studying her closer. When her gaze lifts, she twirls a lock of hair around her finger, an envious look on her face as her eyes trail over the brunette.

No fucking way. Does she believe this tramp is superior to her? I've known the brunette long enough to get a blowjob and for her to start riding my dick. I've known Jordyn for a much shorter span of time, but I'm certain of one thing— there's no comparison. Jordyn has more class in her pinkie than the puck bunny has in her entire body.

"You're not a bother." I hurriedly reassure her before the brunette can open her big trap again and ruin everything. "I'm sure Julie won't—"

"My name's *not* Julie," the brunette snaps, venom in her tone.

Oops. I wrack my brain, trying to think of what her name is. *Jessica? Jennifer? Jenna?* I gulp, running a hand through my hair, panicking that this was happening in front of Jordyn. *She probably thinks I bang anyone who has a pussy. Shit, this is terrible.*

"Sorry, Jessica?" I cringe, shooting in the dark and hoping to score a goal. But from the look on her face, I didn't even make it to the net.

She's fuming so badly, I'm surprised smoke isn't rolling from her ears. "My name is *not* Jessica. It's Janelle," she hisses through clenched teeth. "Un-fucking-believable."

From the corner of my eye, I see Jordyn turn away, shoulders shaking from laughter. *Is she laughing because she thinks I'm such a man whore I have no idea who I'm fucking?*

Janelle shakes her head, then jabs her finger into my chest. "I did this as a favor to Josh, and you don't even know my damn—"

"Wait a fucking minute. What do you mean by 'a favor to Josh?' What the hell did he ask you to do?"

She dismissively waves her hand. "Seriously? You're worried about that? You should be crawling on your knees, begging for my forgiveness for not knowing my name after I gave you amazing head."

Anger flares inside my chest, spreading outward like unrestrained embers from a fire. "Crawling on my knees? The way you sucked my dick wasn't that great. Certainly not enough to make me get on my knees, let alone beg you for anything." Folding my arms over my chest, I glare at her.

She huffs, her face turning red. But I'm not finished with her yet. "Now tell me. What. Favor. Did. You. Do. For. Josh?"

"Um, I'm gonna go get my luggage." Jordyn's quiet voice cuts through the fog of rage that's descended over me. I spin around, opening my mouth to tell her I'm coming with her, but she's already out the door.

"Oh, you didn't know?" Janelle's smug voice grates on every one of my nerves. "He asked me to come over here and fuck you. Said a piece of ass would ease your depression."

My hands curl into fists as the room turns red. I want to punch the damn wall so hard my fist comes out the other side, but I refrain, knowing it'll only worsen Jordyn's impression of me.

I'm gonna fucking kill him. My gaze moves to the closed door, and I sigh. Rubbing my forehead, I've lost all patience with this shitty morning. *What a disastrous first impression I've made on Jordyn. Then I find out my roommate conspired to pimp me out to a puck bunny.*

"Don't worry, Tristan. I would've done it even if Josh hadn't made a bet with me."

"Made a bet?" My mouth drops open as I stare at her, a sick sensation spiraling in my stomach. "What the fuck did you bet on?"

Her smile is arrogant as she examines her nails, playing it cool. "Oh, you know. He bet that I couldn't even get you naked, while I wagered I'd have your dick inside my pussy." Evil eyes lift, glittering with satisfaction. "Guess I won."

My breathing accelerates like I've just run a marathon. Although Josh is nowhere near as close to me as Alex Graves, who's like a brother to me, he's been my teammate and roommate for two years.

Son of a bitch. Josh is dead!

CHAPTER 3

Tristan

Without a word, I spin on my heels, racing for the front door. I need air. The stinging betrayal and volcanic level rage coils through my body like a snake, taking me over. Although Josh and I aren't that close, he knows about the tragedy that stole my entire world in an instant. He knows each day that ticks by brings me closer to reliving that horror and blaming myself.

My hands clench into fists as I step onto the porch. My palms ache from my fingernails digging into them as my bare feet slap down the stairs to the sidewalk. *I should've known better than to trust anything that came out of Josh Fowler's manipulative mouth. That asshole only cares about himself.*

Sucking in a big breath of oxygen as my feet hit the sidewalk, my gaze lands on Jordyn. She places her suitcase on the pavement of the driveway, her eyes lifting to mine. The concern in them as we engage in a silent stare down causes my anger to dissipate. She's like a soothing balm, calming my frayed nerves.

"Jordyn, wait." I jog over to her, my breathing accelerated as I draw to a stop, admiring the way her golden strands glisten beneath the sun. Her lightly tanned skin glows, a pink tinge coloring her cheeks as her gaze moves from my face to my bare chest. Her breathing accelerates as she looks away. I engage in a silent victory of beating my hands over my chest like Tarzan at her reaction to me. I affect her.

"Let me do that." My voice is low as I move closer to her, breathing her in. *Goddamn. She smells like strawberries.*

She stiffens, her grip tightening on the handle of her suitcase. "I got it, Tristan. You focus on—"

"I don't wanna focus on *her*." My words rush out in an attempt to remove the doubts from her mind. "I *want* to help you. And not because—"

My mouth snaps shut as Janelle's heels stomp on the pavement behind me. Tensing, I look over my shoulder, waiting for the tirade I'm certain is coming.

"I can't believe you ran out on *me* to chase after this meek little nerd." Her eyes rake over Jordyn, disdainfully, a disgusted smirk on her lips.

"Don't fucking insult her," I snap, losing all patience with Janelle. "Her name is Jordyn, and she has more class in her pinkie than you have in your entire trashy body."

"Ohhh.... This is rich." Janelle crosses her arms over her chest. "All protective over a little nerd you just met." Her eyes slide to Jordyn, a calculating expression on her face. "Josh's stepsister, right?" She smirks, her snakelike eyes narrowing on mine. "Didn't Josh warn the team that his nerdy sister is off-limits?"

"I'm not his sister," Jordyn straightens, crossing her arms over her chest, an irritated scowl on her face.

"Semantics." Janelle's eyes dart back to mine, a contemplative expression on her face. "I'm pretty sure that wanting to fuck Josh's stepsister is something he won't like." The venom in her voice makes me want to grab her by the hair and drag her to her car.

Nausea churns in my stomach. *I can't believe I let this bitch touch me.*

Grinding my teeth, I step closer, my demeanor threatening. "You're a fucking bully." My cold gaze slides over her disdainfully as I forcefully spit out my next words. "You're *not* going to spread lies about Jordyn and me." Another step brings me toe-to-toe with her. "I have a pretty good story I could tell daddy that involves you and three members of the Wolverines."

Janelle's eyes widen slightly before she shakes it off, attempting to hide the fear flashing in her eyes. "That's just a rumor." She waves one perfectly manicured hand dismissively. "He won't believe it."

I cock my head, a vile smile on my lips. "Is it, though? Because the video I have on my phone says otherwise." Reaching into the pocket of my gray sweatpants, I grab it and hold it up. "Care to watch?"

Janelle takes a step back, her face turning white. "N-Noo. I don't need to see that." She takes another step back. "I-I won't say anything."

"That's right. You won't say a goddamn word, or this video goes straight to daddy. Now, apologize to Jordyn and get the fuck off the premises."

"Tristan, it's fine. She doesn't need—" Jordyn stumbles as she moves toward me, her hands flying out, bracing for a fall that doesn't come because I whirl around and catch her. Soft, warm hands are planted against my bare chest, sending tingles coursing through me. There's a jolt in my chest like I've been hit with paddles to restart my heart. *Goddamn. What the hell is that?*

"S-she doesn't n-need to a-apologize." Her voice is low and shaky, an embarrassed flush stealing over the apples of her cheeks, enhancing her beauty. Her eyes widen before lowering to her hands on my chest, and I inwardly groan as she shivers.

Dazed eyes lift to mine, two liquid pools of desire. My gaze moves to her mouth, nearly growling when her teeth sink into her bottom lip.

Goddamn. I've never been so jealous of teeth before in my life. A strong desire to lift my hand to her face, free her lip from her pearly whites, and then kiss the hell out of her in the middle of broad daylight consumes me. I'm barely able to resist the urge.

Jordyn snatches her hands away from my chest. Despite the warmth of the day, I'm immediately cold from the loss of her touch.

She looks down at her untied shoelace, and I follow her gaze. "I'm such a klutz." She shakes her head before looking up at me. The sadness tingeing her aqua irises steals the breath from my lungs. But her next words shred my insides. "You don't have to defend me. I'm not worth it."

Who the hell made her feel insecure and like she's not worth defending? I wanna beat the shit out of them.

I do my best to keep my anger at them in check as I answer. "I want to defend you, and I will." My voice shakes from the passion in it, surprising us both.

The engine's roar pulls my attention to the car idling on the street. Janelle slams on the gas, racing away. I shake my head, glad she's gone but pissed at the chaos left in her wake. *You helped create the chaos. You never should've touched her.*

My gaze moves to Jordyn, who kneels, tying her shoe before she stands. Casting me a furtive look, she bites her lip before focusing on the lone suitcase in the driveway. "Well, I should—"

"I'll help. *No* arguments." My voice lowers, embarrassed by what she witnessed. "It's the least I can do after the shit show I put you through."

"Please don't feel obligated to help because of... Well, all that." She makes a feeble gesture, emitting a nervous laugh.

"It's a memorable way of meeting your new roommate." She flashes a lopsided small, easing the sting of my humiliation.

"Yeah, this is definitely a first for me." A bitter laugh escapes me. "Not my finest hour."

The smile dies from her lips. "Everyone makes mistakes. I've made my share of them." A shocked look covers her face as though she's embarrassed at the words she just said. "Well, umm... thanks for defending me, although you didn't have to."

"Yeah, I guess we all make mistakes." Stepping closer, I gently touch her arm, noting the goosebumps that immediately spread over her skin when I touch her. "Don't thank me for defending you. You're worth defending."

Her soft expression warms my cold heart. I jerk my hand away as though someone dumped ice water over my skin. *What the hell are you doing? You made a promise to yourself not to get involved with anyone. You have goals to focus on. The last thing you need is to drag anyone else into your darkness.*

Turning away, I move to her suitcase. *Just help her get her stuff inside and leave her the hell alone.*

As I bend to lift her suitcase, her words haunting me, I make the mistake of looking at Jordyn. Her doe eyes stare down the street in the direction Janelle's car traveled. Her shoulders slump in defeat, a wistful look on her face before she looks down at her outfit and frowns.

A protective vibe I haven't felt in a long time rises, taking me over. For so many reasons, I should force it away.

But I *can't*. Something draws me to her, tethering me to her like a rope.

My reactions and movements are raw, unconscious, as I set her suitcase down and straighten. I step into her personal space, my finger sliding beneath her chin, lifting it to mine. "I don't know who failed to defend or protect you, but they're assholes." A lump is in my throat when I see the gratitude shimmering in her eyes. "Janelle had no right acting bitchy to you. She did because she's insecure. She's beneath you, and she damn well knows it."

We stand there, our chests rising and falling in unison, unable to look away. The heat rolling between us and the electricity in the air is something I've never felt before.

The roar of a car engine coming down the street rips us from the moment. The rope tethering us together snaps, and in unison, we step back, averting our eyes. My teeth gnash together as I inwardly berate myself. *What the hell are you doing? You know better than to get involved with* anyone, *least of all* her. *My teammate's stepsister.*

The car continues down the street, and we exhale, relieved that it's not Josh. It's a crude reminder that I need to get my shit together.

The sound of Jordyn's retreating footsteps draws my attention back to her. "I've got this, Tristan," she calls over her shoulder. I hate the coldness in her voice.

She hauls another suitcase out, slamming it on the pavement. My brows furrow as I watch her, silently fuming as she hauls out a duffle bag.

Realization spreads through me. *She felt it, too. That's why she's reacting so coldly toward me.*

I shake my head, irritated by my reaction. Everything was going just fine until Janelle and Jordyn showed up.

CHAPTER 4

Jordyn

Tristan sets my boxes of books on the floor with a soft thud. My body hums from the proximity to him. Inwardly berating myself, I keep my eyes averted from his muscular torso and arms, irritated by how sexy I find his bulging muscles, not to mention the outline of his cock in those gray sweatpants. *Dammit. Knock it off.*

My eyes skip around the room, resting on a floor to ceiling bookcase in the corner of the room. I'm drawn to it, the smell of the wood infiltrating my nostrils as I inhale deeply.

"This bookcase..." I swallow hard, my reverent gaze sweeps over the cherry wood. "It's gorgeous." Stopping in front of it, my fingers lovingly stroke it.

Tristan steps beside me. "Wow. I've never seen anyone stroke wood like that." My head snaps to his and he turns to me, a grin on his face. "At least I didn't say, 'I wish a woman would stroke my wood like that.' Trust me, my friend, Alex, wouldn't have been able to contain himself."

I can't help the teasing smile, a laugh threatening to bubble from me. "From what I saw, your wood was being stroked just fine on the couch."

A surprised laugh bursts out of him. "Oh, burn." He steps closer to me, his expression softening. "Josh said you liked to read and would probably bring a ton of books, so I thought this was practical while adding a nice touch to the room."

My brows shoot up in surprise. "You bought this?"

For a moment, something that looks like embarrassment flashes on his face. "Yeah." He keeps his gaze averted as he pretends to examine the bookcase like it's the most interesting thing in the world. For some reason, his reaction is tugging at my heart strings. "If you don't like it, I—"

"No, I love it." My words tumble out in a rush, my palm flattening over the wood. "This is an amazing gift." A sick feeling washes over me. "It is a gift, right? Or do I owe you money for it?" I barely have enough left to fill my gas tank this week.

"It's a gift." Green eyes lock with mine, seeing too much. "You don't owe me *anything* for it." The gruffness in his voice and the sincerity in his mossy eyes are profoundly affecting me. Almost as much as his touch, which is shooting electric sparks through my skin.

Sucking in a deep breath, I slowly exhale, doubt swimming through my veins. I want to believe he's not a puck boy, but warning bells ring inside my head. *You walked in on him getting a blowjob and fucking a girl. He didn't even know her name. He's definitely a puck boy.*

Pulling myself from my thoughts, I flash him a tight smile. "Thank you."

His smile fades, and I'm instantly filled with regret.

"Tristan, this is amazing." I touch his forearm, ashamed of the jolt of current that flows through me when I touch him. He doesn't look convinced.

Blowing out a breath, I give him an explanation I don't owe him. But I can't stand the hurt look from his face. "I'm not used to people doing nice things for me without expecting something in return."

"Oh." His brows furrow, an angry look on his face. "You deserve to have people do nice things without expecting anything in return." He bows his head, running a hand through his short, dark blond hair. I can't help salivating over the swell of his bicep.

His words draw me back to the present. "Josh mentioned that your stepfather cut your educational funding. I'm sorry, Jordyn." He lowers his arm, shoving it in the pocket of his sweatpants. "It was an asshole thing for him to do."

"Robert Fowler is an asshole." My voice rings with an unusually strong vehemence as the anger swirls inside me like a storm. Surprise lights up Tristan's face, and I immediately backtrack. "Don't get me wrong, it was nice that he was funding my education. I certainly didn't expect him to do that. But taking it away because I changed my major to some-thing he deemed unacceptable is just...."

"Reprehensible?"

What the hell? Puck boy is smart. That doesn't go with the image of jocks that live inside my head.

"Well, yeah. He's a manipulative, selfish man, so I don't know why I expected him to understand."

The silence stretches between us, making me nervous. I begin rambling. "Don't get me wrong. I'm extremely grateful you're letting me live here." *Rent free.* I choke on the words, unable to get them past the lump of pride lodged in my throat.

Clearing it, I continue, "I'm thankful I can pursue my dreams, having the freedom to major in what I want without anyone pissed at me for it. I just..." I grapple for the right words to convey how I feel about it.

"You're infuriated because you were attending an Ivy League school in New York until he pulled his funding, yanking your dreams away, over something so frivolous like your choice of major. He placed conditions on your education, and as soon as you didn't meet them, he yanked the funding, taking everything away, upending your life."

Wow. He's intuitive and understanding, making my opinion of him waver again.

"That's it, exactly." Confusion rolls through me. I can't fathom how he understands what I'm feeling. The sleek SUV in the driveway and this house, which from all I've seen, suggests he doesn't worry about money.

"How did you know I was attending an Ivy League school?"

Tristan cocks his head, intense eyes boring into me. "Umm... Josh mentioned it."

I raise my brows, suspicious of the uncomfortable way he shifts, his eyes darting away from mine. *Hmmm. Why don't I believe him?*

"Did he mention that Robert knows Josh isn't smart enough or interested in taking over his lucrative jewelry business, and I was his backup plan after my mom married him? Did he tell you Robert forced me to spend my summer working in one of his stores, and I was miserable, hating every minute of it?" My chest heaves, anger coiling through me like a heater coil, melting my insides and turning them into a pool of lava.

His mouth hangs open in shock, his brows lifting in surprise. "No... He didn't tell me about that."

God, I'm an idiot. Why did I blurt out that shit?

Tristan nods. "What's your major?"

"English Literature with a minor in Composition and Writing. I plan on getting my master's in library science once I finish my undergrad degree."

There I go again. The nerdy girl with verbal diarrhea and no acceptable social skills.

Surprisingly, Tristan relaxes, seemingly unbothered after

21

my little meltdown. "I have no doubt you'll accomplish your goals, Jordyn. I admire you for not giving up." The genuine look of respect on his face does something to my heart, but I force myself to ignore it.

"Thank you." My voice is softer than I expected, resulting in an uneasy silence.

He raps his knuckles against the bookshelf. "Well, I better leave you to unpack your things. If you need me, yell." Pivoting on his heel, he heads to the doorway, but my voice stops him before he leaves my room.

"Can I have your number?"

He freezes, and I immediately berate myself. But the words hang out there, and I can't take them back.

I rattle on, my words spilling from my lips like a damn breaking. "Only in the event of an emergency." A nervous laugh escapes as I push a lock of blonde hair from my face. "It's not like I'd just be blowing up your phone, sexting you."

Sexting? Where the hell did that come from?

Tristan slowly spins around, a wide smile spreading over his face. "Dammit. I was hoping you planned to text me and ask if you could give me a blowjob, then ride me on the couch." The laughter in his voice and his wink causes me to relax and smile at him.

Pulling his phone from his pocket, the used condom slips to the floor. He doesn't notice, but I do. An uncomfortable feeling wells inside me.

"That's a good idea to exchange numbers, roomie." He hands me his phone so I could input my number.

He grins at me, not noticing the change in my demeanor. "I wouldn't mind if you texted me memes or... whatever."

I smirk as I enter my contact info. "Be careful what you wish for, puck boy." As soon as the words leave my mouth, I'm horrified. My head jerks up to find his smile gone; a hurt looks replacing it before a cold mask slides across his features.

"I didn't mean—"

"No, I deserve that." He glowers at me. "You'd do well to remember that's what I am, Jordyn. It's better that way." He snatches his phone from my hands and strides toward the door without a backward glance.

When it slams behind him, I sink to my knees in front of my suitcases. A long sigh comes from my lips.

"Great start to your new living arrangements."

CHAPTER 5

Tristan

I'm avoiding Jordyn, pacing my bedroom floor while berating myself for my final words to her. The conversation was flowing between us, and I started to feel hopeful that I'd managed to shift the awful first impression I made to something better. She genuinely seemed impressed by my intelligence. And even though I joked with her, she didn't seem bothered.

Then she called me a puck boy. It stung like a nest of bees protecting their hive. Although I deserved it, considering what she walked in on.

I can't take it anymore. I've gotta get out of here.

My fingers pull my phone from my pocket and shoot Alex a text.

> Me: Meet me at the rec for a workout?

Grabbing a T-shirt, keys, and phone, I pace my room as the three dots appear, and my phone dings when he responds.

> Alex: What if I'm in the middle of something?

I smirk as I reply.

> Me: Are you?

> Alex: Nope. See you in ten.

FUCKING ALEX. I grin as I hurry from my room, but it fades as I look at her closed door. *Should I tell her where I'm going?* I start down the hallway, then stop, feeling like an ass. *I'll need to be civil if we're going to be roommates.*

Turning around, I stride to her door and knock. I hear a series of thumps before she whips the door open.

My gaze scans her sweaty face, blonde hair pulled in a ponytail, and the sports bra and spandex shorts she's wearing. *Holy shit, she's beautiful.* She sure as hell doesn't look like a nerd like Josh said she was. Not with a body like that.

Sucking in a breath, my gaze moves over her shoulder. Everything has been unpacked, including her books, which are placed neatly on her bookshelf. She even broke down the boxes and stacked them against the wall.

Yanking out an earbud, she gives me a smile, her breathing heavy. "Sorry, I was unpacking." She gestures behind her. "What's up?"

"I see. You've been very busy." I force myself to focus on her face and not the delectable body in front of me. "I'm going to the gym. Do you need anything before I leave?"

She shifts her weight uncomfortably before she shakes her head. Forcing a smile and an enthusiastic tone, she says, "Nope. I'm good." Her smile doesn't reach her eyes, making me suspicious.

"What is it, Jordyn? You can ask me for things, you know."

She shifts again, her gaze on the floor. "I'm not used to asking strangers for anything."

Leaning my shoulder against the doorframe, I study her, my heart softening toward her. "Good thing I'm your roommate and not a stranger. What do you need?"

She blows out a breath before saying, "Do you have bottled water in the fridge?"

"Of course. I'll get you one."

"No, no. You don't need to do that. I was just thirsty and..." her voice trails off, embarrassment coloring her cheeks.

"I don't mind. And Jordyn, you can eat anything in the fridge, freezer, or cupboards. You never have to ask."

"Thanks." She tugs at her ponytail, her embarrassment lessening but still there.

"Of course. I'll get you a bottle."

Her hand squeezes my bicep as I push off the door frame. "I'll come with you. I feel bad enough—"

"What? That you're asking for water? Come on, Jordyn. It's fine." I lean closer, a teasing smile on my lips. "Lower your pride a little, would ya?"

She smiles, and this time, it reaches her eyes. "Okay. But I'm coming with you to check out the snacks." Her gaze roams over me before she quickly glances away.

She's definitely attracted to me.

"Help yourself to any snack you want." *Goddamn. Why did that sound so suggestive?*

Her musical laugh fills the air between us. "Hopefully, there's some junk food around here." She eyes my physique, and I flex my muscles.

"Of course there is. I work hard and like to indulge when I can."

"Good. Dibs on anything chocolate."

CHAPTER 6

Tristan

Tears roll down Alex's cheeks as he sits on the weight bench, his entire body shaking from laughter. I glare at him, wondering why the fuck I tell him anything. "Are you done?"

He laughs harder, slapping his knee. I glare at him from the weight bench across from him, irritated as hell.

"I'm sorry, it's just..." Wiping the tears from his face, he squares his shoulders, trying to compose himself. "The first time you get any action in what—over a year, and your new roommate walks in and witnesses you getting your dick sucked and fucked." His shoulders shake, but he manages not to howl with laughter like when I first told him. "Damn, that's awesome."

"You and I have very different definitions of awesome." Although my voice drips with sarcasm, Alex completely ignores it.

"Did she run out of the house screaming or ask to join in?"

"Alex." Picking up the dumbbells from the floor, I debate hurling one at him. "She didn't ask to join."

"Did she scream and run upstairs?" He raises a brow, leaning forward, intensely assessing me.

Blowing out a breath, I dare to lift my eyes to his, knowing what's coming. "She stood there and watched."

Alex gapes at me like a fish before he says, "Get the fuck outta here. Stop pulling my dick and tell me what she did?"

"I'm not kidding. She stood there, watching, until her bag slipped to the floor."

"Did she film it?" Wide sapphire eyes stare into mine, shimmering with curiosity and an envious look.

"No, asshole, she didn't film it." I roll my eyes. "Why do I tell you anything?"

"Because I'm your best friend. Actually, I'm pretty much your only friend." He winks as I scowl at him.

"Can we focus on the point? It was awkward as hell, and I made the worst impression in history on this girl."

"No, *we* can't. Maybe *you* can, but I'm still imagining this chick watching you get a blow job before a puck slut jumped on your dick."

"Jesus Christ." I blow out an exasperated breath, running my hand through my hair. "This girl is my roommate."

He smirks. "You lucky sonofabitch. Did you ask her if she wanted to suck and—"

"No. Hell, no." I rub my forehead, a tension headache brewing. Heaving in a deep breath, I slowly exhale. "The point is, I made a terrible first impression on Josh's stepsister. She thinks I'm a puck boy."

Alex snorts, laughter spilling from him again. "She doesn't know you at all, does she?" He reaches down and grabs the weights from the floor. "Did you tell her you were a born-again virgin?"

"For fucks sake. Don't you ever stop?"

He levels me with a look. "Are you seriously asking me that? How long have we known each other?"

"Too fucking long," I joke. "Get serious. What am I gonna do?"

The smile dies off Alex's face, his expression contemplative. With a straight face, he shrugs. "Ask her to sit on your face and then see if she'll blow—"

"Hell no." My dick grows hard as the visual floats through my head before I shove it away. "You know Josh said she's off limits."

"Ahh, so Josh is the only thing standing in the way of you asking her to ride your face. Is she hot? Maybe—"

I glower at him, and he shuts up, barely repressing his laughter.

"Don't fucking finish that statement! Yes, she's hot, but if you go anywhere near her, I'll rip your goddamn balls off."

"Ohhhh, you really like her. She must be gorgeous."

"Alex," I warn, the threat clear in my eyes. "Stop while—"

He holds up his hand. "You're proving my point more and more. You like this woman, and that's why you're so worried about the first impression you made."

A knot forms inside my chest. "No, I don't." Even to my own ears, my tone is unconvincing.

"Uh-huh. That's why you've spent the past hour barely working out, worried about the impression you made on your new 'roommate,' who happens to be hot and forbidden. What a combination. Why can't I get that lucky?"

"Alex, I'm not interested in Jordyn."

"Yeah, right." He raises a brow. "Lemme see your phone."

"Why?"

"Don't you trust me?"

"With my life, yes. My phone, no."

Alex chuckles before he lunges. I'm caught off guard, my mind still reeling from his words, and before I know it, he's pinned me down and has my cell phone. Twisting my hand behind my back, the screen is pressed against my thumb before he releases me and steps back.

"Ahh... lookie here." He holds up my phone, and my search history is displayed on the screen before he moves away. "Jordyn Reese. Pretty name."

I jump to my feet. "Gimme my fucking phone back."

Alex darts away, his movements quick and fine-tuned since he's a goalie. "You stalked her Instagram and TikTok." His laughter fills the weight room, and I'm glad as hell no one else is here but us.

I chase after him, jumping over a weight bench. "Give me my goddamn phone back."

"Nope. This is a goldmine." His reactions are nimble and quick, like the contestants on "American Ninja Warrior." He dodges my attempts to grab my phone again, his eyes lifting to mine. "Tell me the truth, and I'll give it back."

"Fine." I gauge the distance from me to him. "I checked out her social media before she moved in. It makes sense. She's living—"

"Uh-huh." He strolls over and hands me my phone. "You like her. Just admit it."

I refuse. "Josh said she's a nerd. I wanted to see if she looked like one." My defense is weak, and I know it. The gleam in Alex's blue eyes as he cocks his head, his brow raising, has me bracing for his next question.

"You bought something for her, didn't you? A welcome home gift."

"They aren't welcome home gifts. She just moved—"

"*They*? You bought her multiple things?"

I blow out a frustrated sigh, my fingers curling so hard around my phone I'm surprised that it doesn't shatter. "Her bedroom was used for storage. After I cleaned it up, it looked barren and cold. Josh told me she'd been down on her luck, so I figured I'd do something nice."

The urge to punch Alex grows stronger as his smirk widens. He crosses his arms over his chest, leveling me with a look. "What did you buy her?"

I swallow hard, knowing how bad this is gonna look. "Not much." Good. My voice doesn't waver, and my tone is neutral. "New curtains and a comforter set for the bed—"

"You bought her a new bed. There wasn't one in that room, Tristan."

I ignore him. "A desk and chair."

"Holy shit. You bought her more furniture?"

I should punch this motherfucker square in the balls. "So what? It made the room nicer. She's going to be living with two rowdy hockey players—"

"Rowdy? Are you gonna move Bryce, Landin, and me in and throw you and Josh out? Cause the two of you are far from rowdy."

"No, asshole." I blow out a long breath. *Why do I tell this motherfucker anything?* "A book nerd probably thinks we're rowdy."

"She didn't look like a nerd on social media. Course, you know that since you were stalking her on it. Besides, nerds can have a wild side. Remember the professor that Bryce fucked last semester. She was a freak." His eyes light up, and an evil smile curls his lips. "Maybe Jordyn is—"

"Don't finish that fucking sentence, or I'll knock your teeth down your throat."

"Man, you're swearing and making a lot of threats. More than you have in the past six months. She really got under your skin."

"She didn't get under anything. I—"

"Not yet." His smile is arrogant. "But the rate you're going, it's only a matter of time."

I blow out an exasperated sigh. "She's my roommate, Alex."

He shrugs. "Jordyn could be your girlfriend if you play your cards right."

"Did you hit your head on the ice yesterday? I already told you, Josh forbid—"

"Which just makes it ten times hotter. Imagine sneaking around with her. That dumbass is on the couch, playing NHL 23, and you clamp your hand over her mouth and bend her over the table—"

"Shut the fuck up. Right the hell now." *Although, that image is fucking hot.*

"Wow. You're testy. You really have it bad for her." He heads toward the weight bench, motioning me with his hand. "I need to meet this girl."

"The fuck you do. And I don't have it bad for her."

"Uh-huh." He grabs some weights and remains quiet.

The tension drains from my body as I pick up a pair of fifty-pound dumbbells, getting ready to curl them. Maybe he's finally dropping this.

As soon as I curl the weight toward my shoulders, he says, "Book nerd, huh? Did she bring any books?"

My brows furrow. "Yeah. Why?"

"You bought her a bookcase, didn't you, motherfucker?"

I'm so surprised that I nearly dropped a dumbbell on my foot. "What are you, psychic?"

Alex's loud laughter is going to haunt me forever. Rolling my eyes, I pump out some curls with renewed vigor, hoping it will drown him and my errant thoughts out of my head.

CHAPTER 7

Jordyn

S neaking through the patio doors, I listen intently for the shouting that shook the house before I went for a run. When Josh came home, Tristan flew into a rage, screaming about betrayal, puck bunnies, and being set up. Josh laughed until Tristan grabbed him by the neck and slammed him against the wall.

Although my stepbrother annoys the shit out of me, he's the reason I'm not homeless right now, so I intervened, putting my hand on Tristan's arm. Then I gently rubbed his back, my voice calm as I tried to soothe the rage that turned his eyes a deep shade of green. I must admit, when he first turned his head toward me, eyes blazing and baring his teeth, my panties became wet. Dropping my gaze to my feet, I kept talking until he released Josh.

Once I was sure he wasn't going to kill my stepbrother, I fled the room like I was being chased by a ghost and grabbed my running shoes. I needed to calm the hell down before I did something stupid because the image of Tristan's big cock was making me hot and bothered.

For the second time in a day, I was jealous of Janelle.

My gaze went to the trashcan that contained the used condom Tristan dropped earlier. It's a reminder of what he is —a player.

Slipping inside, I tiptoe through the house and up the stairs. I breathe a sigh of relief when I reach my doorway. Until Tristan's door flies open, and there he stands, shirtless, wearing only those damn gray sweatpants.

My eyes immediately drop to the outline of his cock. For the first time, I want to throw caution to the wind and do something foolish. Like drop to my knees and suck his cock.

Horrified by my thoughts, my eyes snap up when his woodsy scent infiltrates my nose. He's so damn close that I could easily reach out and touch the bulge in his pants.

Dear God, what is wrong with me?

"Sorry if I scared you earlier." His deep, raspy voice is like an intoxicating blend of alcohol and seduction, making me drunk and stupid. I want to do really bad things right now, like roll on the bed with him, naked.

Inhaling, I catch the scent of his shower gel mixing with the woodsy scent. Then I notice his damp hair. He must have taken a shower while I went for a run. *I wonder if he thought about me—*

Cutting off my thoughts, I flash him a smile that I hope is reassuring and not seductive. I'm not even sure I know how to smile like that anyway. "It's okay. You had every right to be upset." *God, why does my voice sound breathless? Am I giving him fuck me eyes? His pupils dilated when I spoke.*

"Yeah, but that's the second time I've made a bad impression on you in one day." His eyes drop to my lips, and I swallow hard, wondering what it would be like if he closed the distance and tasted me.

Stop it. He's a jock who fucks puck bunnies. You're not in his league.

"Jordyn." The way he says my name has my attention snapping back to him. "Are you okay?"

No. But your dick could fix what ails me. "Yes. I'm fine," I squeak, causing him to raise his brows skeptically.

Way to go. Now he's really gonna think you're strange.

"Are you sure?"

Goddamn. Did I imagine that he leaned closer, interest flaring in his eyes?

"Uh-huh. I'm sure." *Yeah, that's why my voice sounds like I'm practicing for a job as a phone sex worker.*

"Okay." He leans against my door, trapping me against it. "If you need anything, just ask me."

My mouth is as dry as the Sahara Desert, which is ironic because my pussy is so wet, I'm soaking my panties. If I stripped them off, I could probably wring them out.

Taking a deep breath, I slowly exhale, trying to get myself under control. It's impossible with him leaning over me, his arm propped against the door frame like one of my book boyfriends. My imagination runs wild, picturing him grabbing my throat and devouring my mouth like he owns me.

"Jordyn. I'm gonna need you to say something." He pins me with his intense green eyes. "Use your words."

Oh, I'd like to use my mouth but not to speak any words.

"Umm... O-okay," I finally stammer. "What was the question?"

The flirty smirk that curls his lips makes all reason flee from my head, and I melt into a puddle at his feet. "I said—"

The front door slams and Tristan jumps back. Avoiding my gaze, he runs a hand through his hair before his eyes meet mine. "Guess I'd better go. I just wanted to make sure you're okay."

I nod. "Fine," I squeak out, biting my lip.

"Goddamn, I wish you wouldn't do that," he mutters, eyes locked on my mouth. He looks down the hallway as

Josh's footsteps on the stairs reach my ears. "I've gotta get outta here. See ya."

I slump against my door frame as he walks away, my eyes following his every move. When he steps through his doorway, he looks over his shoulder, and the look he gives me incinerates my clothing, leaving me naked and exposed.

Then he steps inside and shuts the door while I burn into a pile of ashes.

As Josh's footsteps grow louder, I slip into my room, quietly shutting the door. Heading to my laptop, I hit the mousepad, waking it up, and put on some music. Then I grab my cell phone and crawl onto my bed. Pressing the button to dial my best friend, Chelsea, rolling onto my back, waiting for her to answer.

"Hey, blondie. How's life at Weston Heights?"

"Ugh. I don't know how to answer that." Pulling my legs up, my wet panties make me uncomfortable, so I spread my legs slightly.

"Oh, this sounds good." I hear her moving around, then the slam of her door. "Tell me about it as I get a frozen mocha. I have a feeling I'm gonna need it."

"I miss frozen mochas from Katie's Coffees." I pout as I envision the coffee shop across the street from my old apartment.

Chelsea laughs. "Yeah, but from the tone of your voice, you have more than frozen coffee on your mind." The sound of her footsteps descending the stairs fills my ears. "What's Tristan like?"

Hot. Muscular. Sexy as hell. Huge cock. "Complicated," I finally say.

"Complicated, huh? So you wanna fuck him."

"Chelsea Renee Brady. Do you kiss your mother with that mouth?"

"Nah, she kisses my father, and eww. Now that I think

about it, I can't remember the last time they kissed. Or the last time I've seen them."

I frown, hating that her parents are always off, living their best lives, throwing money but not love or attention on their only daughter. As much as Chelsea claims she likes the freedom to do what she wants and the platinum credit cards, I know she's lonely. "Where are they now?"

"Bora Bora. Mom said it was getting too cold in New York." Her brittle laugh makes my heart ache. "Yeah, the balmy eighty-nine-degree temperature is absolutely freezing. I had to get out my winter coat."

"Sorry, sweetie."

"Eh, don't worry about me." Her voice lowers, and I can practically hear the gleam in her eyes when she says, "Tell me about Tristan. I know he's hot—"

"How do you know that?" *Damn it.* Not only did I admit it, but my voice sounded accusatory. Even slightly jealous.

"Ohh, he's really hot." The sound of traffic comes through the line. "What's the hockey team's name again? Wolverines?"

I don't answer. Instead, I stare at the ceiling, irritation spreading like a disease.

"Here he is."

"Are you looking at the team webpage?"

"Obviously, you've checked it out." Her amused laughter makes me want to slap her. "So what happened? How was your first meeting?"

That's a loaded question. I debate what to say, but she squeals in my ear before I can form the thoughts, nearly deafening me. "Oh, my God. Tell me right now, bish."

"Well..." I chew on my lip, still unsure what to tell her.

"Fuuuck! You saw his dick!"

"Chelsea! Are you psychic?"

"Yes. Yes, I am." I hear the smug smile in her voice. "Now tell me."

I recount everything that's happened since I arrived, including how the jolt of electricity raced through me when I touched his chest and how he rattled me in my doorway just a few minutes ago.

"Sounds like chemistry to me. I think you should fuck him."

"Chelsea, he's a puck boy. Weren't you listening when I told you about our first meeting?"

"Oh, I heard it. The best part was you standing there and watching like a voyeur."

"Stop it." I slap a hand over my face, my burning cheek heating my palm. "I know it was wrong to watch...."

"But you haven't had sex in a long time, and when you did, your asshole ex and that one-time fling wouldn't know where to find your clit if you drew them a map."

"Well, yeah," I admit, embarrassed at how well she knows me. "But it's not just that..."

"Oh, he's hung like a horse. Do tell."

"Chelsea," I squeal. "You're terrible."

"But you didn't deny it. If he were a short dick man, you would've instantly denied it. Spill the tea."

Laughing, I shake my head and stick my tongue out at her, even though she can't see me. I'm glad I didn't Face-Time her. This conversation is humiliating enough. "I mean, yeah, he has the biggest one I've ever seen. But it's more than that."

"So he knew how to fuck even though you interrupted them."

"God, Chelsea, you make it sound so sordid. I mean, I guess it was since I watched. But my bag hit the floor before the grand finale, so I don't know how good he is."

"You did not just call it the grand finale."

"I'm trying not to be crude. The point is, I didn't watch the whole performance, so I—"

Her loud laughter cuts me off. "Please stop talking about performance and finales like you were watching a damn circus instead of a hotter-than-hell hockey god fucking some busty bitch."

Her laughter is irritating, as is her commentary. "You're so damn annoying."

"You know what I think? That you're jealous because he was fucking someone else, and you like this guy already." I open my mouth to interrupt, but she raises her voice, continuing before I can. "You're trying to convince yourself he's a stereotypical jock who fucks puck bunnies, but the truth is, he makes your head spin, and your panties explode. Not a bad combo, if you ask me."

"First, I didn't ask you. Second, you're wrong."

"Yet, you called me and spilled your guts. Clearly, you wanted my opinion. Second, I'm right, and you know it." Her voice drops to a conspiratorial whisper. "Your panties are soaked, aren't they?"

"Chel-sea." I drag out her name, frustration welling inside me. The ringing of the bell above the coffee shop door as she steps inside causes a pang in my chest. *I miss her and New York.*

"I'm right. And the lady doth protest too much." Her giggle grates on my nerves like nails on a chalkboard. "You like him, and that's why you're feeling confused. It's easier to push him away if you think he's a puck boy rather than a sweet man who bought you a floor-to-ceiling bookcase. By the way, any man who does that is marriage material."

I can't help the giggle that escapes my lips. "The bookcase was super sweet. But I'm not marrying him."

"Yet. Hold on a sec while I order."

I stare at the ceiling, my thoughts whirling with all that's happened since I arrived. *I wonder what Tristan is doing right now?*

"Okay, I'm back. Sorry, it took so long. I had to douse the fire you ignited with a long drink of coffee. Hot damn, girl." The bell rings again as she pushes through the door, the sound of traffic filling the line. "Living with a hotter-than-hell hockey player who's into you."

"Wait a minute. I never said he was into me."

"You didn't have to. I can tell. Come on, Jordyn. He pinned you against the door frame and did the infamous book boyfriend lean. He's not only dying to get into your pants, but the bookcase proves he likes you."

"You're incorrigible."

"I'm right."

My heart pounds faster beneath my sternum, though I do my best to ignore it. "Doesn't matter. We're too different. And he's too much of a risk."

"Whatever you say, Jordyn." The gloating tone in her voice irritates me even more.

"Whatever, bish. I miss your face."

"I miss you, too. I promise to come visit soon so I can hear all about how good Tristan fucked you."

Rolling my eyes, I don't say a word. *I'll have to prove to her that Tristan and I will never be more than roommates.*

CHAPTER 8

Jordyn

I hurry up the steps of the Weston Grove building, heading to my first class of the day. As I grab the door handle, I pause to wipe the sweat from my brow, excitement and nervousness pumping through my veins.

Pulling the door open, I exhale a happy sigh as I smell the familiar aroma of higher education. Oddly enough, it smells like my former New York campus.

Taking a sip of the iced coffee, I spot a sign pointing to the stairs. Pushing through the door, I enter the stairway and take the stairs to the second floor, my heart beating with anticipation.

Exiting the stairwell, a song is in my heart as I walk down the hallway, taking the first step toward my dreams. Anticipation courses through me because I'm starting my day with the class I most look forward to this semester and the one I'm offering tutoring in—English Literature.

My eyes roam around the room when I step through the door, stopping when they clash with mossy ones. My excitement dims, turning to shock. *Oh my God. Why the hell is Tristan in my class?*

A spark of recognition and something else is in his eyes, but I quickly turn away, not wanting to analyze it. He did a great job distancing himself from me the rest of the weekend. Josh nonchalantly mentioned Tristan texted, saying he was staying with their teammate, Alex, at his house.

I busied myself as much as possible, trying not to think about Tristan. I met with the Learning Center Director and the other tutors on Sunday afternoon. It was informal, a chance for us to meet and bond. Dr. Marshall, the director, divided us into groups. I enjoyed my group, and by the time we left, Jessica, Felicity, Matt, and I were chatting and laughing like old friends.

Shaking my head, my gaze moves to a seat on the opposite side of the room, and I realize someone is waving at me. A relieved smile is on my face as I spot Jessica, one of the tutors in my group. I hurry toward her, not sparing another look at Tristan.

"Hey, Jordyn." Jessica greets me as I slide into the seat beside her. "I'm so glad you're in this class."

"Me too." Unzipping my backpack, I pull out my class materials. "I was afraid I wouldn't know anyone here." I don't tell her that I know Tristan, but I sneak a peek at him as I open the lid of my laptop. Twinkling green eyes glance over me, briefly locking with mine, before I look away, a blush heating my cheeks.

A muscular guy with short dark hair slides into the seat beside Tristan. I look over at him, and he meets my gaze head-on, a smirk curling his lips.

Oh, God. Is that Tristan's friend, Alex? Did Tristan tell him about our first meeting?

I turn to Jessica, desperate for a distraction. "What other classes do you have?"

As she rattles off her schedule, Tristan's eyes bore into me.

I nod as she talks, happy that she and I have a writing class together after lunch. She asks me about my schedule, and I hand her my phone, the picture on my screen. Anxiety courses through me as I feel Tristan and his buddy staring at me.

When the professor walks in and begins class, I glance over at Tristan again. His eyes are already on me, a smirk curling his lips. I look away, anger filling me as I pretend to follow along as Professor Martin reviews the syllabus. Meanwhile, I'm seething as green eyes continue to bore into my profile.

The asshole avoids me all weekend, but now he can't take his eyes off me. Yeah, no thanks.

"I know you can't wait to do this," Professor Martin's voice draws me from my thoughts. Dread fills me at the look on his face. I know what's coming, and I hate the idea already. "We're gonna go around the room. Please stand, tell us your name, what you're majoring in, and any minors."

My palms are sweaty when the person in front of me sits down, knowing it's my turn. I exhale and stand. "Hi. I'm Jordyn Reese, and I'm majoring in English Literature with a writing minor." I practically fall into my seat, relieved that's over. My heart pounds as I stare at my screen, my cheeks flushed.

With an exhale, my gaze moves to Tristan. He flashes me a smile and a thumbs up, and I can't help the grin that spreads over my face.

The introductions continue, and I pretend to pay attention. But it's hard when a sexy-as-hell six-foot-tall hockey player lounges in his seat, staring at me like he's starving and I'm the only thing on the menu.

A chat box pops up on my laptop screen. Curious, I click on it, my breath accelerating when I realize it's a private chat from Tristan Harrington.

> Tristan: You did amazing. I'm sorry I've been MIA this weekend. Will I see you later tonight?

I stare at his message, debating how to respond.

> Me: Thanks. I'm sure you'll do great, too. No worries about this weekend. I had things to do as well. I'll be home later tonight.

I search his profile as he reads it, noting the tick in his jaw. He turns his head, brows lifted skeptically as we silently stare one another down.

The guy beside Tristan gets to his feet, looks around the room, and says, "I'm Alex Graves. Most of you know me as the goalie for the Wolverines and this guy's best friend." He jerks a thumb at Tristan and the class cheers. "I'm majoring in Sports Management with a minor in Coaching. Yeah, I'm ruining the jock stereotype. I'm athletic and smart." He bows before he sits down, and the class erupts into laughter.

My muscles are tense as Tristan gets to his feet. *Why the hell is he so damn attractive?*

"My name is Tristan Harrington and—

Before he can get another word out, Alex and a bunch of students in the class punch their fists in the air and start chanting, "Captain. Captain."

I exchange a glance with Jessica, shrugging my shoulder. She leans closer to my ear so I can hear her over the ruckus and says, "Tristan is the captain of the Wolverines hockey team. Clearly, he's well liked."

I nod, slumping in my chair as I swallow hard, intimidated by the reaction of my classmates. Tristan gestures with his hands for the students to calm down, and they immediately obey. The room goes silent as he graciously says, "Thanks for that, but please, don't do it again." He lightly punches Alex's shoulder before chuckling. "I'm double majoring in Communication and English Literature with a minor in Coaching." His eyes zero in on me, a smirk on his face, before he sits down.

My mouth drops open in surprise. There he goes, ruining the jock stereotype again.

I'm stunned by his majors and minor, but the uneasiness swimming through my veins has nothing to do with that. *We are too different. There's no way Tristan would ever be interested in me.*

Professor Martin begins lecturing, and I force myself to concentrate on class, especially since I'm offering tutoring services for this and his other section. I begin taking notes, even though my heart isn't in it.

A new chat message appears on my screen, and my fingers still as I see Tristan's name.

> Tristan: Hopefully, what you learned about me today will help change the horrible first impression I made.

Irrational anger swirls through me. *Why is he doing this?* It's more obvious than ever that we are complete opposites.

> Me: I should be impressed that you're a smart jock. Probably makes you better at being a puck boy.

> Tristan: Ouch. I'm not a puck boy, blondie. Nice try, though.

> Me: Shouldn't you be paying attention instead of messaging me, smarty pants?

> Tristan: Shouldn't you?

I bristle as I read his message. My gaze sweeps over him,

frowning as he flashes me an arrogant smile. *What is his deal? He has avoided me all weekend, but he won't leave me alone today.*

Discreetly slipping my cell phone from my backpack, I text Chelsea to update her. I need some sympathy and advice.

My phone vibrates, and I quickly look at it, anticipating Chelsea's response. My eyes widen when I see it's from Tristan.

> Tristan: Now you're texting in class, too. Tsk, tsk. You aren't fitting the stereotypical bookworm behavior.

I roll my eyes, about to respond, when I get a response from Chelsea.

> Chelsea: You have class with Tristan? This semester is going to be full of drama. I can't wait!

I frown at my phone. *Not helpful, Chelsea.*
As if she's a mind reader, another text message appears.

> Chelsea: He missed you, so he can't leave you alone.

I sigh but answer Tristan's text instead of responding to Chelsea.

> Me: So you can deviate from typical jock behavior, but I'm not allowed to deviate from bookworm behavior?

> Tristan: I love your feistiness. It's cute and sexy, just like you. BTW you look hot in that outfit.

My mouth falls open as I read his text. I glance up at the

professor, who isn't paying attention to me, before looking at Tristan. He's staring at me, a challenging glint in his eyes.

Determination coils through me as I give him a smirk.

Two can play this game.

It's on, puck boy.

CHAPTER 9

Tristan

How the hell am I supposed to concentrate in class when Jordyn is dressed like a sexy librarian?

My gaze moves from her black button-down shirt to her plaid skirt. Her long, lightly tanned legs are crossed. She swings one sandal clad foot nervously. My eyes roam back up her body, slowly drinking her in before landing on her crimson cheeks. Her eyes lock with mine before darting away.

"You've got it bad for her, captain." I hate the smugness in Alex's low tone as his eyes follow mine to Jordyn.

My eyes narrow at him. "Shut up."

"Oh... I'm scared by that comeback." Alex rolls his eyes. "Why don't you march over there, flip up her skirt, and fuck—"

"Don't finish that statement," I hiss, unadulterated rage rolling through me at the thought of anyone seeing her naked except me. I tried like hell to get her out of my system by hiding out at Alex's house this weekend.

It didn't work. *At all.*

"If you didn't like this girl, you wouldn't be so pissed off."

His smug smile makes me want to punch him, but I know that would only prove his point. Instead, I clench my jaw and fists, remaining silent.

"Whatever, Alex." I stare straight ahead, pretending to pay attention to Professor Martin. I nod in the instructor's direction and hiss, "Pay attention."

He chuckles, and I turn my head, scowling at him. He's completely unbothered, which is typical of Alex. "You mean, like you? All I've seen you do is stare, message, and text Jordyn."

I punch his arm, and he rubs the spot, laughing at the expression on my face. "You've got it bad for her, Tristan. Doesn't matter how much you run and hide at my house. Won't change your feelings." He faces the front of the room, leaving me to stew over his words.

My gaze drifts to Jordyn. Her fingers move rapidly over the keys of her laptop, her gaze on the screen. I take a moment to appreciate her beauty.

Jordyn's eyes meet mine, and I don't miss the heat that flares in her eyes before she looks away.

A jolt of satisfaction blooms inside me before it changes to worry. I promised myself I wouldn't get involved with a woman this year because I needed to focus on the draft. The second I looked at her, I was ready to throw that rule out the window.

I'm in so damn much trouble with this woman.

❧

Sweat drips down my back as Coach Jensen blows his whistle and screams, "Again."

My teammates groan, exhausted from the brutal practice. We have our first game this Saturday, and Coach is determined that we will have a strong start to the season.

49

My gaze slides to Alex. When I see the irritation and frustration on his face, I skate over to coach, sending shavings of ice his way as I stop in front of him. I slide my gloves off and spit my mouth guard into my hand. "Come on, Coach. We know the damn drill. We've done it so often we're gonna have nightmares about it." Removing my helmet so he can see my eyes, I plead with him for their sake and my own. "The team is exhausted, and the risk of one of us getting injured is high."

Coach's face is stern, his arms crossed over his chest as he silently weighs my words. A smile tugs at his lips before he grows serious. "Good of you to be looking out for your guys." He turns toward the rest of the team and blows his whistle. His voice carries around the rink as he says, "I'll tell you what. You can hit the showers if Tristan can score a goal in five minutes or less."

Fuck. I exhale a deep breath, turning my weary eyes toward Alex, reading the challenge in them. Alex practices like he plays, and I know this isn't going to be easy. But when I look around at my exhausted, sweaty teammates, I know I must find a way to score.

Alex pops his mouthguard back in before placing his hand inside his goalie glove. He skates to his position in front of the goal, then bangs his stick on the ice.

Challenge accepted.

Shoving my mouthguard between my lips, I slide on my mask and gloves, determination settling in my spine. As I skate across the ice, I pass the puck back and forth, moving around invisible players as my teammates cheer me on. Alex readies himself in a position to block my shot. I pull my stick back, setting up to take my shot. But I fake it, which sends Alex to the left side, and I immediately take advantage of the opening. Swinging my stick back again, I send the puck flying into the net as my teammates erupt into cheers.

Alex pulls off his gloves and spits his mouthguard in his palm. "You're lucky I'm exhausted, Harrington," he quips.

I skate over to him, removing my glove and spitting my mouthguard in my palm. "That was all skill, Graves." Patting his padded shoulder, I give him a smug grin. "Let's hit the showers."

Alex nods. "Maybe I let you score a goal because we're all fucking exhausted. Coach is pushing us like we're machines."

I chuckle. "Noted. And true."

We pull off our helmets simultaneously, sweat matting our hair and running in rivulets down our faces. "What's up, Tristan? You have that *look* on your face."

I wave my hand dismissively. "Nothing's up." *Please don't ask any questions or bring Jordyn up.* "Wanna come back to my place? I'll order pizza... And you can help me do some research."

He raises a brow, a smirk settling on his lips. "On blondie?"

"Why are you asking when you already know the answer?"

He chuckles, shaking his head. "Tryin' to get you to admit your feelings for this woman is worse than pulling teeth."

"And how many teeth have you pulled?"

"None. But I have knocked some out on the ice during fights. It's easier to remove teeth than getting you to confess you're head over heels for Jordyn."

Lowering my voice as we step into the locker room, I shake my head. "Good to know."

I PUSH through the library doors, my backpack over my shoulders, giving the illusion I'm there to study. In reality, the only thing I plan on studying is Jordyn.

I nonchalantly cut through the Learning Center, where

Jordyn works. Jessica, the girl Jordyn sat beside in English Lit, also works here. Since I couldn't sleep last night, I stalked Jordyn on social media and the school website.

As I round the corner, I spot her standing at the counter, talking to one of her coworkers. Her back is to me, and I unabashedly check out her tanned legs, short plaid skirt, and black shirt. She laughs at something her co-worker says, oblivious to me checking her out.

I can't take my eyes off her.

The girl she's chatting with looks over Jordyn's shoulder, her eyes widening. She reaches out, shaking Jordyn's arm, who turns around to see what her coworker is looking at.

Her eyes widen, and her face pales as she looks at me. "Tristan. What are you doing here?" My presence flusters her, and it turns me the fuck on.

I just stand there, not saying a word.

The electricity in the air between us is palpable. I know Jordyn feels it when she shifts her weight from one foot to the other. Her curious gaze never leaves mine. Her breathing becomes heavier, her chest straining against the buttons holding her shirt together.

Gritting her teeth, she pushes off the counter and stomps my way, her cheeks flushed from anger.

Oh, Jordyn. You have no idea what you do to me. The sexy librarian look is making me feral.

Her strawberry scent engulfs me when she stops in front of me. She cocks her head, irritation blooming over her face. In annoyance, she puts her hands on her hips and taps one heeled foot. The urge to grab her and kiss the hell out of her until she surrenders to me is almost impossible to ignore.

"Did a puck smash you upside the head and cause you to lose your hearing? I asked you a question."

Oh, shit. She's a feisty little kitten, hissing at me.

My smile widens as I gesture to my backpack. "Just passing

through to head toward the study lounge." I point to the large corridor on the left, which leads to the lounge.

Her gaze narrows. "Why cut through the Learning Center? It's longer than—"

I step forward so our shoes are toe to toe. She stops talking, her aqua eyes widening in surprise. I'm so close she's forced to tip her face up to mine. What she sees on my face causes her to suck in an audible breath and hold it.

A sense of satisfaction rolls through me. "I saw you here and thought I'd come over and say hi."

Jordyn exhales, her irritation disappearing. She scratches her cheek, looking uncomfortable. "Oh." She runs a hand down her shirt before it travels to her skirt, smoothing her clothing. "Well, hi," she finally says, her voice high-pitched and unnatural.

"Hi," I rasp, breathing her in. *God, she smells good.* All the tension drains from my body, the aches and pains from that brutal practice disappearing in her presence. The boulder that has been weighing down my chest for the past couple of weeks lifts, allowing me to breathe again.

The girl she was talking to approaches us, curiosity on her face. "Aren't you going to introduce me to your boyfriend?"

Jordyn's eyes widen as she looks from her coworker to me. "Oh, h-he's—"

I immediately extend my hand. "Hi. I'm Tristan. And you are?"

Jordyn gapes at me as the girl shakes my hand. "Felicity. It's a pleasure to meet you."

"Likewise." Felicity's gaze slides to Jordyn, who stares at me like aliens have taken over my body.

Before either of them can say another word, I hurriedly offer an explanation. "Just thought I'd come in and say hi to Jordyn before heading to the table to study." My voice lowers as I look around the quiet Learning Center. "I'm also here to walk her out to her car. I don't like her walking to her vehicle alone at night. It's unsafe."

Jordyn opens her mouth, her face red from anger. Before she can speak, Felicity says, "Oh, that's so sweet. You're right, it's unsafe." She turns to Jordyn and pats her shoulder. "You have one of the good ones. Lucky girl."

I wink at Felicity. "I keep trying to remind her of that." Jerking a thumb over my shoulder, I smile at Jordyn. "Well, I better let you get back to work." My gaze moves to Felicity. "Nice to meet you. I'm sure I'll be seeing you again."

She giggles and waves. "You too, Tristan. I'm sure we'll cross paths since I work with your girlfriend."

As I walk away, I chuckle to myself. Jordyn was so mad that steam was coming from her ears, rendering her speechless. While I appreciate that I had her so on edge she couldn't speak, I'd much rather use my lips to shut her up.

If the opportunity arises, I'm not wasting it.

CHAPTER 10

Tristan

I've barely cracked open my English Literature textbook when Jordyn stomps over, a very pissed off expression on her face. I do my best to keep my expression neutral and pretend I don't know she's flying toward me like a bat out of hell.

I bite the inside of my cheek, trying not to laugh as she gets closer. Every one of my nerve endings sizzle, waiting for the confrontation.

I wait until she's right beside me before looking up. "Oh, hey, Jordyn—"

"Don't you 'hey, Jordyn' me," she snaps, her chest heaving from frustration and anger. "Do you have any idea what you did back there?"

I feign innocence, raising my brows with a bewildered expression. "Said hi to you and met Felicity." I shrug. "What's the big deal—"

"That's not what I'm talking about," she hisses. "You let Felicity believe you were my boyfriend." Her eyes dart around nervously, although we are alone.

"Oh, that." I wave a hand dismissively. "No big deal—"

"No big deal," she screeches, her eyes so wide I can see the whites the whole way around them. "It's a very big deal. What if she tells Josh?"

I level her with a look. "Does she hang around Josh? Because he sure as hell doesn't set foot in the library unless he has to, let alone come to the Learning Center."

Jordyn huffs, her anger dimming slightly. "That's not the point."

Pushing my chair back, I stand, towering over her. She trembles before she takes a step back, then another. Heat flares in her wide eyes, her breath hitching when her ass hits the edge of the table behind her.

With two steps, I'm pressed against her. I place one palm on either side of the table behind her, the wood cool against my sweaty hands. My body overheats being this close to her. "I like it when you get worked up, kitten."

"I-I'm not worked up. And my name isn't kitten."

I lift a hand to her face, inhaling her fear mixed with the sexual tension that hangs in the air between us. "Yes, you are. And it's a cute-as-hell nickname for you." Our lips are inches from one another.

When her gaze drops to mine, her teeth sink into her bottom lip.

"Tristan. We shouldn't." Her voice is breathless as her hands flatten against my chest. I wait for her to push me away, but she fists my shirt instead.

"Are you sure about that, kitten?" I glance down at her hands on my chest before my gaze lifts to hers.

She trembles against me, heat blazing in her aqua irises, unsure what to do. I wait her out, looking for a sign to proceed, hoping she hurries the hell up before I die. I'm exercising so much restraint right now that sweat trickles down my back from my efforts.

"Fuck it," she says before her lips slam against mine.

Holy hell. She's kissing me.

Jordyn Reese is fucking kissing me.

I'm stunned, my brain a few seconds behind, trying to process what is happening. What I've been dreaming about all weekend is happening, only instead of me kissing her, she's taking the lead.

My body comes to life beneath her mouth. My blood rushes through my veins like a raging river as my heart rate rapidly increases, the tempo beating in my ear like the pounding of drums at a concert. My arms wrap around her, one around her lower back while the other fists in her silky blonde hair.

She moans against my lips and my cock twitches in response. I'm so hard inside my jeans it's painful, but I'll endure it to feel her lips against mine. Hell, I would walk barefoot over hot coals to feel her in my arms like this.

Jordyn's hands slide up my chest and to the back of my neck. She lifts onto her tiptoes, pressing herself flush against me as she continues kissing me with a desperate hunger that suggests I wasn't the only one craving this.

My hand slides to her ass, squeezing it with a growl. Her skirt is too short and—

I forget what I was thinking when she grinds against me. "Tristan," she murmurs against my mouth.

Keeping my lips against hers, I whisper, "Yeah, kitten?"

"We shouldn't... But I can't seem to stop."

"Then don't. Right now, it's just me and you. No one else." Then I take over the kiss, tilting her head and licking her bottom lip. She tastes so fucking sweet, like the most decadent strawberry. When I lick the seam of her lips, she parts, and my tongue slides inside, tasting more of her.

My head spins as our tongues dance together. I want more. Everything she's willing to give, I want it.

I want *all* of her.

She moans again as I squeeze her tight little ass. It would be so easy to touch her right now, but I don't want to rush anything.

I slowly pull back, wanting to see what she's feeling. Fear grips my heart, and I expect to see a horrified look on her face before she pushes me away, telling me this was a mistake.

But she surprises me when she whispers, "Kiss me again."

Hell yes. I grab the back of her head, pulling her mouth to mine. The kiss is passionate, full of a hunger and need I've never experienced before. But another feeling has me both thrilled and a little scared. It's indescribable. It feels *right*, like everything I need but wasn't aware I'd been craving.

The fear dissipates when she rocks her hips against me and murmurs, "My God, you feel so fucking good." She kisses me again, another confession slipping from her lips. "All weekend, I wondered what it would be like to kiss you."

Anticipation threads through me, knotting my stomach as I wait for her to continue. When she doesn't, I pull back slightly, worry festering inside me. "Did it live up to your expectations?"

A sexy smirk lifts her lips. Her gaze drops to my mouth, tongue gliding over her bottom lip. When her eyes meet mine, a glimmer of mischievousness mixes with the fire and longing burning in them. "It's better than I imagined."

Groaning, I cup her face. "Kissing you is a fucking dream, kitten. It's everything I craved but didn't know I needed." My lips crash against hers like the ocean waves pounding against the shore, our arms clinging to one another like a life raft as we drift into unfamiliar seas.

I can't help but wonder if we'll swim or drown.

CHAPTER 11

Jordyn

Excitement thrums through my veins as I hurry to class, wearing a blue and black plaid skirt that's shorter than the previous one, paired with a low-cut black top. I can't wait to see Tristan's reaction. I'm certain he'll be pissed, and for some reason, that gets my blood pumping.

I'm halfway to class when a hand latches onto my arm and slaps over my mouth before I can scream. I struggle against whoever it is, but it's futile. He's too strong, and there's no one around.

He drags me into a closet, closing the door behind us, shrouding us in darkness. I sense his hand moving, and a bright light infiltrates the room.

I'm breathing hard against his hand as he whispers, "Kitten, retract those claws. It's me."

His hand moves from my mouth, and I immediately look over my shoulder, staring into a pair of familiar mossy eyes that are tinged with humor and anger. "Tristan." His name is a relieved sigh that fills the small custodial closet.

He pulls my backpack off as he spins me around to face him. His hot, fiery gaze drifts over me, his brows furrowed as he takes in my outfit. "What the hell are you wearing?" he snaps, a vein in his forehead throbbing.

"Don't you like it?" I grin, grabbing the edge of my short, pleated skirt and curtsy.

He steps closer, gripping my chin. "Hell no. Unless we were alone in my bedroom."

My hand wraps around his wrist, my thumb stroking his furiously pounding pulse. I stick my lip out in a pout, victory pumping in my chest when his eyes soften. "I wore it for you."

"Stop pouting." His tone is soft, but his hold is aggressive when he throws me over his shoulder and carries me to a small desk, depositing my ass on it. "I should punish you for wearing this."

I clench my thighs together, my mouth going dry at the thought. *Why does that turn me on?*

He steps between my legs, spreading my thighs wider. "You like that, don't you, kitten? The thought of me spanking you makes you wet." His lips move close to mine, and goosebumps scatter over my skin as he teasingly runs his fingers over my inner thighs.

I can't form words as I wiggle closer to him, desperate for him to touch me. A voice screams inside my head, reminding me of how we first met. But my hormones overrule it, shutting down the doubts.

"Words, kitten. Use them." His voice is commanding, his face dark and stern, just like the hockey clips I've seen on the Wolverine's website. A shiver runs through me as I spread my legs wider, inviting him to touch me.

"Yes." I lick my lips, never breaking eye contact. "Please touch me. I'm soaked."

The feral groan that comes from him speaks to a part of me that I didn't know existed. My feminism slinks to the floor, arms folded and glaring. I've always prided myself on being a strong, independent woman, but right now, the idea of him taking control of me is heady.

He cocks his head, reading the signals I'm sending. His lips meet mine as his fingers graze over my panties, lightly stroking my aching pussy. "Mmm. You're right. Your panties are soaked."

I grip the back of his neck with one hand, holding him against my lips. He chuckles while continuing to torture me. I arch against him, a desperate whine leaving my lips, anxious for him to slip his fingers beneath the fabric and touch me.

"Don't worry, kitten. Wild horses couldn't drag me away from you." His lips press against mine, full of need and desire. His fingers slip beneath the edge of my panties, and I moan, arching against his hand.

"Please, touch me," I beg, feeling my femininity pound her fists against the floor. But I'm floating in a haze of lust, uncaring how pissed she is.

He slides a finger inside me, and the moan that leaves his lips is louder than mine. The sound makes me wetter and hungrier for him. "Fuck, you're so tight." He pushes deep, then slowly slides out. "So hungry for me." His pace is driving me mad, so slow and teasing that I almost beat my fist against his back. He groans, his voice raspy and filled with awe. "The way your pussy grips me." He inserts another finger, and I whimper his name.

"Please. Faster." I breathlessly whisper.

He moves his fingers faster, but not nearly fast enough. I open my mouth to protest, but he shuts me up with his tongue. His other hand pins my hip against the desk so I can no longer arch against him, taking control of my pleasure.

When he pulls back, he gives me a devious grin. "This is what happens when you wear short skirts." His head lowers, raining kisses down my throat and to my cleavage. My head falls back, a moan slipping free as the bliss takes me over.

He grazes his fingers over my shirt, fingers teasing my nipples through the material while his other hand continues its maddeningly slow thrusts in and out of my pussy.

"Tristan, please."

He lowers my back to the desk before sliding my shirt up, exposing my lacy black bra. His eyes bore into mine as he nips at my hard nipple through the fabric. "Nope. It's slow torture for you, little kitten."

I groan until he moves my bra, exposing my breasts. His mouth wraps around my nipple, licking and sucking on it while he continues moving his fingers deep inside me, then slowly out. "You taste so good, kitten."

His thumb moves to my lips, pulling the bottom one down. My tongue pokes out, licking the tip. His eyes heat, and he curses, his fingers finally moving in and out of my pussy faster. Wrapping my lips around his thumb, I suck the tip, pulling a feral groan from him that melts my insides.

"Fuck. I need to taste your pussy." His thumb leaves my mouth as he shifts, dropping to his knees between my legs. He roughly pulls my panties to the side, his tongue swirling around my clit to the rhythm of his fingers. Whimpers and moans fall from my lips as he sucks on it hard.

"Tristan," I moan, my head thrashing from side to side. "Oh, God. Don't stop."

"Mmmm..." he hums against me. "Your pussy tastes so fucking good. I could spend every day eating you."

"Shit." My nails dig into his scalp from his sexy, possessive tone. I arch up, riding his face and fingers.

His growl of approval is too much for me. Every nerve is on fire as my legs shake. "I'm gonna—"

He curls his fingers toward him as he sucks my clit hard. My body convulses, my orgasm slamming over me so hard I see stars. Even my lips are trembling as I lose all control of my body.

"Fuck, you're gorgeous when you come." He continues licking me, dragging my orgasm on and on. I've never felt anything so powerful before.

When my body stops tremoring, Tristan gives my clit a few more lazy swipes with his tongue while he slides his fingers from me and adjusts my panties. I open my eyes, completely sated and still dazed, watching Tristan stand.

God, he's the finest specimen of a man I've ever seen.

As though he can read my thoughts, he gives me a cocky grin and shoves the two fingers that were inside me in his mouth, sucking my orgasm from his fingers. The bliss on his face makes me shutter, butterflies swarming inside my stomach.

He holds out his hand, and I take it. Pulling me to a sitting position, he flashes me a smile that melts my insides. "Come on, kitten. We need to get to class."

Panic fills me as I look toward my backpack. *Oh, shit. Are we late?*

Tristan points to a clock on the wall. "Relax. We still have a couple of minutes." Lifting me from the desk, he sets me on my feet. He tugs at my skirt with a frown before fixing my top so I'm covered again. When his eyes meet mine, he gives me a lopsided smile. "Your skirt is too short, but goddamn, you're beautiful. And *mine.*"

"Thanks," I whisper, blushing at how much I like everything he said.

"You're welcome." He intertwines our hands, lifts them to his lips, and kisses my hand. I melt, amazed that this tough hockey player is gentle and sweet with me.

He leads me to the door, then slowly opens it, poking his head out. "The coast is clear." I hurry into the hallway, hearing the flick of the light switch before he follows me out.

We don't touch as we head toward the classroom, but we keep sneaking peeks at one another. He gestures for me to enter the room first, and when I do, my heart pounds as I see someone sitting next to Jessica. The only available seats are beside Alex.

"Don't worry. We don't bite," Tristan whispers, nudging me toward the chair. "But we are fun."

"You had something to do with this," I hiss over my shoulder.

"Did I? How, when I was in the closet with you?" He whispers back.

I sigh, my gaze meeting Alex's. A knowing smile spreads across his lips, and his eyes twinkle.

Fun, huh? More like I'm about to endure fifty minutes of torture.

CHAPTER 12

Jordyn

Tristan holds the door as I step outside, laughing at Alex, who's in front of me, arguing he's the better hockey player. "Everyone knows the goalie is the most important person on the team, captain. It's just a fact."

Tristan falls in step with me. "Oh, please. I faked you out during practice and kicked your ass." Tristan launches into the story, finishing with, "Alex is an excellent goalie. But he needs the team to help protect the goal."

"Whatever, asshole." Alex's lips curl into a smile. "I bet voyeur believes me, don't you?"

"Voyeur?" My hackles raise as I stare him down. He has an "Oh shit" expression on his face, his gaze sliding to Tristan, who glowers at him.

My eyes flash at Tristan. "You told him."

Alex immediately defends him. "We're best friends. We tell each other everything." He levels me with a look. "That was one helluva unforgettable first meeting."

My face heats, and the sudden urge to flee winds its way through me, cutting off my air.

"Hey." Tristan's hand squeezes my arm, his touch more

comforting than it should be. "I'm sorry. I needed to get it off my chest." The pain in his voice causes me to lift my eyes to his, studying his expression. "I made a terrible first impression, and it bothered the hell outta me."

Sympathy rolls through me. He looks so hurt that I can't help but feel bad. *He cares about my opinion of him.*

"I'm not a puck boy. I cut off women after—"

Grief and devastation war across his features. He runs a hand through his dark blond hair, bicep rippling as he does. "Anyway, that's in the past."

Before I can say a word, Alex jumps in. "He's not kidding. That was the first time he'd been with a woman in over a year." A smirk curls his lips as we walk toward the coffee shop. "His palm is probably worn the fuck out. I'm surprised he hasn't needed wrist surgery."

Tristan punches Alex's shoulder, laughing. "Oh, and you're suddenly Mr. Stud now? Exactly how many people have you been with since you and Natasha broke up? Zero."

Alex smirks at Tristan, then me. "I haven't found anyone to drag into a custodial closet yet."

I gasp, my accusing gaze sliding to Tristan. "You told him?"

The look on Tristan's face is perplexed. "When did I tell him? You've been with me since the closet."

Alex's howl of laughter reaches my ears "You two are easy. You can't keep a secret for shit."

Oh, God. Is he right? Will Josh take one look at my face and know what Tristan and I did?

Alex laughs harder, patting my left shoulder. "It's not that obvious, voyeur. Only to me, because I pay attention. That's why I'm the best goalie the Wolverines have had in two decades."

"Don't touch her," Tristan growls. His green eyes lower to mine. "Alex isn't exactly known for his modesty."

Alex shrugs. "Why be modest when it's the truth?" His twinkling eyes drop to mine. "Don't worry about Josh. That guy isn't the brightest star in the sky. More like the dimmest." He leans closer, his voice a loud, conspiratorial whisper. "Tristan knows I'd never do anything, but he's afraid you'll want my dick."

A low, threatening growl comes from my right side. "I'm not threatened by you or your dick, asshole."

"Oh, really? Lemme just find a puck girl to blow me in front of voyeur—"

"Stop." A burst of laughter rolls out of me as I shake my head. "The two of you are crazy. It's like being at a comedy show."

Alex grins proudly, puffing out his chest like he's a superhero. "It's a gift."

Tristan snorts. "Nothing about you is a gift."

"I beg to differ. You've seen my dick."

Tristan rolls his eyes. "Everyone on the team has seen it. You parade it around like you just took Viagra and are experiencing the four-hour erection side effect."

I'm howling with laughter at this point. Without thinking, I look up at Tristan and blurt out, "I'm surprised you don't walk around with yours hanging out. I've never seen one that big—" I cut myself off, my cheeks burning from embarrassment, as both guys stare at me, smirking.

I immediately begin backtracking. "It's not like I've thought about it since I saw it. Not that I really saw it..." *Oh, God. Shut up.*

"Sure you haven't, voyeur," Alex smirks at me before looking at Tristan. "I think she wants you to walk around naked so she can see it again."

Oh God. This is humiliating.

Luckily, I'm saved by the aroma of coffee wafting from the

coffee shop as a group of students walk out. One holds the door while the rest greet the guys like they are superstars.

When they finally move away from us, Alex bounds up the steps, slapping hands with the guy holding the door. I dare to peek through my lashes at Tristan, who is looking down at me with a smug smile on his face. "I'll show you my dick anytime you want, kitten," he whispers.

I turn away, not saying a word as I hurry up the steps where Alex is waiting just inside the coffee shop. As I pass by him, he murmurs, "I don't know what Tristan said, but your face is fucking priceless."

Can the floor open and swallow me, please?

CHAPTER 13

Jordyn

I'm sweaty, and my muscles ache in a good way from the pole dancing class I just finished at the recreation center. Walking to my car, I slip inside, turn the key, and blast the air conditioning. Grabbing my phone, I pull up a playlist, driving home to the beat of a Dua Lipa song.

Arriving home, I'm relieved that neither Josh nor Tristan's vehicles are in the driveway. I don't want questions about my whereabouts and the resulting lies I'll have to make up. There's no way in hell I want to confess I'm taking classes at the rec center, training for my new weekend job at Sinful Sirens.

I worked last Saturday when Tristan pulled his disappearing act. I lied to Josh, telling him I was going to visit a high school friend. Instead, I drove forty-five minutes to another town where I moonlighted as an exotic dancer for money.

A long sigh comes out of me. I started dancing in New York in July as a means of staying in New York. Although I was making good money, it wasn't nearly enough to cover the $57,000 tuition at Cornell. Everything in New York was expensive and consumed a chunk of my money. The rest I used for books, fees, and a meal plan at Weston Heights.

Ray Carbaugh, the owner of Sinful Sirens, gave me a trial and hired me on the spot, asking me to work that night. Desperate for money, I readily agreed. Like the club I worked for in New York, Sinful Sirens is an upscale gentleman's club, so dancers don't strip completely.

Raven Starling, a dancer working at Sinful Sirens for three years to pay for nursing school, was in the dressing room backstage when I walked in. She eased my nerves with her infectious smile, and the pep talk she gave me was like a balm to my frayed nerves.

Once the music started, I lost myself in it, stripping off the skimpy dress to reveal the sexy bra and panties I had the foresight to put on before heading there.

I made good money that night, so it was worth it.

As I wearily climb the steps to the front door, a wry smile curls my lips. *Who would believe that a nerdy girl who loves books and wants to be a university librarian is stripping on the weekends?*

Once inside the house, I wearily climb the steps and head to my room. Tossing my bag onto the floor, I immediately turn around and head to the bathroom. The massaging shower head is screaming my name right now.

Once inside, I shut the door and move to the shower. Turning the handle, I adjust the water temperature, then peel the sweaty clothing from my body, dropping them onto the floor.

Stepping beneath the warm spray, I close the shower door, relishing the feel of the water beating against my fatigued muscles. A moan comes from my lips at the sensation. *God, this is amazing.*

I duck my head beneath the spray, tilting it back to get it wet so I can shampoo it. Grabbing my favorite shampoo, I lather it up, washing away the stress I've been under. After thoroughly rinsing, I apply conditioner, letting it soak in while I wash.

My mind goes to my conversation with Tristan and Alex yesterday and the embarrassing shit I said about Tristan's dick. I groan, humiliation washing over me as I lather up my skin with my favorite strawberry-scented body wash. *God, why did I say that?* Just because he has the longest, thickest cock I've ever seen doesn't mean I need to make a damn fool of myself in front of him and his friend.

Thinking of Tristan immediately sends my mind to the custodial closet. No one has ever made me come like he did. The orgasm was so damn intense....

My blood runs faster, my heart pounding as the images roll through my head. I can feel his touch, even though he isn't in the shower with me. But damn, that would be so hot.

A moan falls out of me as my fingers slide to my nipples, pinching them just the way he did. Within seconds, the fantasy takes over.

TRISTAN IS in the shower with me, his finger teasing my nipple while his hot mouth sucks on the other one. My pussy throbs, aching for his touch. When I moan, his eyes flick to mine, the mossy green darkening from desire.

Releasing my nipple, his gravelly voice washes over me. "Do you want me to touch that pretty pussy, Jordyn?"

"Please. Touch me," I beg, arching toward him.

A smirk curls his lips before his hot mouth moves back to my breast as his other hand slides to my pussy, slipping between my wet folds. I whimper, grinding against his hand, wanting him so damn much I'm ready to explode.

"Tristan," I whine. Before I can get another word out, his finger sinks deep inside me while his thumb rubs over my clit.

"Oh, fuck." *My head falls back, hitting the shower wall. "Yes. Just like that. Don't stop."*

He releases my breast and drops to his knees. "I need to taste you. I'm fucking starved for your sweet pussy."

My fingers run through his wet hair. "Y-Yesss."

His mouth seals over my clit while his finger pumps in and out. I moan and gyrate my hips against his face, wanting everything he'll give to me.

Grabbing my leg, he throws it over his shoulder. "Ride my face until your juices drip from my chin."

Fuck me. *I immediately comply, the feeling of his tongue deep inside, fucking my pussy, driving me insane.*

When his mouth seals over my clit, my head rolls against the shower wall. He plays my body like a masterful musician. I grind against his face, our rhythm in tandem, pushing me closer to the edge.

"Fuck, Tristan. I'm gonna cum on your face."

He curls his fingers, his tongue flicking over my clit so fast that I explode like a bomb. His name is on my lips as my hand twists in his hair, nails digging into his scalp so hard I'm probably making it bleed.

PULLING my hand from between my legs, I open my eyes, and still as a pair of familiar green eyes stare at me through the glass shower door.

"That was the hottest damn show I've ever seen. Mind if I join in on the fun?" Tristan says as he opens the shower door.

I'm not myself as I peel my back from the wall. "Get in here, hockey god."

As he quickly strips and climbs inside, I whisper, "How the hell are you here?"

"You left the door unlocked. And before you ask, Josh isn't home, and I shut and locked it." He smirks at me, backing me against the shower wall. "After I heard you moaning my name, I couldn't resist—

"Oh my God. I was that loud?"

"I may have pressed my ear to the door and listened." He winks at me. "I'm glad I hurried home after practice to see you."

"You missed me?"

"Of course. You're all I can think about." He lifts me, and I wrap my legs and arms around him, clinging to him like a koala bear in a tree. His hardness presses against my pussy, and I immediately wiggle against him. His answering moan into my mouth sends shivers down my spine. "Damn, kitten. My control is hanging on by a thread."

I grin against his lips. "Good."

He moans again before he grabs my arms from the back of his neck and pins them overhead against the shower wall. He holds my wrists with one hand while the other trails down my body. "You got yourself pretty worked up for me." He hungrily kisses me again, his hand cupping my pussy. "So fucking wet after your orgasm."

I stare at him through lust-filled eyes, a whimper coming from my lips. "I need you, Tristan. I wanna feel you inside me."

"Jesus, kitten." He wraps his hand around his cock, sliding the tip against my clit, making me moan.

"Fuck. I need to grab a condom. They're in my room." He releases my wrists. My hand wraps around his arm as he starts to move away. Tristan stills, staring at me with a question in his eyes as the water pelts his back.

"I have an IUD." A sudden shyness takes me over. "If you're okay with that?"

His eyes widen, flickering with something I've never seen. "I've never done it without a condom."

"Oh. That's good. Very responsible." My nerves are taking over. "If you want to use one, that's—"

He cuts me off. "No. I *don't* wanna use one. Not with you." His hand cups my face. "You're special to me."

Currents of electricity roll through me from the way he's looking at me. Like magnets, our lips gravitate toward the other, crashing together in a kiss that leaves me breathless. We grind against one another, his hard cock feeling amazing against the slickness between my legs.

I break the kiss, staring into Tristan's eyes. Without a word, I reach between us, heat flaring in his mossy irises. The hiss of air when my hand wraps around his cock, stroking the smooth skin, makes me feel sexy and confident. His head falls back, a deep, guttural moan falling from his lips. His neck is so appealing that I lean forward, peppering it with kisses that end at his shoulder.

Pulling back, I stroke him faster, earning a groan. His head lowers, a pleading look in his eyes. "You need to stop before I embarrass myself."

"I can assure you that you won't embarrass yourself with me." With a grin, I guide the tip of his cock to my entrance. I hesitate, fear coiling into my belly because I've never been with a man the size of Tristan.

Tristan chuckles at my words before growing serious. He sees the fear in my eyes. His thumb strokes my cheek. "It's okay, kitten. I won't hurt you. I promise." He intently watches my face as he pushes his hips forward, slowly entering me.

"Holy shit," I pant. "You feel... This feels... Amazing," I finally croak, my nails digging into his shoulder.

"My thoughts exactly." He gives me a heart-stopping smile, making my breath hitch as he keeps sinking until he can't go any further.

"Jesus," I murmur, my forehead falling against his as he remains still, allowing me to adjust to his size. "You're big."

He pulls back slightly, alarmed. "You okay?"

I nod vigorously. "Perfect. Please fuck me."

The huge smile on his face makes my breath hitch. "Be careful what you wish for." Then he pulls out and pushes back inside, his pace steady. We moan in unison before our lips crash together. He keeps steadily thrusting, driving me to the brink of madness.

"You take my cock so well. Like you were made for me."

His words make me feral. "Go faster. Please."

But he doesn't, keeping the same steady pace, irritating me.

"I'm not a fragile piece of China. You—ohhh."

He smirks at me, slamming my back against the wall from his hard thrust. His arm bands around my waist as he pulls out, then does it again, pounding hard and fast inside me.

"Fuck. That feels so fucking good. Don't stop, Tristan." I arch my hips, taking his cock deep. Lust barrels over me as I fuck him back, his powerful thrusts pushing me closer to the edge.

"Is this what you want, kitten? To be fucked hard until you come so hard you see stars." Water beats down on his back, rivulets of sweat trickling down his face, making him look sexier than hell. "No fucking way am I stopping. This pussy is too good." He pounds into me, our skin slapping together.

My head falls against the tile, and my legs begin to shake. "Tristan," I moan, my fingers slipping against his back, seeking purchase but unable to find it.

He squeezes my ass cheek as he continues thrusting. "I know, kitten. Soak my cock with your juices. I wanna feel it."

Shit. His words are a magical elixir that causes me to detonate. I whimper and moan his name as he continues thrusting through my orgasm. He doesn't let up, only slowing his thrusts as I convulse around him, and when I stop trembling, he picks up the pace again.

"I've never felt anything like this before." He swallows hard as we move in unison, our eyes locked together.

"Me either," I whisper.

My thighs tighten around him, and his answering groan makes me feel desirable and powerful. "Jordyn," he rasps, squeezing his eyes closed. "I'm gonna come."

"Yesss..." I tighten around him. "I wanna feel your cum inside me."

"Fuuuucck." His forehead falls against mine as he begins fucking me so hard and fast, I slide up the shower wall. "I'm gonna give it all to you."

A shiver runs through him before he pulls out and thrusts once more, releasing deep inside me. His warm cum fills me, making me moan as I squeeze him, milking every drop from him.

With a groan, he falls against me, his lips against my neck. His heavy body is warm and comforting as our heavy breaths mix with the water spraying from the shower.

Tristan lifts his head, a small smile curling his lips. "I'm not done with you yet."

CHAPTER 14

Jordyn

M y eyes widen even as the pleasure builds inside me. "What?"

"Don't talk. Just feel." His lips crash against mine, preventing me from saying a word.

My heart pounds wildly from the physical sensations of being fucked by him after two orgasms and the connection we share. I know it's wrong. Josh would flip out and throw me out on my ass. But I can't stop these feelings that crash over me like waves.

Tristan pulls back slightly, a smile on his face as his thumb reverently strokes my face. "So fucking beautiful," he grits out, thrusting wildly. My pussy constricts around him, squeezing like a vice. He shivers around me, and I know he's about to come again.

"Give it to me, Tristan. Every drop." My words are the trigger that detonates the bomb. He groans as he spills himself inside me. Watching him lose control of himself sends me over the edge. He reaches between us, rubbing my clit, as I convulse around him before I collapse in his arms.

The water flows over us as our breathing and heart rates

gradually return to normal. Tristan holds me against him, peppering kisses over my neck until he sighs and lowers my feet to the floor. "We better wash up and get out of here. Your skin is like a prune, and mine is getting there." He chuckles, his lips meeting mine.

I nod, kissing him a few more times as I trace the stubble on his chin with my fingers. "Yeah, we better." Reluctantly, I reach for my body wash and mesh sponge.

A loud knock on the door startles me, nearly making me drop it. "Jordyn? Is that you in the shower?"

My wide eyes lock with Tristan. He nods, whispering, "Act normal."

"Yeah, it's me," I yell.

"Have you seen Tristan?"

Wide-eyed, I stare at Tristan in horror, nearly losing my cool. *Oh, shit. Does he suspect he's in here with me?*

Tristan and I share a look as I yell, "No. I've been in the shower. I didn't know he came home."

"Oh, okay. I'll text him to see if he wants anything from the pizza shop."

Tristan's eyes widen as he points toward his sweatpants on the floor. I receive the message loud and clear. If Josh texts Tristan, it will beep, and Josh will hear it and know he's in here with me.

I need to distract Josh. "Wait, what about me? I'm hungry. Why don't you get my order and then text him?"

"Yeah, sure. What do you want?"

Tristan silently opens the shower door, grabs a towel, and wraps it around his waist before exiting. Fishing his phone from his sweatpants, he slides the button, turning the sound off.

Meanwhile, I'm rattling off my order, then changing it again to buy him time. When Tristan gives me a thumbs up, I say, "A ham & cheese sub. That's what I want."

"Sheesh. Okay. Is that your final answer?"

"Yes."

Josh laughs. "Okay. I'm gonna go text Tristan now."

I exhale as his footsteps retreat. I shut the water off, and Tristan hands me a towel and extends his hand to help me out before he dries off.

"How are you gonna get out of here without him seeing?" I hiss, panicked.

"Don't worry." He hurriedly steps into his boxers and sweatpants. "I have a plan." He quickly kisses me, muttering, "Stop worrying," before he opens the bathroom door, peeks out, and slips out, silently closing it behind him.

Stop worrying. Yeah, right. My future hangs in the damn balance because I lust for a hockey player.

CHAPTER 15

Tristan

Slipping my feet in a pair of sneakers, I sneak out the back door. I was able to avoid Josh as I snuck to my room, waiting for him to go to his. Then I slipped down the hallway and outside for a short run to make my lie believable.

Leaning against the siding and out of his view if he'd look out the window, I respond to his text before slipping my phone into the pocket of my sweatpants. I head around the side of the house and jog to the sidewalk, adrenaline pounding through my veins as I run.

Lost in the images of what happened in the shower, I grin like an idiot as I run. But like a black cloud, the doubt creeps in. My ex-girlfriend, Tamara, and I broke up our freshman year of college when the distance and limited time to focus on a relationship pulled us apart.

My mind races with negative thoughts. *What happens when you're drafted? You won't have the time to devote to a relationship, especially if you live in different states. And what about Jordyn's plans after she gets her bachelor's degree? She has two years until she's done, and then what? Does she plan to stay here for her master's or return to New York?*

My heart clenches beneath my ribcage at the thought of giving her up. Although Jordyn and I haven't known each other long, she's already captivated me more than any woman, including my ex-girlfriend. The thought of not being able to kiss, touch, or hold her again causes my stomach to knot.

I don't realize how fast and far I've been running until the agony tightens my chest, and I stop, my hands on my knees. My breaths rasp out of me so fast that I'm lightheaded.

When my vision clears, I straighten, tilting my head to the sky. *Fuck. This is gonna hurt when it ends. And you'll be right back where you started.*

Lowering my head, I take off running again, trying to outrun the grief inside me. It's been manageable lately because I've spent so much time around Jordyn. But she's not here now, and I'm drowning.

When I focus on my surroundings, I realize I'm at the one place I had no intention of going. Dread fills me, my stomach hardening as their tombstones on the hill come into focus. I should turn around, but I can't. It's as though their voices are beckoning me, and I can't resist their call.

Each step draws more air from my lungs as I travel the road leading up the hill and to their gravesites. The emptiness and pain inside my chest make me gasp for oxygen as I stumble toward their graves, sinking to my knees in front of their tombstones. Tears freely flow down my cheeks as the grief pours from my aching heart.

"D-Dad," I rasp through quivering lips, the pieces of my heart breaking again. "I-I miss y-you so fucking m-much." My gaze slides to my mom's name beside his. "M-Mom. I've been trying, b-but..." My hands go through my hair, fisting the short blond strands.

Weakness overwhelms my muscles and bones, and my body crumples to the ground. The grass is cool against my overheated skin, the long shadows from nearby trees blocking the late afternoon sun. Rolling to my side, I curl in the fetal position, tears sliding down my face as my gaze moves to my sister's grave. "Elaine. I'm so s-sorry. Y-You were too y-young."

My hand slides over the cool grass, reaching for them, but they aren't there. They're gone, and I'm here, struggling and alone.

My fingers fist the blades of grass as though I'm clinging to the ground, afraid I'll slide into the abyss. Squeezing my eyes closed, I struggle to breathe through the unrelenting tightness in my chest. Memories roll over me like raging ocean waves, making me dizzy. I close my eyes as the world spins.

When it calms, I open them. Through blurry eyes, I stare at their tombstones, blame, and guilt warring inside me. "I'm so fucking sorry," I sob, my throat aching. "I was so fucking selfish. I'd give anything to go back to that moment..."

My voice cuts off. No one can save me. Nor should they. My selfishness cost me my entire world.

I'm unsure how long I lay there, staring at their graves. Reality sets in, and realization swells over me like a punch to the stomach. *I'm going to drag Jordyn down. I'm nothing but bad luck.*

Climbing to my knees, I stare at my father's grave. "I'll make it up to you, Dad. I'll do whatever it takes to get drafted by the Penguins. I'll continue your legacy and make you proud. I promise you."

The wind blows, and goosebumps pebble across my skin. *It's a sign. I know what I must do.*

"You brought me here. I was confused until you showed me what I must do." My heart twists inside my chest, and I can barely breathe. "I have to end whatever this is with Jordyn. I'll only destroy her and myself."

I stand there a few more minutes, allowing the numbness to take me over. "I love you," I whisper before wiping the tears from my face and the dirt from my skin and clothing. Turning, I square my shoulders and blow out a shaky breath, resolve filling me.

I won't destroy Jordyn like I did my family.

CHAPTER 16

Tristan

I slip through the back door, quietly closing it. When I look up, I meet familiar aqua eyes lined with worry. I'm sinking into their depths, nearly forgetting my promise to my family at the gravesite. When she smiles, doubt rears its head, and a war begins inside my head.

My spine stiffens as I cock a brow at her. "Hey."

"Hey. That's all you have to say to me?" she hisses, hurt and anger on her face. "I texted you, but you didn't answer."

I shrug. "I was busy."

Her eyes narrow as she frowns, glaring at me. She's mad as hell, but I remain stoic, not reacting to it. I'm acutely aware of the weight that lifts from my chest simply from her presence.

Hurt flares in her irises, but I don't crumble. It's best that this ends now before we fall any deeper. "Where's my food?"

Jordyn points to the refrigerator, not saying a word. I turn my back on her so I don't have to hide the ache that permeates every part of me. It's persistent enough that I almost want to break my promise to my family, grab her in my arms, and hold onto her forever.

"Hey, Tristan." Josh's voice comes from behind me,

pulling me from my musings. I look into his bloodshot eyes, frowning as he staggers into the room. "We missed you at the bar tonight."

I grab my sandwich and plaster a fake smile on my lips. "Hey, Josh. How's it going?"

"Great, man." His bloodshot eyes reveal how much he had to drink, and he stumbles as he tries to take a seat on the stool.

Jordyn scowls at him, folding her arms over her busty chest. I take a moment to drink in her cut-off jean shorts and black tee. *Why does she have to look so fucking gorgeous?*

"How much did you drink tonight?" She snaps, clearly out of patience. I can't help but wonder if a part of that is directed at me. But I continue as though I'm unbothered, unwrapping my sandwich and taking a huge bite before setting it on the counter beside me while I watch them.

"Don't you worry about it, lil sis."

"I'm not your sister," she hisses, eyes narrowing. "I'm your *stepsister.*"

He waves his hand. "Semantics." His gaze slides to me before giving me a sloppy grin. "You should've come with us, T. It was a blast. Puck bunnies all over the place. I ended up fucking Janelle in the bathroom."

Jordyn scoffs as she brushes past me on her way to the fridge. She grabs a bottle of water and takes a long drink, bristling at the mention of Janelle's name. Luckily, Josh is busy chattering about the night and doesn't notice.

Images of Jordyn and me in the shower fill my head. As I swallow the bite of the sandwich in my mouth, Jordyn bends over to pick up the napkin she dropped, and her shorts ride up, exposing her ass cheeks.

I choke at the pornographic thoughts inside my head. *How the hell am I going to stay away from her?*

"You okay, Tristan?" Josh leans forward, the stool wobbling precariously. Jordyn looks concerned by my coughing, hurries to the refrigerator, and then hands me a bottle of water. I take it, downing half the bottle before I answer.

"Yeah. Wrong hole," I rasp out.

"Speaking of the wrong hole, you missed out with Janelle. She's a damn good time. I don't know how the hell you couldn't get your dick up with her."

Jordyn nearly spits out her water. I level her with a look before I take another bite of my sandwich, unbothered by missing a shot with Janelle.

Josh is oblivious and continues rambling. "I fucked her pussy and then her ass in the bathroom of the bar. Boy, she loves dick in her ass."

Jordyn rolls her eyes, disgust on her face. "Please, Josh. I just ate. I don't wanna lose my dinner."

My laugh sounds hollow as I lean forward, feigning interest and excitement. "She likes it in the ass, huh?"

Jordyn stiffens, pained aqua eyes latching onto my face, but I pretend to ignore her, even though I'm acutely aware of her every reaction.

This is for your own good, Jordyn.

"Oh, man. She loves it. She was screaming, 'Fuck my ass harder, Josh.' I think the whole damn bar heard her."

Jordyn's eyes narrow. Her voice is full of suspicion when she asks, "How are you allowed in a bar? You're only twenty, just like Tristan and me."

"Kevin, the owner, is a huge hockey fan. As long as we get an Uber to take us home, he'll serve us."

"Does your daddy know?"

Josh glares at her. "No, and he won't find out." A threatening look is on his face as he leans closer to her. "My image stays pristine. Got that?"

His outburst pisses me off, and I'm about to intervene when Jordyn scoffs, unbothered by his threats. "Like I'd tell your asshole father anything. Besides, he'd never believe me if I did."

Josh relaxes and turns back to me. "Anyway, if you ever change your mind, Janelle would be down for it. Hell, she'd probably let us both fuck her." He gives me a sloppy grin. "Have a go at her ass. It's fucking tight."

The stool scrapes the kitchen floor as Jordyn jumps to her feet. "This conversation is disgusting. Janelle has no self-respect, and neither do either of you." She's shaking as she storms past me. "I have homework to do. Don't interrupt." Her eyes simmer with anger, but I see the hurt in them before she turns away.

Josh shakes his head. "She's wound too tightly. You know what she needs? To loosen up and have some fun. Maybe find some nerd to bang."

I grip the water bottle so hard that some shoots out onto the counter and floor. "Uh-huh," I say through clenched teeth. The thought of Jordyn fucking anyone else makes me want to destroy the whole fucking town.

Josh laughs. "Anyway, I'm gonna join the guys for a round of NHL. Wanna play?"

Shoving the rest of the sandwich in my mouth so I don't say something I'll regret, I shake my head. Once I've chewed and swallowed, I speak. "I need to shower and write a paper for English Lit."

Josh shrugs. "Sucks to be you. That's why I chose an easy major, man." He stumbles as he gets up, and I shake my head, irritated as hell by him. "Hey, my nerdy sister is taking that class. You should ask her for help."

Yeah, there's no way she's helping me. But I nod at him so he's not suspicious before I turn toward the stairs.

As I head to my room, the ache inside my chest is nearly unbearable. *This wasn't supposed to be so hard.*

I can't resist looking at her closed door, wondering what she's thinking. She probably hates me now.

It's what's best, my brain argues.

But my heart has doubts.

Grabbing a clean pair of sweatpants, I whirl around and head toward the bathroom, knowing one thing for certain. Jordyn will be on my mind the entire time I shower.

CHAPTER 17

Tristan

I can't concentrate on anything except her.

Shoving away from my desk, I forget about writing my English Lit paper and head to my window. The irony that my thoughts remain with her is humbling and ironic, considering I'm the one who pushed—no, more like shoved her away. The hurt look on her face when I feigned interest in Janelle pierces me like a knife through my heart.

Shoving my hands in my pockets, I stare into the darkness. I have no desire to be with Janelle or any other woman. There's only Jordyn. She's the only one I want.

Am I doing the right thing by pushing her away? I have no idea. But the pain that engulfs me every time I think about that period of my life is enough to make me believe it is.

A few weeks after Tamara and I broke it off, my family was killed, and the heartache was unbearable. I was so miserable I gave up everything. Hell, I almost lost my spot on the team. And I would have if my dad wasn't Christian Harrington, former distinguished alumni of the Wolverines who turned pro-hockey and became the star center for the Pittsburgh Penguins.

The air in my room is stifling as regret wars with doubt. *I can't breathe.*

I quietly exit my bedroom and slip downstairs, then through the back door. My bare feet cross the deck until I reach the railing, gripping it until my knuckles hurt as I suck in giant gulps of air.

Breathe, Tristan. Look at the stars in the sky. Which is the brightest?

Focusing on the night sky calms me. My breathing evens out as I stand there, basking in the cover of darkness. For once, I can be myself and not have to hide behind the public persona I've created to survive. Others see a high-achieving student, star center, and team captain of the Wolverines. The only son of a legend.

On the surface, I appear to be all those things. Inwardly, I'm a broken mess of fragmented pieces. A shell of who I once was.

My life is divided into two periods: pre-death and post-death. Before their deaths, I was a happy-go-lucky guy who thought he had the world at his feet. And post-death, I became a broken man who lost everything. Someone who knows how easily love can be ripped away from you. One moment to snuff out the flames and leave behind charred ashes.

A faint voice pulls me from my thoughts, and I immediately back against the side of the house, becoming one with the shadows.

Jordyn's melodic voice floats through my ears, and all the pressure in my chest eases. Her tone is low, her phone pressed to her ear as the light from inside the house illuminates her like an apparition.

"I feel like a fucking idiot, Chelsea. What the hell was I thinking? I don't make rash decisions like that." She pauses, listening to whatever Chelsea is saying, before she continues pacing. Her voice is exasperated. "Yes, we had sex in the shower. That's not the point of the story."

She's quiet again before her gaze darts to the house. "I was foolish. We didn't use a condom. He... I... Well, I told him I had an IUD."

My shoulders are by my ears. *Oh, shit. If she lied, I need to get her the morning-after pill ASAP.*

"I know the IUD is effective. I'm not worried about pregnancy," she snaps, pinching the bridge of her nose. "I slept with the hockey player who was fucking a puck bunny when I arrived. I probably have ten different STDs because I'm stupid and fell for the bullshit story that he hasn't been with anyone in a year."

It isn't bullshit. My hands curl into fists, hating that she doubts me now. I understand why, but I fed her a false narrative to get her to distance herself from me.

She shakes her head, a brittle laugh coming from her. "Yeah, right. I mean, I know he didn't finish with Janelle, and yeah, he wore a condom with her, but how many others..." Her voice breaks. "I can't do this." Her shoulders slump, and I hate that when she lifts her face, the light reveals silvery tears glistening on her cheeks.

Wiping her cheeks, she exhales a long breath. "Making matters worse, I have to go to their stupid hockey game on Saturday. Mom called me earlier and Robert is insisting we get there early to support Josh."

She bites her lip, pacing back and forth. When she speaks again, her voice is a soft plea. "Can you come with me to the game?"

More silence ensues before her face lights up. "Tomorrow is amazing. But I have a class and then work."

She's quiet, driving me crazy as I wonder what her friend is saying. When she finally speaks, her words cut like a knife.

"Yeah, there's a health center on campus. I'll get tested, and then we can hang out."

Irritation causes my hands to curl into fists. I *don't* have an STD. I barely fucked Janelle, and I used a condom. After Tamara and I broke up, I had one brief fling where I used protection, but it was apparent she wanted a relationship, and there was no way I could do that. I broke it off, went to the health center, and got tested. I received a clean bill of health and have been celibate until Janelle and Jordyn.

The sadness in her voice pulls me from my thoughts. "I'm such a fucking idiot." Her chin and lips wobble before tears slide down her cheeks again. "I thought Tristan really liked me, Chelsea. He said I was special, and I believed him. He probably says that to everyone..." She clamps a hand over her mouth, unable to continue.

My heart twists and shatters into pieces inside my chest as I watch her. *You are special. I never considered coming inside a woman without protection until you.*

"I know. You're right. It's just... I haven't been told I'm special by any man since my dad died. And the way he said it, he seemed so sincere."

Fuck. My mouth is hanging open as I stare at her. *Her dad is dead?* Josh never mentioned that. *What happened to him? When did he die?*

But I can't ask her those questions. *I have no right. No claim over her...* My limbs shake, and it spreads until my entire body is vibrating. *I want to claim her. Hell, I'm fucking desperate for her to be mine, despite the promise I made.*

I feel like shit as she quietly cries. "I know, Chelsea. Since my dad died, I've built walls around myself, keeping others out. As soon as I found a man I thought was different, I let them down. Now I'm hurting while he's probably in his room, thinking about banging that slut Janelle in the ass." The humiliation and hurt roll off her in waves that wash over me, making me feel like utter shit.

God, I'm a fucking asshole. I never wanted to hurt her.

"I know, Chelsea. I just... Well, it doesn't matter how foolish and used I feel." She heaves out a long sigh. "I need to change the subject. This is too much." Taking a deep breath, she blows it out. "Has anything strange been happening there? Any more details about Lucas? Is he still in the facility?"

She's quiet, her brows furrowed as she paces a few feet from me. "I'm glad you're coming here tomorrow. I'll feel better when I see you." She turns and heads to the door, so close to me. I remain perfectly still, holding my breath as she says, "Love you, too."

She ends the call and heads inside without noticing me.

Exhaling a long, mournful sigh, the sad reality isn't lost on me. Once again, I'm alone in the darkness with my despair.

Sweat runs in rivulets down my chest as I bolt upright in my bed, my chest heaving. My wild eyes search the room, reality sinking in. *It was only a nightmare.*

The haunting images of my parents and sister's charred bodies dissipate. Only this time, Jordyn was with them. The haunted look in her eyes before the flames engulfed—

No! I cut the thought off and swung my legs over the side of the bed.

Running a hand through my hair, I pace the floor, trying to forget the horrific dream that makes me wish I could climb out of my own damn skin.

My breathing is ragged, and my pulse pounds in my ears. I grab a bottle of water from the mini fridge in my room, slurping it down before I toss the empty plastic bottle in the trash. I feel marginally better.

Exiting my bedroom to use the restroom and splash water on my face, I stop and stare at her closed door. I tiptoe to it, pressing my ear against the wood. I listen for a few beats before turning the handle and opening the door.

I need to make sure she's okay.

Stepping inside her room, I quietly close the door behind me. I reach the foot of her bed, staring down at her. The moonlight filtering through her window gives her a silvery glow, making her appear otherworldly. She's curled on her side, long lashes resting on her flushed cheek. She steadily breathes in and out, and I breathe with her, feeling my chest fully expand and contract from being near her.

She's a fucking angel. I don't deserve her.

Although there is so much to learn about her, tonight, I learned we have more in common than I imagined when I overheard her mention her dad's death. It makes me long to ask her questions I have no right asking, desperately seeking a connection to someone who understands what losing a parent feels like, especially when you're supposed to be in the prime of your life.

Sadness infiltrates me as I study her tear-stained cheeks. *I did that.* I inflicted pain on this beautiful woman, and she has no idea why. She believes I'm a pucking male slut rather than a twenty-year-old man terrified of love.

It pains me to be so close and unable to touch her, but I suspect she'll raise hell if she wakes and finds me in her room after what happened earlier. Yet, I'm so relieved she's okay, her steady breathing bringing me a peace I haven't known since my family died, that I stand there like an idiot, feet glued to the floor.

I should leave.

Turning my head to try and get the courage to go, my gaze lands on a picture and a Strawberry Shortcake doll behind it on her bookshelf.

I move toward it, a smile curling my lips. As I lift the picture frame, I see a younger Jordyn wrapped in a man's arms. They are laughing, and she clings to the doll on her lap.

Sadness engulfs me. Strawberry Shortcake was my sister's favorite, too.

I grab the doll before setting the picture frame back where I found it. My finger traces over the adorable ragdoll with red hair and big green eyes, a permanent smile stitched onto her face. Memories of my sister with her doll fill my head.

My finger brushes over something on the back of her dress, and I spin the doll around. A tiny note is pinned to her back.

Jordyn,

You'll always be my strawberry shortcake. Hug her whenever you're hurting, and know that I'm hugging you back, even though you can't feel or see me. I live inside your heart.

Love Always,

Dad

I look over at Jordyn's sleeping form, my heart squeezing painfully inside my chest. I want to gather her in my arms and hold her tightly. To ease her pain.

But I can't.

Still holding the doll, I sit on the chair by her desk. My past and present collide as the pain grips me. I'd be in agony if I weren't sitting in her bedroom.

Sighing, my gaze slides to her. I watch her chest's steady rise and fall, my breathing syncing with hers.

You're being selfish. If you care about her, you'll walk away. Why is walking away easier said than done?

CHAPTER 18

Jordyn

I stare in disbelief at Tristan's body, slumped in my desk chair, fast asleep. I close my eyes, counting to ten while rubbing them again. But when I open them, he's still there.

Why the hell is he here? Did he watch me sleep all night?

It's barely daylight, and I have no earthly idea what woke me, but here I am, wide awake at the ass crack of dawn on a Friday morning with a fucking puck boy slumped in my desk chair, fast asleep.

Tossing the covers back, I get to my feet and stomp over to him. When I see my Strawberry Shortcake doll clutched in his hands, something inside me snaps. It was a present from my dad on my fifteenth birthday.

I loved and cherished that doll as a child. When we moved into a smaller house closer to the hospital, she was lost in the move. I was devastated. Strawberry Shortcake symbolized some of the best memories of my childhood, and I clung to that doll for strength and comfort. Witnessing my dad so sick and frail from battling an aggressive form of cancer were some of the darkest days of my life.

Then she was lost, and I couldn't breathe.

When I opened my gift from my dad on my fifteenth birthday and pulled the doll from the box, dread settled into my heart. When I met his exhausted, distraught eyes, I knew we were on borrowed time, especially when I saw the note he'd pinned to the back of her dress.

He died two days later.

Tristan is holding my world in his arms, and considering the way he acted and the things he said yesterday, it infuriates me. He doesn't deserve to hold the doll who means everything to me. And he doesn't deserve me, either.

He's a puck boy who fooled me into believing he was different. Just like my ex-boyfriend, Joey, who broke my fucking heart when he lied to me.

I glare at Tristan, clenching my fists. I refuse to be anyone's dirty little secret again. I'm not a plaything he can just use and toss aside.

Leaning beside Tristan's ear, all the wrath I'm feeling rolls out of my lips like a thundercloud. "What the fuck are you doing in my room, holding my doll?" I scream.

Green eyes fly open. He blinks at me, disoriented and confused. Realization slowly dawns on his face when he straightens in the chair, shame etched onto it.

"Tristan," I snap, out of patience. "Put the doll on my desk and get the fuck outta my room."

His brows draw in as he looks at the doll, then at me. "I didn't mean to fall asleep in here. I had to see if you were okay and—"

A brittle laugh rolls out of me as I cross my arms over my chest. "You're pretending to care about me. That's rich, especially after last night."

He blows out a breath, lifting his hand and running it through his hair. I hate that my body heats as his bicep ripples, and I have to force my eyes away. "I know it sounds bad, but—"

"Sounds bad?" A bitter taste is in my mouth from the venom spewing from my tongue. Leaning over him so I don't wake Josh, I hiss, "You fucked me in the shower, then disappeared and ghosted me. When you returned, you acted like an asshole and seemed interested in fucking that slut, Janelle." Rage makes my hands shake. "Get your ass up and march it the fuck out of my room. You aren't welcome in here ever again."

He stares at me, not saying a word. It infuriates me.

I grab the Strawberry Shortcake doll, but he refuses to let go of her. Anger burns in his eyes, but mine is more potent right now. It's laced with the bitter sting of broken trust and betrayal.

"Just let me explain," Tristan says through clenched teeth.

"No. I'm not listening to any more of your lies. Let go of my doll, dammit."

"I need you to listen—"

"I don't *need* to do anything, jackass." My chest heaves as the words spill out of me, laced with the bitter sting of betrayal. "I gave you a piece of me in the shower, and you know damn well what I'm talking about." My mouth is as dry as cotton, and I choke out, "I foolishly believed you when you said I was special and..."

His grip on the doll loosens as pain contorts his face. I snatch her away, clinging to the one thing that's always been there for me. She represents the one thing I desperately want but can't have right now—a hug from my father.

"*Get out*, Tristan, and don't come back." I whip around, turning my back to him as I carry my doll to the window and stare blankly at the yard, trying to keep my trembling body from breaking right in front of him. He's stolen enough from me. He doesn't get to see me break.

I hear his footsteps moving to the door. His voice is low and full of regret. "I'm sorry, Jordyn. I... I d-didn't mean for things to turn out like this."

I don't turn around. The thought of looking at him sickens me.

Gathering my strength, I spit out words I don't mean. "Go fuck Janelle in the ass, Tristan."

When the door closes behind him, I break, sobbing into my doll's hair as I slump to the floor.

CHAPTER 19

Jordyn

Chelsea's long, brown hair gleams beneath the sun and her legs look impossibly long in the short skirt she's wearing as she climbs out of her vehicle. Pushing her sunglasses on top of her head, blue eyes assess me intently before a warm smile breaks over her face.

I'm already running toward my best friend before she opens her arms.

Crashing into her, I sob, all the agony bursting out of me like a broken dam.

Chelsea hugs me tightly, rocking me like she's comforting a child. "Good God, Jordyn, do I need to commit fucking murder? Just say the word, and I'll cut off Tristan's cock and balls and deliver it to you on a silver platter." She pulls back slightly, a glimmer in her eyes. "Then we'll light 'em on fire and watch 'em burn."

A laugh bursts out of me as I wipe my eyes. "I can always count on you to make me feel better."

"I'll kill anyone who hurts you. Then I'll love all your broken pieces back together. That's my promise as your bestie." She steps back, holding up her pinkie. I wrap mine around hers, the bond between us as strong as ever. "I know something happened after we talked. You look fucking miserable."

I sigh. "I am miserable. I'm blowing off class today. Let's go to the clinic, and I'll explain what happened."

Chelsea holds up her keys. "I'm driving. You're too upset." Her red lips curl into a wide smile. "Plus, when I run over that bastard, it'll be my car that sustains damage instead of yours."

"No arguments there. I learned my lesson." After fastening my seatbelt, I grin at her. "Remember the last time I drove when I was upset? I knocked over the drive-thru speaker at McDonald's and almost ran over the guy putting air in my tires."

Chelsea laughs loudly as she starts her car. Checking her mirrors, she puts her car in reverse. "Of course I do. That dude throwing the hose in the air and running was funnier than hell."

"God, we almost pissed ourselves from laughing so hard."

"Good times, girl." She looks over at me. "There will be more of them now that I'm here. I'll be damned if I'm gonna let some puck boy bring my bestie down." She lowers her sunglasses as she drives toward campus. "Not on my watch."

～

FIFTEEN MINUTES LATER, Chelsea and I walk across campus toward the clinic. Her long brunette locks tumble around her shoulders as she shakes her head. "I don't get why he was in your room."

"Neither do I. It was so—" My voice cuts off as my eyes lock with a pair of sad, mossy ones. I freeze, anger and hurt rolling inside me as I stare him down.

Chelsea looks back and forth between us, then shoves her

sunglasses on top of her head, marching toward him like a one-woman army.

Oh, this won't end well. Tristan better duck and cover.

"Yo, ass wipe." She stops right in front of him, ignoring Alex, who stares at her in awed fascination. "Jordyn told me what happened."

"Chelsea, don't. He's not worth it."

I feel Tristan's eyes boring into me, but I ignore him, focusing on Chelsea. But there's no way to talk her down now. He hurt me, so she's going for the jugular.

She snaps her fingers. "Eyes on me, jackass. You don't deserve to look at her."

Alex snorts, turning his head away. His shoulders shake with silent laughter as Chelsea glares at him before turning the full force of her anger at Tristan. "You fucked up. You'll be damn lucky if you're not talking in permanent soprano when I'm through with you."

Tristan's eyes drop to her, and he blinks like he's struggling to process her words.

Chelsea folds her arms over her chest, flipping a lock of dark hair over her shoulder. "It'll be hard to get drafted by the NHL if every time you open your mouth, you chirp like a damn canary because I fucking ripped your dick and balls off and set them on fire."

Alex groans, cupping his private area in the middle of campus. "Jesus. Dark angel is fierce as fuck. Why the hell is that so damn hot?"

I grip Chelsea's arm to pull her away, but she's already set her sights on Alex. "Listen, hockey boy. You may be hotter than hell, and normally, I'd wanna ride you like a bull in a rodeo. But your friend ruined that when he fucked with my bestie."

The smile dies on Alex's face. He turns his head, shooting Tristan a murderous glare.

Chelsea doesn't miss it. "You look awfully pissed, hockey boy. Maybe you'll rip his dick and balls off before I get the chance." She shrugs. "Have at it. But give 'em to me when you're done so Jordyn and I can burn them."

I'm shocked at the dark look on Alex's face. He steps forward, his eyes roaming down Chelsea's body, then back to her face. He smirks before he crosses his arms over his chest. "Don't flatter yourself, sweetheart. I have a long list of women wishing they could fuck me, and you're at the end of that long line, aging while you wait."

Before Chelsea can say a word, Alex turns his attention to me. "There's a lot of shit you don't know, Jordyn. I know you're hurting, and trust me, I'm pissed at Tristan. I gave him hell for it." He lowers his voice, but his words are like darts shooting into my heart. "For the record, he's not a puck boy. But he is a broken man."

My gaze moves to Tristan's face. Even though I see the pain in his eyes, the way he acted after we had sex in the shower hurt.

Stepping into Tristan's space, I unleash my pain, hoping it cuts him to the bone. "Instead of running away and doing God only knows what after our shower, you should've talked to me. When you returned, you acted like a complete ass." Tears sting my bloodshot eyes. "You really fucked up."

Tristan swallows hard, his Adam's Apple bobbing. "You're right. I really fucked up. I should've talked to you, especially after I visited..." He stops, shame coloring his cheeks as his eyes drop to his feet. "I regret my actions after our shower. I was really fucked in the head and—"

I hold up my hand. "I'm not interested in hearing it now, Tristan. It's too late."

The pain on his face nearly takes my breath away. But my self-preservation kicks in. *I can't look at him anymore. I'll cave*

*and get my heart trampled. It'll be the Joey situation all over
again.*

Hitching my purse higher on my shoulder, I straighten my
spine. "Puck right off, asshole."

I grab Chelsea's arm and start moving away, but the accusation in Tristan's voice stops me. "Are you going to the
clinic?"

How the hell did he know that? I slowly turn around, one
brow raised questionably. "Why does it matter if I am?"

He crosses his arm over his chest, glaring at me. "I hope
you didn't lie about being on birth control."

My patience snaps. Releasing Chelsea's arm, I march over
to Tristan, not stopping until we're toe to toe. "I didn't lie
about that. I'm getting tested to make sure you didn't give me
any diseases."

The muscle in Tristan's jaw ticks as he stares at me
contemptuously. "I don't have any fucking diseases."

"Yeah, well, I believed you when you said I was special, and
you obviously lied about that, so...."

Tristan snorts. "I believed you when you said you have an
IUD. Was that a lie so I'd get you pregnant and you could
trap me?"

My mouth drops open. His words stung. "If I didn't have
an IUD and remotely thought that was possible, I'd have
already gotten the morning-after pill." I glare at him. "I do
have an IUD. But you believe whatever you want. I'm not the
liar here."

Tristan's voice is hollow. "I don't have any diseases,
Jordyn. But go get tested. See for yourself." His gaze moves to
Alex. "Come on. Let's go."

As Alex walks past Chelsea, he winks at her and whispers,
"You're feisty as fuck. I like that."

She stares at him for a long moment, her expression giving

away her lust. When she feels my gaze, she straightens her spine. "Puck off, asshole."

A cocky grin spreads over his face. "You can puck me anytime. Are you free tonight?"

I tune their banter out, my eyes locking with the man I didn't want to fall for. It's painfully clear to me that I've done the one thing I never thought I would—fallen for a jock.

Tristan stares back at me, his face stony. I can't read him. Maybe I never could.

Grabbing Alex's arm, Tristan gives me one long lingering look before he turns and walks away.

Despite the sun beating on my skin, I shiver, crossing my arms over my chest. The last time I felt this cold and empty was when my dad died.

CHAPTER 20

Tristan

I hoped that I'd have a chance to talk to Jordyn in English Lit, but she failed to show, which fucked me up in the worst way. I obsessively worried she changed to the 1:00 p.m. section Martin teaches, which conflicts with another class I'm enrolled in.

Alex rolled his eyes when he saw me logging into her schedule, repeatedly refreshing my screen throughout the class to ensure she hadn't dropped it and switched to the other section.

I couldn't focus on anything, and I could barely eat.

When I skated onto the ice for the final practice before the first game of the season, my mood and concentration were shot. I'd be lucky if Coach Jenson didn't bench me at tomorrow night's game.

Coach Jensen blows his whistle. "Harrington. In my office. The rest of you hit the showers." He gives me a long look before he spins on his heels and exits the rink.

Alex skates over to me, ice shavings flying when he stops beside me. "It's cool. Don't get anxious. Coach probably just wants to go over last-minute stuff for tomorrow's game." His

106

tone is unconvincing, as is the look on his face, but I don't call him out on it.

"Yeah, sure." My tone drips with sarcasm. "Probably a pep talk." I roll my eyes, heading toward the locker room and Coach Jensen's office.

"Chin up, captain. Coach is a fair man." Alex is looking at me with too much sympathy in his eyes for me to believe what he's saying.

"I know." *But his patience with me may have run out after that shitty practice.* "I'll see you later." With apprehension tingling inside my chest, I turn in the direction of Coach Jensen's office, bracing myself for a verbal lashing.

I hesitate in the doorway, gauging Coach's mood as his fingers move across his keyboard. He looks up, gray eyes meeting mine. "Ah, Harrington. Come in and shut the door."

There's a huge lump in my throat as my mind frantically races, but I have no good excuse to give him for my distraction but the truth. I brace myself for the disappointment I'll see when I tell him I can't get my head right because of a woman.

Coach gestures toward a chair, and I slide into it. I squirm in the chair, anxiety racing through my veins.

His intense gaze is on me as he leans back in his chair. "I couldn't help but notice you were struggling during practice." He leans forward, folding his hands on his desk. "It concerns me."

Swallowing hard, I open my mouth, then shut it. I really admire Coach Jensen, and in the two years we've worked together, he's really improved my game. My respect for him increased tenfold when he was supportive after my parents and sister's deaths. If not for him, I would've given up hockey. Hell, I would've given up on life.

The silence stretches between us as he waits me out. My heart bangs like a drum as I search my non-functioning brain for something to say to excuse my behavior during practice. But I've got nothing.

Finally, I say, "I'm fine, Coach. Just some personal stuff. I won't let you down tomorrow night." My leg bounces uncontrollably.

He stares at me, saying nothing.

"I'm just having an off day. I'll be fully focused when we play the Bears tomorrow night." Forcing a weak smile on my face, I give him a salute. "Scout's honor."

Coach Jensen doesn't even crack a smile. My anxiety doubles as I glance at the clock. *I need out of here before I pass out.*

"Harrington." Coach leans forward. "I'm gonna be frank. I already know your distraction has nothing to do with hockey. Before practice today, you've been focused as hell, playing better than ever."

His words sink into my brain. The truth slaps me in the face. The reason I've been focused and played better than ever was because of Jordyn. She renewed my passion for hockey and improved my life.

And I threw it all away.

I'm pulled from my thoughts by Coach's stern voice. "I don't talk about personal stuff with you guys, but in your case, I will make an exception."

Oh shit. This is gonna be bad.

CHAPTER 21

Tristan

Coach drums his fingers on the desk, then heaves out a long sigh. "I focused solely on the game when I first started playing college hockey. I firmly believed women and relationships were a distraction that would ruin any chance I had of playing professional hockey. I had flings, of course..." The side of his lip pulls up in a smirk. Coach is good-looking for his age, so I can only imagine how wild the women went over him when he was in college.

He grows serious, his eyes distant. "I was wrong."

I lean forward in my chair, shocked by his words.

He runs a hand through his hair, his distress evident. "I met Kacie during my freshman year of college. She hit me with a door when she was exiting Stevenson. Her face turned bright red, and she apologized profusely."

Clearing his throat, he says, "There was something about her. I was hooked. She was like a drug, and I couldn't stop thinking about her. But our worlds moved in different directions. Until I started struggling in psychology."

My hands twist together, anticipation thrumming through me, wanting to know more.

"I was doing great in all my classes except that one. I went to the professor's office hours and felt more lost than ever. It was too late to drop the course, and I was too stubborn to withdraw since that felt like giving up. The professor suggested I go to the Learning Center. Guess who ended up tutoring me?"

"Kacie."

He nods. "Not only did she break the course material down in ways I could understand, but I earned an A by the end of the semester. Although I thought Kacie and I were complete opposites, we were the same in everything that matters—values, views, and morals."

I blink, his story oddly like Jordyn and me. We are opposites, but we share similar values and morals.

Coach takes a deep breath and slowly exhales, shifting in his chair. "I was infatuated with Kacie the day she hit me with the door. I fell in love with her during our tutoring sessions. She tried to resist me since I was a jock...."

A laugh bursts out of me. *Sounds familiar.*

But the smile dies off my face, a wave of fear coursing through me. I lean forward in my chair, desperate for the answer to the burning question inside me. "Did she fall in love with you?"

A wide smile splits his face, which is all the answer I need. "We were engaged by summer and married over winter break." His face fades, and the grief that transforms his face is like looking in a mirror. His voice is hollow, his gray eyes full of heartache as I stare at a man as broken as me.

"Seventeen amazing years together before Kacie passed away from cancer." He rubbed his hands together, the wedding ring on his finger gleaming beneath his office lights. "She was the love of my life... I've been alone ever since."

Ouch.

I close my eyes. And there it is. All good things come to an end.

"I know you've been through your share of loss."

My eyes snap open. I'm barely breathing as I wait for him to finish.

"If you asked me if I'd do it all over again, knowing the outcome, I wouldn't hesitate for one second to say yes. And I'd mean every goddamn word. I'd go through her illness and death all over again to hold her in my arms."

While my heart breaks for him, the confusion churning in my stomach baffles me. "You mean the whole better to have loved and lost...."

He chuckles. "Kinda."

His fingers drum over the wooden desk as he gathers his thoughts. "What I mean is love is worth it. Life isn't worth living without love, Tristan. Does it hurt when you lose it? Of course, it fucking does. When you love someone so much, and death steals them from you, it can make you so bitter that it sucks all the joy from the world, making it a terrible place to live. Sometimes, you consider the possibilities of ending things just so you can join them."

I suck in a breath. It all makes sense now. Coach so easily understood my grief and loss because he'd been through something similar. He was instrumental in helping me, sometimes dragging me into the land of the living again when all I wanted to do was give up.

"I went through a terrible depression after Kacie died. My dad and sister nagged at me to see a doctor because they were so worried about me. The doctor prescribed pills for it." He bows his head in shame. "I ended up drinking while taking the pills, although I wasn't supposed to, and nearly died."

My palms are sweaty, and my heartbeat is sluggish. I understand that feeling all too well. Had my grandma not intervened, I may have wound up dead the night I got drunk off my ass and tried to ride my dad's motorcycle.

"We're kindred souls, Tristan. It's why I kept reaching out to you after your family died. Why I refused to let you give up. I had people who cared about me, and they were there, pushing me when I needed them to, refusing to give up on me. I did the same for you."

I'm an emotional mess as I nod, too choked up to speak.

"I'm not benching you, Tristan. Get that thought out of your head. This isn't about that." He smiles. "I saw you near the clinic, arguing with a very pretty blonde. The tension and electricity between you reminded me of Kacie and me."

"Yeah and look what happened. I played like shit today. I couldn't focus."

"That happens when you love someone."

My head snaps up, and my movements still. "I-I'm not in l-love, coach. Jordyn and I... well, it's complicated. We're roommates, and her stepbrother is my teammate."

Coach frowns. "Who's her stepbrother?"

"Josh Fowler."

Coach raises his brows. "That surprises me. The two of them seem like complete opposites."

"They are. There's a lot of tension between them. But her stepfather cut her education funding, and she didn't have a lot of options."

"Ah, I see. You have a beautiful, forbidden roommate living with you." He gives me a knowing look. "She seemed pretty into you, too."

I raise my brows. "We're opposites."

Coach leans back in his chair, a shit-eating grin on his face. "Opposites attract."

"Yeah, well, I haven't exactly put my best foot forward. First, she caught me with another girl—"

"She saw you with someone else?"

I squirm in my chair at the look on his face. "Well, um... yeah. It was stupid. Josh told me to fuck the pain away since it's near the anniversary..." My voice shakes, and I swallow hard before forcing the words out.

"The anniversary of your parents and sister's death," He finishes. "It takes a while to say it without breaking down, Tristan. Three years for me."

I do the math. "You're thirty-nine?" I'm shocked. He sure as hell doesn't look thirty-nine. He could easily pass for much younger.

He chuckles. "You seem surprised."

"Sorry. It's just... You don't look it."

"I'll take that as a compliment." He shoots me a wink, then leans back, crossing his hands over his stomach. "Tristan, we're a lot alike. And our life experiences are similar. You see, I didn't believe in love at first sight. I thought that a relationship would destroy my hockey career. Course, that didn't keep me from having flings, so please don't think I'm judging you. I can't help but laugh at the image of you and Jordyn meeting like that."

I snort. "Most embarrassing moment of my life. I hadn't been with anyone in a long time. Of course, she was skeptical. Alex and I convinced her otherwise... Until I fucked up."

Coach arches a brow. "What did you do? Sleep with another woman?"

"God, no." I shudder at the thought. "I nearly got caught in the shower with her. By Josh."

Coach laughs, shaking his head. "Sorry. I've been there. The fear of getting caught heightens the experience."

"It should've." Slumping in the chair, I sigh. "I went for a run afterward. The fear of my relationship with my high school sweetheart dissolving started creeping into my head while I aimlessly ran. When I looked up, I realized I was near the cemetery."

"Lemme guess? You ran up there, broke down, and vowed to focus solely on hockey?"

"Am I that obvious?"

"Yes, but only because I did the same thing. After Kacie and I had a big fight, I visited my mom's grave and vowed to end things with her and focus solely on hockey."

I lean forward, my interest piqued. "What happened?"

"I was fucking miserable. My game sucked. I fought with the guy on the opposite team who'd been flirting with her while she sat in the stands. Got benched for two games by my coach, who wasn't nearly as cool and understanding as me." He gives me a smirk and laughs.

"It was my dad who set me straight. He could tell I was nuts about Kacie. And yeah, I barely knew her, Tristan. But she was different. It was like my heart and soul instantly knew she was the one. Once we made up and got back together, I played better than ever. Seeing her in the stands, cheering me on... She's the reason I was drafted."

His words sink in. "But when you fought... Or things went wrong in your relationship...."

"Tristan, things are going to go wrong in life. Hell, you could get the flu and play like shit because of it. But I knew, no matter what, I had someone who loved me, whether I played hockey or not. It was the same for your parents. They fell in love at first sight, and both went on to marry, have kids, and juggle demanding careers."

I nod. "Yeah, I remember them talking about how complicated things were."

Coach grins, leaning forward. "Describe your family in one word."

I don't hesitate. "Love."

"They supported one another. When your mom got injured and couldn't skate anymore, your dad convinced her to teach, right?"

I nod. "Yeah. Mom said she wouldn't have done it if not for Dad."

"And until your dad retired, didn't your mom attend every one of his games?"

"Yes. We went to every game. My grandma would often come along in case she needed to take me and Elaine back to the hotel so Mom could remain at his game."

"Exactly. They supported one another. I had the pleasure of meeting the two of them. They were amazing people with an incredible love that reminded me of what I had with my wife..."

"What are you saying, Coach?"

"Love is always worth the risk."

CHAPTER 22

Jordyn

C helsea looks around as we step inside Sinful Sirens. "Nice facility, although not nearly as posh as the one in New York."

"It's not sleazy, which is what matters to me. Ray Carbaugh, the owner, is amazing. Wait until you meet Gary. He's my favorite security guard. He doesn't tolerate any bull-shit, but he's as sweet as pie to the dancers."

Chelsea gives me a sad smile. "I'm sorry you have to do this. Your stepfather is such an asshole. I'm gonna hit him in the nuts and make it seem like an accident when I see him at the game tomorrow."

"I won't stop you." I hitch the bag on my shoulder higher. "Come on. I have Ray's permission for you to be backstage with me. Gary will stay with you while I dance."

"If Josh or your stepfather knew you were doing this, they'd shit."

I roll my eyes. "They're the reason I'm doing this. But it must remain a secret. I can't get kicked out of Tristan and Josh's house. I'm not paying rent."

"Like I'd ever tell those assholes anything." Chelsea levels me with a look when I stop in front of the door. "Does Tristan know you dance here?"

"Hell, no. Why?"

A huge smile lights up her face. "Even though he's an ass, I'd love to see his face. He'd be so fucking pissed."

My heart accelerates at the thought before I mentally scold myself. "I don't care what that asshole thinks." Yanking the door open, I stomp inside, angry at myself because I'm lying.

"Yeah, I see that," Chelsea mutters.

I don't say another word as I throw my bag down. "Will you do my hair and makeup?"

"Of course." She's already rummaging through my bag, pulling out my makeup and curling iron. Envy flows through me as I watch her. I wish I could be that excited about something. I'm hoping the fake smile on my face hides my misery.

"What do you know about Alex?" Chelsea's attempt at casual is about as subtle as a bulldozer. I smirk as I take off my street clothes, watching as she pretends to focus all her attention on my makeup palette.

"He seems nice. Hasn't made any comments about ass fucking anyone."

Chelsea jerks her head up. "As mad as I am that Tristan hurt you, saying and doing are two different things, sweetie. Could there be another reason he said that?"

My brows draw in. "What happened to wanting to rip his cock and balls off?"

She levels me with a look. "That was before you said he went for a run, and when he returned, he had dirt on his face and grass stains on his sweatpants. You also said his eyes were bloodshot."

I shrug. "Yeah, that's true."

"You assumed he was doing something awful, like fighting or fucking someone. But could it be something else?"

Scooping up my clothing from the bag, I begin dressing for tonight's performance. "Like what?"

"I don't know. But he wasn't acting like a puck boy when the two of you were fighting in front of the clinic. He looked more like a broken-hearted man."

"Chelsea." My heart squeezes inside my chest. "I don't wanna think about this right now."

"Okay, I'll drop it." She plugs in the curling iron before turning to me. "But maybe you should give him a chance to explain."

For a minute, I nearly cave. But then I picture the arrogant smirk on his face when he was talking to Josh and the conversation about Janelle, the puck slut. "No, he doesn't deserve it. The first impression I had of him was correct. I just need to avoid him as much as possible until I can save up enough money to move out."

Chelsea nods. "I support whatever you wanna do, love. You know that."

I finish dressing, then walk over to her and give her a hug. "Thanks. I know you do."

I CHANGE BACK into my street clothes but don't bother removing my makeup. I just want to go home.

The drive seems to take forever. Relief fills me when Chelsea finally pulls up to the house. This has been a long, exhausting day, and I'm ready for bed.

"You really don't mind me sleeping with you? I can sleep on the couch or floor. I really don't mind." Chelsea says as she steps beside me on the sidewalk in front of the house. The lights are on, indicating someone is home.

"Of course, I don't mind." I picture Tristan slumped in

my desk chair asleep when I woke up this morning. I'm not ready for a repeat performance of that incident.

Waving my hand, I change the subject. "Finish telling me about Dr. Grayson. Was he really having an affair with a student?" As I step onto the front porch, I crash straight into a hard chest. Strong arms grip me as I stumble, but he steadies me.

"Tristan." His name leaves my lips as a breathy whisper, making me hate myself.

"Where the hell have you been all day? And why haven't you responded to my texts or calls?"

"Oh, so that's why you turned the volume of your phone off," Chelsea says from behind us. "Is Josh home?"

"No, he's at a party. I told the asshole we have a game tomorrow and that he shouldn't go, but he doesn't fucking listen." Beneath the porch light, Tristan's angry green eyes turn to me. "I've been worried about you."

"Tristan, what the—" Alex stands in the doorway, a frown on his face as he takes in the scene before him. "Jesus Christ. I went to the fucking bathroom, and you disappear." His gaze slides to Chelsea and a wide grin splits his face. "Hello again, gorgeous."

"Tristan, let go of me. It's none of your business—"

"You skipped class." He loosens his hold but doesn't release me. His eyes narrow as he examines my made-up face and curly hair. "Why are you wearing so much makeup? And your hair is curly."

Chelsea puts her hand on his. "Let's take this inside so you don't wake the neighborhood. It's late."

Alex steps behind Tristan. "I agree with legs. Let's go inside."

"Legs?" Chelsea gives him a puzzled look.

"They're a mile long, sweetheart. And the nicest pair I've seen."

Chelsea laughs, tossing her hair back flirtatiously. "I appreciate the compliment. Help me get these two inside so they can talk."

"You heard the woman." Alex grabs Tristan's arm. Although he lowers his voice, I still hear him. "It's a bit chilly tonight. Your girl looks cold."

His words have a magical effect. Tristan immediately wraps his arm around me and ushers me inside.

"I'm not his girl," I snap at Alex.

Chelsea follows, rolling her eyes. Alex brings up the rear, shutting and locking the door behind him.

Tristan starts on me again. "You didn't answer my question. Why—"

"I don't need to." I yank my arm away, reaching a breaking point. "I can't do this right now, Tristan. Just leave me the hell alone." I whirl around, running up the stairs.

As I flee, I hear Chelsea say, "Tristan, give her some space."

Running into my room, I slam the door behind me and throw myself on the bed. *I wish I never would've come to WHU and met Tristan Harrington.*

CHAPTER 23

Jordyn

I changed outfits three times before settling on a pair of skinny jeans, heeled booties, and a black, long-sleeved t-shirt. The entire time, I inwardly lectured myself for caring what I looked like.

Chelsea, wearing a similar outfit, eyes me skeptically. "I can't believe you don't have a jersey or some type of Wolverines attire."

Shooting her a glare, I turn back to the mirror, critically examining my appearance. "Whose jersey would I wear? I'm sure as hell not wearing Josh's since I can't stand him."

"I know one guy who wishes you were wearing his." She gives me a smile that makes me want to throttle her.

"Whose side are you on?" I turn away from the mirror, critically studying her as I move closer. "Exactly what happened last night? You seem to be a bit more pro-Tristan than you were yesterday."

Chelsea gives me a look. "Listen, Jordyn. You know I'm always on your side. But maybe you should listen to him."

I glare at her, folding my arms over my chest. "No. It's over between us."

Chelsea steps closer and places her hand on my shoulder. "Then why do you still seem so miserable? And why, after I came to bed, did you spend half the night crying?"

I blink at her, irritation coursing through me. "I'm tired of his hot and cold behavior. I wish he'd just act cold like when he returned from his run."

"If you don't care about him, then why do you care about how he acts? And why do you want him to be cold? Is it because it makes it easier for you to be mad and pretend you hate him?"

"Who says I'm pretending?" I snap, turning around and grabbing my purse. "Come on. We need to go. I promised Mom we'd get there early to wish Josh good luck. Robert was nagging her to make sure I complied."

Chelsea nods. "You look amazing. Let's go knock 'em dead."

A genuine smile curls my lips. "Thanks, bestie. You're hotter than ever." I nudge her in the side. "I heard Alex calling you legs last night. He looked pretty smitten."

My God. Did my best friend just blush? I've never seen that before.

The genuine smile lighting up her face makes me happy and a tad envious. "He has a great ass."

I snort, shaking my head. *That's such a Chelsea thing to say.* "Is his ass the only thing great about him?"

"I'll let you know after tonight's game." She winks and hooks her arm through mine. "Come on. Let's go."

CHAPTER 24

Tristan

Despite Coach Jensen's pep talk and the private conversation we had in his office, I'm nervous as hell about tonight's game. It has everything to do with seeing Jordyn again.

"Hey, captain." Alex slides on the bench beside me as I glumly stare at my locker. "Nervous?"

I slowly turn my head to his. "Yeah, but not for the reason you think."

"Does it have to do with the blonde voyeur that stomped off last night and refused to talk to you?"

A long mournful sigh is my only response.

"Look, Tristan, the entire situation sucks. Especially since you've finally gotten your head on straight in time for her to shove hers up her ass."

Despite being down, Alex's words make me chuckle. "Ironic, isn't it?"

He shrugs. "She's hurt. If she didn't care about you, she wouldn't be acting this way."

"You think?"

"I know she does. I've been around the two of you." He slings an arm around my shoulder. "Let's head out. Chelsea mentioned they were arriving early to wish Josh good luck. Stepfather's idea."

Hope flares in my chest. "Let's go."

I hurry from the locker room, Alex beside me. My eyes scan the people waiting outside the locker room until I spot her long, blonde hair. She's leaning against the wall, arms folded over her chest, and a pinched expression indicating she's uncomfortable. Her eyes move back and forth between Robert and Josh.

I hear Josh bragging to Robert and the blonde woman standing beside him about how well he's been playing. Alex and I exchange a look and I nearly snort aloud. "He's a damn liar," I say to Alex.

"And a lazy motherfucker." Patting my shoulder, his voice is low. "Go talk to your girl."

Sliding up beside her, I lean down in her ear. "He's such a pompous ass."

Jordyn momentarily tenses before she snorts. "Which one? They're both pompous asses."

I chuckle, my muscles relaxing. She's not screaming at me or ignoring me, so that's progress. I open my mouth, about to tell her how gorgeous she looks when a jovial voice interrupts.

"Hey. You're Jordyn Reese, right?" Bryce Gardner, the right defenseman, approaches her, a smile on his face.

I stare at him beneath lowered brows, wishing I could tell him to fuck off. If he looked at me, he'd see it on my face.

"Yeah. Why?" She eyes him suspiciously.

"Hi. I'm Bryce Gardner." He sticks his hand out and she stares at it for a moment before he continues. "You're an English Lit tutor, right? I'm struggling with that class, and Professor Martin suggested I talk to you about tutoring."

A smile splits her face as she grasps his outstretched hand. "Oh, yes. I offer tutoring for his class." As she animatedly launches into the specifics of tutoring and explains how to schedule an appointment, my fury mounts. I don't fucking like this one goddamn bit. I know Bryce is up to something, but I haven't figured out what.

When their conversation finally ends, Bryce gives her a big smile. "I'll be in touch soon, Jordyn." He looks up at me, a challenging look in his eyes that makes me want to kick his ass. But I can't do a goddamn thing in front of her stepfather and stepbrother.

"Jordyn. Come here a second." Robert beckons her over.

She blows out a breath, panic on her face when her eyes dart to mine. "Gotta go. The asshole beckons." Grimacing, she hurries away before I can say another word.

It's thirty minutes until the puck drops, and the people are filling the arena. As I skate around the rink, I wave to a few people screaming my name, holding signs above their heads, and wearing my jersey.

My attention moves to the player-reserved seating section. Jordyn sits in the middle, with Chelsea on her right and her mom on her left. She's laughing at something Chelsea said. When her head turns toward me, her smile dims before she smirks. She makes a point of standing up, and my heart skips a beat when I see she's wearing a jersey. She turns as I get closer, offering me a clear view.

What the actual fuck. My body vibrates with rage, and I jerk to a stop in front of the glass, sending shavings of ice flying around me. I'm so fucking pissed that I want to slam my customized hockey stick over my knee, breaking it in half before stomping over to her, yanking that jersey off her, and turning her over my knee.

She's fucking wearing Gardner's jersey. Rage causes me to shake. *She'll pay for this stunt.* I slam my hand against the glass, causing her to jump. I gesture with my fingers for her to come closer.

A smug smile is plastered on her face as she adds an extra swagger to her hips, taking her time moving toward me. The number 27 and *his* name mocks me as she stops in front of the glass.

"Walk over to the back of the rink." I gesture to the location with my hand, my furious gaze never leaving hers. "Now." Then I skate away, heading in the direction I told her to go.

Jordyn stares at me for a couple of beats, her brows furrowed. She looks over her shoulder at Chelsea, shrugging, before she heads toward the last bend in the rink where I told her to go.

I'm practically climbing out of my skin from the irritation coursing through me when she finally arrives. I point to the steel handle on the board. "Turn it. It swings toward you."

The second I hear the lock click, I barrel through the door, not giving her a chance to move. My body towers over hers, and the height distance is more noticeable with my skates on. She cranes her neck, blinking in surprise as I get in her space.

Ripping my helmet and gloves off, I throw them on the floor. "Take that fucking jersey off. Now." My eyes drop to the offending jersey, wishing I could light it on fire and hold it up in front of her face so she could watch it burn.

"What? Who the hell do you think you are?"

Something inside me breaks. I can't take this distance between us. Coach's words roll through my head. I know I'm fucked up. A broken shell of who I once was. But dammit, I want to be a better man for her. I can be a helluva lot better than what I've been.

My hand cups her face, my thumb stroking her cheek. "I'm a broken man who doesn't deserve you. A man who fucked up, acting like an asshole and pushing you away. I led you to believe I was interested in what Josh was saying about Janelle when I don't give a fuck about her."

Encouraged by the softness in her eyes, I continue. "Since the day we met, you're all I see. There's only *you*, Jordyn. And I'm scared as hell because I know what it's like to lose those you love the most." My mouth is dry, and there's a giant lump in my throat. But I keep going, my voice cracking with emotion. "My parents and sister died in a tragic accident, and it fucked me up. My entire world imploded, and I haven't been the same since." My body overheats, sweat streaking down my back as I try to get this out before she walks away. "I shut down, not letting anyone in until you. I've built walls around my heart, but you knocked them down and climbed inside."

Tears shimmer in her eyes. "Tristan." She breathes my name like a reverent whisper. "I'm so sorry about your family."

I give her a shaky smile. "I can see it in your eyes. I hate the pain there. I've caused you so much the past few days. All because I'm a fucking coward who let his fears take over." I bow my head, shame washing over me.

Her soft hand moves to my chin. "Tristan, look at me."

I comply with her request, letting her see me. Raw and unfiltered. I'm not the hot-shot hockey player, the son of a legend, or the driven student who works his ass off academically and on the ice. I'm simply me. A damaged soul.

"I think your heart is fractured, like broken pieces of glass, but you can be repaired. You're not broken beyond repair."

My breath comes out in a rush. I'm shocked she can see what no one else can. Her words cause my sluggish heart to pound faster, giving me hope.

"I'm glad you told me. I wish you would've done it sooner, but the important thing is, you opened up to me." She takes a step closer, our bodies nearly touching. "We have a lot to work through, but I'm willing to listen."

Moisture fills my eyes. "I missed you, Jordyn."

A slow smile spreads over her face, bathing me in her light, warming my cold, fractured heart. "I missed you. I'm still mad, and all isn't forgiven... But I missed you."

"Well... You're gonna have something else to be mad about." I grab the hem of his jersey and yank it over her head. Tossing it onto the floor, I slam my skate into the fabric before reaching behind me and pulling my jersey over my head.

"Tristan! What the hell are you doing?" Large aqua eyes dart in the direction of her stepfather and mom. "I can't wear your jersey."

"The fuck you can't." I hold it out to her, watching as she swallows hard, heat blazing in her eyes. *She likes it when I'm possessive and demanding.* It makes her hot, causing her breathing to accelerate, a flush spreading over her cheeks.

"You don't wear anyone's name and number but mine," I growl as I pull my too-large jersey over her torso, smoothing it over her hips and thighs. I slide my hand up so it's cupping her pussy. Her resulting gasp and the heat radiating through her jeans tell me what I'm desperate to know. "You're fucking soaked for me, aren't you, kitten?"

She grips my padding, a squeak coming through parted lips.

"God, I'd love to lick your pretty pussy until you explode onto my face." Reluctantly, I remove my hand before someone sees us.

Her hands slide from my padding as I step back. I give her an appreciative look. "You look sexy as fuck wearing my jersey."

She wrinkles her cute little nose. "I smell like your sweat."

"Just like you did in the shower." I wink at her, chuckling as she gasps. The sound heads straight to my cock.

"You're an ass." She spits, folding her arms over her chest and glaring at me like an angry kitten.

"Maybe, but I'm your ass." Reaching out, I gently push a strand of her hair away from her face, intentionally grazing my finger over her cheekbone before tucking a silky curl behind her ear. "You're so damn beautiful." My knuckles graze her neck, goosebumps pebbling in the wake of my touch. "And you're mine. All mine."

Her eyes heat as she snaps, "I'm not yours. And I haven't forg—"

My finger over her lips stops her. "I'm running out of time and need to return to the ice. But, kitten, you're mine. Just like I'm yours. *Only yours.*"

She stares at me, her expression softening. "Give me a chance to grovel for being an asshole. Please."

"I'll hear you out—"

I shake my head. "I need you to listen and understand. I want you to understand me."

She searches my pleading eyes before she finally nods and whispers, "Okay."

A smile breaks across my face. "Good. I'll see you after the game?"

"Yes."

"Enjoy the game." Stepping back, I quickly bend and pick up Gardner's jersey. As I straighten, her voice makes me still.

"Aren't you going to get in trouble for this?" She gestures at my jersey she's wearing before her eyes move to my padding. Her gaze slowly travels down to my skates and then back to my eyes, cheeks turning scarlet.

"Worth it." I tilt my head, speaking the words inside my

heart. "You're worth any amount of trouble I'd get in." Then I wink before putting my helmet and gloves back on, heading for the ice.

I feel like I'm floating as I skate across the ice. Alex catches my eyes, a shit-eating grin on his face as I skate by him.

But I don't give a shit. *Nothing can bring me down.*

CHAPTER 25

Tristan

C oach Jensen gives me a strange look as I head toward my locker, taking in my missing jersey. I see his lips twitch before he says, "Get a fucking jersey on, Harrington."

I salute him and head to my locker to do as he instructed, throwing Gardner's jersey inside to deal with it later.

Slipping another jersey over my head, I head to my usual spot beside Alex on the bench for the pre-game speech from Coach Jensen. He moves to the center, commanding our attention with his presence alone. I sure as hell hope I look as good as he does when I'm thirty-nine and can command a room like he does.

Feeling eyes boring into me, I look up. Josh is staring at me, suspicion in his eyes. Gardner sits beside him, a smirk on his face, with Landin Walker, the right winger on the team, on his left.

A silent stare down ensures between Gardner and me. I smirk when he drops his gaze to the floor.

Alex leans closer, his voice low. "I may need to find new roommates after this war, killa."

"Good. Move in with me, and Josh can live with them." My eyes meet Walker's, who shrugs and gives me a smile. He's tight with Gardner, but he'll defer to me and show respect because I'm the captain.

Alex chuckles. "Throwin' down before throwin' the Bears down on the ice. I like it, killa."

I smirk at Alex. "You know it."

"Nice job claiming your girl by putting your jersey on her."

"Her best friend is wearing yours."

He groans, grabbing his dick. "Don't remind me. I've been hard as fuck since I spotted her in it." A pained hiss comes from him as he shifts. "Christ, I'm thinking about it again. If my pants rip and my cup shoots across the room, it's all your damn fault."

I chuckle. "I may join you." I shift on the bench, my dick thickening as images of my kitten wearing my jersey run through my mind.

"I'm surprised you didn't jizz in your pants when you put your jersey on voyeur."

"How do you know I didn't?"

Alex laughs as Coach looks in our direction. I brace myself for the public lashing Alex and I are about to receive for talking while he is speaking. Instead, he gives me a brief smile. "A few words from your captain to get you fired up. Harrington, the floor is yours."

Adrenaline pumps through my veins as I stand. Alex and I do our typical fist bump before I move to the center of the locker room, confidence oozing from me as I pump up my guys. My speech has never been so passionate and inspired. The blonde wearing my jersey is responsible for that.

"Let's wipe the ice with these assholes," I conclude, earning a round of sticks pounding against the floor as my teammates whoop and yell.

As we exit the locker room, Alex gives me a huge smile. "Inspirational as fuck, killa. She's good for you." His look is loaded with meaning. "Work things out with her after we take care of these guys."

A confident smile spreads across my face. "You know it, Graves."

We do our extensive pre-game handshake, which Alex developed during our freshman year. "You kill 'em, I bury 'em," he says, referring to my nickname, killa, and his last name, Graves.

"Killa and Graves are gonna take care of business like we always do."

The roar of the crowd reaches my ears as we head to the ice. "I live for this," Alex yells over the noise, a glimmer in his eyes.

"Hell yes."

My gaze moves to the stands, easily spotting Jordyn, still wearing my jersey. I figured she'd take it off as an act of defiance, and the fact that she didn't makes my heart pound faster than when I'm on the ice.

Alex may live for the game, but I have something far more important to live for: her.

CHAPTER 26

Jordyn

It's deafening as the Wolverines, who have home team advantage, file out from the locker room. The crowd leaps to their feet, screaming and yelling, as they skate across the rink.

"This is insane," I scream into Chelsea's ear, on my feet with the rest of the crowd.

Her face glows with excitement as she screams back. "I know."

When Chelsea sees Alex's jersey, she yanks on my arm so hard I nearly topple over. "Graves. Number 34. The goalie." She jumps up and down, still hanging onto me, screaming his name. He looks up at her and pumps his fist in the air before he points at her. Chelsea mimics she's going to faint, and I burst into laughter.

"Get up, Juliet. You might miss Romeo stretching and doing splits again if you pass out."

She looks horrified. "Dear, God, no. I can't miss that."

I giggle, my gaze roaming over the players. When I see Tristan, I instinctively grab Chelsea's arm. "I should be so mad at him. But my heart is racing just seeing Harrington and the number 33 on the back of his jersey."

Chelsea laughs. "You want to be mad at him so the two of you can have smoking hot makeup sex. Don't lie."

I blush furiously, images rolling through my head. "Thanks for that visual," I scream in her ear over the roar of the rowdy college fans and parents in the arena.

"Welcome." She winks at me, her eyes moving back to Alex. I turn to the ice right as Tristan skates by, his piercing green eyes locking on me. He gives me a wink that causes butterflies to swarm inside my stomach, frantically fluttering their wings.

"Wow. I just got fucking pregnant from the way he looked at you. And that wink... Girl. Holy hot damn!" Chelsea dramatically slaps the back of her hand across her forehead. "If a man looked at me like that, I'd marry him."

I laugh, but nervous apprehension rolls through me. My gaze moves to my stepfather, then to Josh, bracing for their accusing eyes to burn into me, telling me they know the secret I've been harboring. But neither are paying me the slightest attention.

Blowing out a breath, I can't take my eyes off Tristan as the game starts. I'm impressed by the way he seamlessly dodges and dances around the other players, in complete control of himself and his stick, his movements powerful and smooth. I'm also impressed by Alex, who is fast and flexible despite all the padding he's wearing.

"Mmmm. Did you just see that split Alex just did when he caught that puck?" Her nails dig into my skin through my shirt. "Goddamn, that man is flexible... and so am I." She gives me a wink and we burst into laughter. "I think I'm pregnant with his baby and he hasn't touched me yet."

I howl with laughter, shaking my head. "Oh my God, girl. You're crazy."

The first period has me biting my nails as I look at the clock, watching as it counts down. The Bears scored a questionable goal and Tristan is currently discussing it with the referee.

Play resumes and the Wolverines are playing more aggressively. The seconds are ticking down when Tristan slams the puck into the Bear's net, scoring a goal and tying the game.

Leaping to our feet, Chelsea and I jump and scream with the rest of the fans. The buzzer sounds and the team celebrates. Tristan looks up at me right as Gardner, the guy whose jersey I was wearing, sticks his foot out and trips him. He tries to make it look accidental, but the smirk he gives his other teammate says it was anything but.

"What the fuck was that?"

"Oh, that was a mistake. Just wait. He'll get his revenge."

I bite my lip as Tristan gets in Garnder's face in front of their bench, and the Coach comes up, saying a few things and separating them.

As Tristan plops onto the bench, removing his helmet and gloves, his green eyes latch onto mine. He gives me a sexy grin, winking at me, and goddamn, my heart stops before it begins furiously banging inside my chest.

"Damn. Why don't you two go fuck on the ice," Chelsea murmurs.

"Chelsea." I slap her arm, shaking my head. "Stop. Why don't you worry about Alex."

"Oh, I am. I'm over here dreaming of all the ways that flexible man can do all kinds of unspeakable things to me. The only reason I can't talk about them in detail is because of all these fools. But I'll tell you later—"

"No, thanks. Keep your unspeakable thoughts sacred by keeping them to yourself."

Sitting back, I shake my head. But I get caught up in

daydreaming about Tristan and me in the shower, making me squirm in my seat.

My mom leans over to my ear. "Nice jersey, baby girl. Looks like a certain captain has it bad for you."

I stare at her, wide-eyed. "Oh, no. We're just—"

Before I can lie and say friends, the roar of the crowd overwhelms any conversation as the players head back to the ice.

The game resumes, and I'm beginning to think Chelsea was wrong about Tristan getting revenge. The Bears have the puck and are moving it toward Alex, who positions himself, ready to prevent the puck from getting anywhere near the net. My gaze is locked on Tristan, who looks like a tornado barreling down on Gardner. He chucks Gardner into the boards before stealing the puck from the Bears player. The refs immediately blow their whistle, calling a penalty on Tristan.

Tristan winks at me as he heads to the penalty box, seemingly unbothered.

Chelsea nudges me with her elbow. "Told you Gardner made a mistake." I shake my head at the glimmer in her eyes. "Oh, don't tell me you're not hot and bothered by Tristan's actions out there. It's clear he was jealous of you wearing another guy's jersey. And Gardner is aware of that and is fucking with him."

It's extremely hot seeing him so jealous, but I don't say a word. I feel bad as I watch Tristan clapping and yelling at his team, his leg bouncing.

My gaze slides to Josh. I'm even more worried that Josh will figure out something is going on between us. Right now, he's oblivious as the coach screams at him. Tristan is glaring at Josh, shaking his head. I read Tristan's lips as he yells, "Focus on the game, Fowler."

Josh turns away from him, a smug smile curling his lips as he looks up at the stands. I follow his gaze and roll my eyes when I see Janelle stripping off Josh's jersey, revealing a massive amount of cleavage in her low-cut top.

As if she senses me looking at her, she turns her head to me, curling her lip in disgust as her gaze moves to my jersey. When her eyes lift to mine, they flash with anger, and I give her a victorious grin.

"Wow. What's going on between you and the big-titted skank."

Jealousy swirls inside me, burning my stomach, my eyes not leaving hers. "Remember how I met Tristan? She's the girl."

"Did he lose a bet and have to fuck her? She doesn't seem like Tristan's type at all."

Janelle turns her head away, her gaze moving to Josh. I turn my head to Chelsea, my brows furrowing. "How do you know what Tristan's type is?"

"After you stomped to your room, I hung with Alex and Tristan downstairs for a while." She gives a slight shrug, trying to play it off as no big deal.

My heart pounds inside my chest. Jealousy tinged with desperation threatens to engulf me. "Did Tristan talk about me?"

She wiggles her brows. "Oh, yeah. Judging by the way he couldn't stop talking about you, you live rent-free in his head."

I grip her arm. "Chelsea. Tell me what he said."

"Nope." Her eyes sparkle. "You'll just have to ask him."

I sigh, turning my attention back to the penalty box where Tristan is poised to jump onto the ice. The crowd roars as his skates hit the ice and he races down the rink, intent on going after the Bears player who just skated around other players, steering the puck in the direction of the Wolverine's goal.

I hold my breath as Tristan gains speed, and when the Bears player loses control of the puck, Tristan deftly steals it, taking it down the ice toward the Bear's goal. Players surround him as he deftly hits the puck to another Wolverine player. The player is under attack and shoots it to Tristan, who fakes left and then shoots the puck straight into the net.

I'm on my feet, hugging Chelsea and cheering with the rest of the crowd. The Wolverines are in the lead.

This is turning out to be a great game. Who knew I'd like hockey so much?

My eyes follow a certain hockey captain as he celebrates with his team. *It's because of him.*

CHAPTER 27

Jordyn

Since it's intermission, I tap my mom and tell her that Chelsea and I are going to get a drink. Before I get up, she grabs my arm, a smile on her face. "Hold up. I need to know about the guy whose jersey you're wearing."

My mom leans over and whispers something in Robert's ear. He gets up and heads down the aisle. Once he's gone, my mom says, "Spill it, baby girl."

"I-I... Can't."

Chelsea leans forward. "A hot hockey player who is obsessed with her."

I smack Chelsea's arm with my other hand. "Chelsea."

"So what's the problem? Why haven't you told me about him, Jordyn?"

Oh, hell. I bite my lip, debating what I should say.

"Cause he's her roommate."

I'm gonna kill Chelsea. What the actual fuck? My face flames as I turn to my mom, worry knotting my stomach.

"Don't worry. I won't say anything to Josh or Robert." She squeezes my hand, then lowers her voice. Her eyes have a mischievous sparkle in them I haven't seen in a while. "You know, I was dating your father's best friend when I met your father."

I sit there in stunned silence, slowly blinking at her.

"What? I was your age once." She sighs, a wistful expression on her face. "There was something about your father. I kept trying to resist him, but every time we were around one another, sparks flew."

I'm hanging on her every word. "What happened?"

"I started realizing how incompatible I was with my boyfriend when he'd ask your father to take me places. For example, my boyfriend was supposed to go to the poetry reading with me but came up with a lame excuse and asked your father to step in. Of course, your dad agreed. Your dad always paid so much attention to me. He figured out that I'd written poetry and kept taking me to the weekly readings until I had the courage to stand up there and read mine."

Wow. That's really sweet and I can definitely see my dad doing that. He's always been supportive of my mom, and vice versa. "So what happened?"

"We kissed at the end of the night, and I felt guilty as hell. I tried avoiding your father and was miserable. Plus, since he was my boyfriend's best friend, avoidance was hard without confessing what was going on. Anytime I was around your father, my resistance weakened. We started sneaking around, going on dates out of town. Your father wooed the hell outta me, trying to convince me to break up with his friend. I was concerned I'd ruin their friendship, but your father said, 'If I had to choose between him and you, it would always be you.' Kinda hard to resist that." Her face is the most adorable shade of red.

A pang goes through my heart. I miss my dad so much. I always assumed my mom stopped missing him when she married Robert, but the look on her face clearly indicates she's still in love with him.

She grabs my hand and squeezes it. "You never get over that kind of love, sweetie. The kind of love I shared with your father... I would run barefoot over glass and through the fires of hell to get him back."

This is the frankest conversation I've had with my mom since high school when it was just her and me struggling together. Life was simpler before Robert came along. "Why did you marry Robert?"

A pained expression is on her face before she lowers her head, her blonde hair curtaining it, obscuring my view.

"Mom?"

She looks up, tears shimmering in her eyes, shame burning her cheeks. "To give you back what I'd taken from you. I used your college fund, depleting it so we could survive. I've always felt guilty. So when Robert needed a wife to look good to his business partners—"

"You didn't marry him out of love?"

She shakes her head. "No. I married him to give you a college education, not realizing he'd be such an asshole and put strings on your education." She looks around, her spine stiff and her muscles tense. "Grab your purse," she hisses.

"What?"

"Do it. I've been planning this for a while." She opens her purse, pulling out a wad of cash. "Robert gives me an 'allowance' and I've been saving money since he quit funding your education. It's not enough to cover your return to New York, but it will help you this semester." Her blue eyes meet mine. "Although, I hope you stay around here. Even though things have been tense between us, I've missed you."

My fingers tremble as I hold my purse in my lap. My mom grabs the zipper, opens it, and then shoves the cash inside and zips it. "Don't let Robert or Josh know. Josh will tell him." She rolls her eyes. "Be careful with that one. He's a wolf in sheep's clothing."

I nod, having a newfound respect for my mom. Guilt washes over me. I resented her for moving on with Robert without asking her any questions and making a lot of assumptions. I've distanced myself from her and rebuffed her efforts to be close again.

"Mom?" I squeeze her hand. "Thanks. And not just for the money, which I appreciate and feel bad taking..." She gives me a warning look and I hold up a hand. "But I will since it came from *him*." We both laugh, and it feels amazing. "But for your sacrifices after dad..." My voice breaks, and I look away, sucking in a breath. "Thank you for telling me that story about you and Dad. I'd love to hear more."

"How about over breakfast or dinner sometime? We'll go somewhere to get away from Robert." She winks and my smile grows.

"I'd love that."

Chelsea tackles us in a big hug. "This is such a beautiful moment. It's even distracting me from thoughts of Alex doing splits and stretching on the ice."

My mom and I burst into laughter at her antics. "This is why I love Chelsea," I grin as Chelsea releases us, and I sit back, grabbing both their hands.

"It's why I also love Chelsea. She keeps you guessing." My mom winks at us.

"Always, Momma Fowler."

"Please call me Abigayle."

"Yeah, I don't blame you. I wouldn't wanna use that asshole's name, either." Chelsea shudders and my mom and I burst into laughter.

We sit in comfortable silence for a few moments before I say, "Mom. Since you and Dad ended up marrying, I'm assuming you dumped your boyfriend?"

She laughs. "More like I was caught in a compromising position with your father. My boyfriend made one helluva scene, and he and your father got into a fistfight. It was obvious I was cheering for your father. I dumped my asshole ex and your father and I were official after that." A wistful smile is on her face. "It was worth every damn minute. I'd do it all again in a heartbeat."

"Everything? Even sneaking around and the anxiety of being caught?"

"God, yes. Sneaking around made it hotter."

We laugh as Chelsea pumps a fist in the air and shimmies in her seat.

"Love is always worth it, baby girl." She looks toward the rink, a smile on her face. "I pretended I wasn't paying attention but I couldn't help but notice how jealous the captain was that you were wearing another man's jersey."

I fist Tristan's jersey, my heart pounding faster at the memory of the possessive look on his face.

"You know, your father played football in college. He was the same way. I wore my boyfriend's jersey, and he'd seethe. Boy, he was so aggressive on the field." A wistful smile curls her lips. "Once we were official, he immediately burned my ex-boyfriend's jersey and gave me his, telling me I'd never wear another man's jersey." Tears shimmer in her eyes. "He was right. I never wore anyone else's."

Raising an eyebrow, I stare at her, stunned. "Dad acted like that? I mean, I've seen him get a little jealous over guys in the store and he'd glare at them, but it's hard for me to picture him losing control."

"Once we were married, he knew I wasn't going anywhere, so he calmed down. But if a man flirted with me, he shut it down quickly."

"That's hot," Chelsea says, leaning forward and fanning herself. "God, I'd love to have a man act like a caveman when another man got near me." Her expression darkens. "Well, one who isn't unhinged and tries to end my life."

My mom looks shocked and then angry. "Listen, Chelsea. If a man hurts you in any way and/or is unhinged, he's not the one for you. But acting possessive and protecting what's his is fine if the man treats you like a queen and showers you with love. Remember that."

Chelsea grins. "You're so wise, Momma Abby."

My mom grins. "It comes from experience. I have a few years on you."

I grin at my mom and Chelsea, feeling like I have two best friends. "One more group hug before Robert returns." We squish together and Chelsea grabs her phone, taking a selfie of us.

When we part, the players are on the ice. I turn my head, feeling Tristan's intense stare boring into me. My body floods with warmth at the look in his eyes. He looks around and quickly does a heart sign with his hands.

Grinning, I look around and do the heart sign back.

Yup, it's official. I'm head over heels for a hockey player.

CHAPTER 28

Jordyn

Robert returns with drinks and snacks, an annoyed expression on his face since the game is underway. He huffs as he throws himself into his seat. "That took way too damn long. And I had to carry all this shit through the crowd."

As my mom hands me and Chelsea our drinks, her voice radiates fake sympathy. "Awe, so sorry, Robert." She rolls her eyes, and I can barely contain my giggle. "Such a hardship." She pats his arm in a placating gesture, and I nearly lose my composure. All the resentment is building up and one of these days, Robert will feel her wrath. I hope I'm there to see it.

For now, he remains oblivious. Emitting a grunt, he takes a drink of his soda, his eyes on Josh. "I hope he gets his fucking shit together. His distraction is going to cost them the game."

I meet my mom's eyes. As much as Josh irritates me, I wouldn't want to be in his shoes if he costs them the game. And it seems likely when he allows the Bears to score again.

Tristan and Alex are beside themselves. Alex slams his fist against the ice, while Tristan skates over and gets in Josh's face. The coach starts yelling, and the referees blow their whistles as

Josh turns around and flips Tristan off, which causes Tristan to lose his shit and get in his face. It's chaos for a few minutes when one of the Bears yells something and a Wolverine player attacks him.

When things calm down, Josh leaves the ice and heads for the bench, throwing his helmet and gloves in a fit of rage.

The pressure is on, as the Wolverines struggle. The next goal attempt is stopped by Alex, sending the crowd to their feet and sparking life into the team. The game is fast and furious as tempers rise.

I'm biting my nails, my eyes moving from the scoreboard to the ice. The game is tied with only thirty seconds left. Tristan steals the puck and deftly skates around a Bears player. I watch in horror as a Bears defenseman comes at him from the side. I jump to my feet seconds before the hit, screaming, "Watch out," to Tristan, but it's too late. Tristan slams against the boards, hitting the ice, while the player steals the puck.

I hold my breath, fear in my heart that Tristan is hurt. He jumps to his feet and skates off after the player, determination on his face.

Alex blocks the shot by catching it with his left-hand glove, and Chelsea and I jump up and down, screaming.

The game moves at lightning speed. I grip Chelsea's arm as Tristan gains control of the puck. The Bears surround him, and we're a man down because Walker got into a fight with a Bears player.

Tristan has no one to pass it to, but he doesn't seem ruffled as he skates toward the goal. The goalie readies himself, but Tristan fakes right, then slams the puck into the net, winning the game one second before the buzzer goes off.

The crowd leaps to their feet, screaming and cheering. Mom, Chelsea, and I have our arms around one another and are jumping up and down, much to the horror of my stepfather. He tugs on my mom's shirt, hissing at her to stop being an embarrassment, but she ignores him.

"Ignore him. Robert's such an asshole. Such a buzz kill." When my mom pulls back, she winks at me before Robert grabs her arm, saying they need to go see Josh. Chelsea and I follow them but for different reasons. The blood is humming through my veins at seeing Tristan.

Robert reaches Josh and immediately launches into a tirade. Josh extracts himself, slinking off toward the showers. Robert's face is red as he screams at his retreating back. "I'll see you at the house. You're staying there until Monday." He stalks off, not even bothering to wait for my mom.

My mom shakes her head before turning her attention to me. She hugs me and whispers, "I don't know Tristan Harrington, but I like what I've seen. Go get your man, sweetheart."

Laughing, I hug her tighter. "Thanks, Mom. Let's meet for breakfast or something soon."

Pulling back, she gives me a wide smile. "My schedule is open. Text me when you're free." She moves to Chelsea and hugs her, then whispers something in her ear, before waving and reminding us to be safe.

"What did she say to you?"

"That woman is magic. She said, 'Just because you had an asshole mistreat you in the past doesn't mean Alex will do the same. Give him a fair shot and get to know him. See where things go.' She also told me I could call or text if I needed any advice."

"Yeah, um, I may have told her that your parents were rich assholes who were too busy with their own lives to be concerned about you. She obviously remembered."

"I'm glad you did."

My attention is pulled away by a sexy-as-sin, dark blond-haired captain coming toward me, a panty-melting smile on his lips. Chelsea pats my arm as she moves away, giving us privacy.

"Nice winning shot, captain." I step closer to him, not caring that he's all sweaty and wrapped in layers of padding.

"Thanks. Nice jersey." He smirks at me, his eyes moving to his jersey. When he looks up at me, the heat burning in his green eyes incinerates me.

"Some random hot hockey god gave it to me. Know anyone with this last name?" I spin around, showing him the back of the jersey, before facing him.

"If you're looking for him to give him a kiss, then I'm him. If you wanna scream at him because he acted like an asshole, he's over there." He points at Alex, who is too busy flirting with Chelsea to notice.

Since the crowd around us has dissipated, I throw my arms around his waist and squeeze him. He hisses out a pained breath and I immediately loosen my hold and try to step back, but he refuses to let me go, pinning me against his sweaty body.

I tilt my head back, concern swirling through me. "Oh, fuck, Tristan. Are you okay?"

"Yeah, just my ribs from being slammed into the boards. I'm gonna get it looked at." He jerks his thumb in the direction of the locker room. His voice lowers as he says, "I wanted to see you first."

"Did I ever tell you that you're a sweetheart?"

"Just now. And you can keep saying it." His voice is gruff and sexy as hell. As he brushes a lock of hair from my face, shivers of pleasure roll down my body. I want to kiss him so damn bad but I can't risk it. We can explain a hug, but our lips pressed together... Not so much.

Chelsea bounces over, tugging Alex behind her. "Hey. You going to the party to celebrate your win?"

Tristan immediately shakes his head as I shrug and say,

"Sure." My brows draw together as we stare at one another. "Don't you wanna go and celebrate your win?"

He slowly shakes his head. "I'd rather be with you. Unless you wanna go?"

I reach up, stroking his jawline, shaking my head. "I'd rather spend it alone with you. Josh has to go home, per my stepfather's rant."

Tristan grins, catching my hand and placing a quick kiss against my knuckles. "I heard." His eyes sear me the whole way to my soul as he rasps, "We'd be alone for the night, huh?"

"Jesus Christ. I just became pregnant watching the two of you." Alex's boisterous voice interrupts, making us laugh.

"Well, not exactly." I look over at Chelsea, who threads her arm through Alex's.

Chelsea wiggles her eyebrows up and down suggestively. "Why don't the two of you go 'talk' and I'll go to the party with this hot goalie whose jersey I'm wearing."

"Oh shit. I just became pregnant," Alex mutters, one hand over his crotch.

"Jesus, Alex. How many times have I lectured you about the way male and female bodies work?" Tristan shakes his head. "Dumb jock," he says, sliding his arm around my waist as I shake my head, my earlier misconceptions about jock and intelligence blown to shreds by Tristan and Alex.

"Shit, I became pregnant when he stripped off that other dude's jersey and replaced it with his." Chelsea points at Tristan. "Then you started humping the ice and doing splits, and now there's twins."

Tristan and I howl with laughter as Alex chuckles. "First, I wasn't humping the ice. It's called stretching. Second, I'm very flexible." He wiggles his brows, causing Tristan and I to laugh harder.

A twinkle is in Chelsea's eyes as she holds up her keys. "Take these. I'm going wherever goalie goes."

Tristan snatches her keys. "Good thing Alex drove me here." He winks at me before his gaze slides to Alex. "Behave yourself tonight." He and Alex do a weird fist bump, causing Tristan to wince from the movement. Alex inquires about his ribs, and Tristan shrugs, saying they may be bruised.

Chelsea moves beside me, linking our arms together. "Hot hockey players. Who would've thought we'd end up here?"

"Not me." As my eyes meet Tristan's, my nerves sizzle and dance, my heart pounding like a drum. *I've never felt like this before.*

CHAPTER 29

Tristan

Holding Jordyn's hand as I drive, I'm grinning like a fool. I can't believe I'm this happy, especially as we inch closer to the anniversary of the tragedy that ripped everything from me.

It's all because of *her*.

My gaze moves from the road to Jordyn as we stop at a red light. Her smile matches mine as she searches my eyes. "I'm really sorry for the way I've acted."

I lift our joined hands, kissing her knuckles. "I'm the one who started it, Jordyn. You have no idea how much I regret the way I acted when I returned from my run." Blowing out a breath as the light turns green, my gaze flits to the road before I accelerate, then back to hers. "I'll explain more when we get home."

"Home. That sounds nice."

We grin like lovesick fools. When I reach a stop sign, I squeeze her hand. "I know I was an ass, but I never stopped caring for you."

Her eyes are luminous in the darkness. "I never stopped caring for you, although I wanted to hate you. Especially after

152

Josh brought up Janelle and..." Her lip trembles and she turns her head away.

"Look at me, kitten." My voice is commanding yet full of emotion. Her eyes lift to mine. "You don't have *anything* to worry about with her. She means nothing to me." I pull into the driveway and park Chelsea's vehicle. Turning to her, I whisper, "I never meant to fall for you. Didn't think I deserved to love after the tragedy. But you... You're *everything* to me, Jordyn."

She rips her seatbelt off and throws herself onto my lap. I wince as she crashes against my ribs, which after the trainer checked me over, are bruised.

"Sorry. I'm so sorry. I didn't mean to hurt you." She tries to pull back, but I won't let her.

"Kitten, you can hurt me like that anytime. I don't care if I'm in fucking traction. Lay on me. I can take it."

She laughs before I silence her with a kiss that has her moaning into my mouth and her hands fisting my shirt. My hands rub over the back of my jersey that she's still wearing.

Mine. She's all fucking mine.

When I finally pull back, I whisper, "What kind of books do you like to read?"

Her cheeks flame red. "Why?"

I smirk. Although many of the books on her bookcase have discreet covers, I took photos of them and read the blurbs on Amazon. I didn't tell her I bought a Kindle Unlimited subscription. "Do you have any smutty books?"

She's blushing to the roots of her hair as she fidgets with the hem of my shirt. "Ummm... why?"

"Cause if you do," I tilt her chin so she's looking into my eyes. "I'd like you to read me a scene while sitting on my face."

Her pupils blow wide with lust, her body trembling. "Good, Lord." Raising a shaking hand to her forehead, she mutters, "I think I'm overheating."

"Good. You can think about which smutty scene you wanna read to me while we walk to the house."

"But I thought you wanted to talk?"

"Oh, I do. But after I grovel and then tell you my sad story, I intend to worship every inch of my bookworm thoroughly and properly."

"Oh, fuck," she mutters, grinding herself over me. "Are you sure we can't start with that?"

"Positive. I don't only want your body, Jordyn. I want *all* of you."

THIRTY MINUTES LATER, Jordyn is lying on my bed, wrapped in my arms. I told her about the conversation with Coach Jensen that helped get my head on straight.

Jordyn's apologetic face lifts to mine. "Before you begin... I just want you to know. I never went to the clinic after I saw you. The things you said before you left and the look in your eyes... I knew you were telling me the truth."

A smile curls my lips. "Good. And can I tell you one more thing? Please don't be mad... But I overheard you outside talking to Chelsea after my run." She blinks at me, her mouth forming a little O shape. "I didn't mean to. I was thinking about my family, and I couldn't breathe. I went outside and before I knew it, you were coming around the corner, on the phone. I didn't have time to go inside."

She shakes her head. "As if you would've gone inside."

I chuckle, squeezing her against me. "You know me better than I thought." Kissing the top of her head, I laugh as she swats my arm.

Pulling back slightly, I tip her face to mine. "After I'm finished telling you what happened to my family, will you tell me about your dad?" *Providing you don't believe I'm nothing but a dark cloud of bad luck and run away, screaming.*

"Of course."

"Okay," I brush a strand of hair away from her face and blow out a shaky breath. "I hope this doesn't change your opinion of me."

"It won't, Tristan. I already know it won't."

We stare at each other, the silence lingering between us as I lie there on the bed, choked by grief and guilt. Fear reaches out, dragging a cold hand along my spine. Everything is on the line.

I take a deep breath, then quickly exhale as pain shoots through my bruised ribs. Jordyn lightly rubs her finger over them. My breath hitches from the gentle, caring way she touches me, and a pained hiss shoots out of me.

"Sorry."

I give her a grin. "Don't apologize. That hiss was worth it. The way you touched me..." Tears fill my eyes from the thought of me telling her about my family and her leaving me, never touching or looking at me like she's in love with me again.

"Tristan. Stop it. Telling me what happened won't change things." Her eyes widen. "Oh, God. Did you have a girlfriend, and she broke up with you because of what happened with your family?"

I stroke her hair, chuckling. "No, that's not it. Tamara, whom I'd been dating since high school, and I called it quits during my first year of college. She was attending the Art Institute of California in Los Angeles, and I was here, playing hockey. The distance proved too much, and when she came to visit me one weekend, she called it quits. We parted on good terms, though."

"I'm sorry, Tristan. Did she fly here to see you play when you were together?"

I stare at her, shocked. "No. She claimed that leaving campus meant missing out on clubs, parties, and activities that ultimately helped her make connections and aided her future career."

Jordyn looks puzzled. "She couldn't have done that during the week? I mean, I get it if it's an occasional thing, but didn't she come to any of your games before the two of you separated?"

"A couple." I'm flabbergasted at her expression. "Would you do that?"

This time, she's the one staring at me in disbelief. "Of course. Your goals would be as important to me as they are to you, and I'd be willing to make sacrifices to help you achieve them. I mean, my goals would still be very important, and I'd continue working on them. But if you're committed to someone, you find a way to make it work."

I pull her against me, my lips capturing hers before she can get another word out. She kisses me back with just as much passion and intensity.

When we finally part, I grin at her. "You're pretty damn amazing, kitten. You know that?"

She grins. "I don't know why that makes me amazing. I'm just... me."

"And you're fucking amazing. All of you."

Her finger runs down my face. "You're amazing, too."

I swat her ass. "Let me get this out before you distract me."

"Yes, captain." A flirtatious grin covers her lips.

"Not helping." I wiggle my brows at her, as she laughs.

"Okay, I'll get serious. Now, tell me what happened."

CHAPTER 30

Tristan

"My parents were amazing people. My mom was a professional figure skater until a knee injury ended her career. My dad played hockey for the Wolverines before being drafted by the Pittsburgh Penguins. After he retired, he became the coach of my high school hockey team, so I was fortunate enough to be coached by him."

"He taught you how to skate and play hockey?"

"Both my parents taught Elaine, my sister, and me how to skate. Elaine was two years younger than me. She was driven and dedicated to following in my mom's footsteps. My mom started coaching Elaine after her injury. She was my mom's first student."

Sadness overcomes me as the memories assault me. "Elaine was tired and run down all the time. She kept telling us it was from pushing herself so hard on the ice and trying to finish high school. She was a senior in high school, and it was my sophomore year here. It seemed logical until she collapsed on the ice in the middle of a competition. She was rushed to the hospital, undergoing various tests. After she was discharged, Elaine was sent to various specialists."

"God, how awful." Her finger lightly strokes my chest. "Scary, too."

I nod. "It was. I somehow made myself believe that whatever it was, she'd be okay. Elaine was strong." As if I'm living through it again, my throat constricts, and my mouth is dry. I swallow several times before continuing. "My parents were exhausted from worry and travel. They were also coming to all my hockey games, as was Elaine when she was feeling up to it."

"What an amazingly supportive family."

I nod. "They were the best." Swallowing over the lump in my throat, I look away, not wanting to cry yet. I take a few breaths in and out, and once the sensation eases, I continue. "The team had a game in New York against our biggest rivals. I was so excited. I wanted to make my dad proud. I had huge shoes to fill, but I felt like under Coach Jensen, my game was really improving."

"My parents and Elaine flew to Colorado to see a specialist three days before the game in New York. Elaine had been diagnosed with two autoimmune disorders. My mom found a doctor who specialized in immune-mediated disorders that were confounding most of her doctors because of the symptoms Elaine was experiencing."

"I'm glad they figured it out, but so sorry she was going through that."

"Me, too." Lifting her hand from my chest and kissing her palm. "The three of them planned to fly to New York to see my game, then home so they could prepare to go back to Colorado for however long it took to help Elaine."

With tears in my eyes, I stare at the ceiling, reliving it again. "My parents booked an earlier flight because of a massive snowstorm set to hit Denver. But the storm hit earlier than expected, grounding all flights. I was beside myself at the thought of them not being there."

"Tristan." Her hands cup my face, sympathy in her beautiful irises. "It's not your fault."

My eyes dart to hers, my voice bitter. "It's not? I wanted them there, Jordyn. I practically demanded they figure out a way to get to New York. That's the reason they booked a flight on a small, private plane. I was selfish and horrible to them, and that was the last time I ever spoke to them." The grief overtakes me, breaking my heart into pieces all over again. I hold onto Jordyn, sobbing for all I've lost.

She holds me for a while, stroking my back. When my sobs lessen, she pulls back, wiping my eyes. "Stop blaming yourself. You're haunted by something that's not your fault."

"It feels like it is, Jordyn. I practically demanded they get to my game—"

"They wanted to, or they wouldn't have tried so hard, Tristan."

Deep down, I know that. Yet, it doesn't assuage the relentless guilt.

"I was furious at them, Jordyn. When I got on the ice and they weren't there, I was so fucking angry. When the game started, I was ruthless, getting slapped with penalties for the way I'd been playing. Coach even threatened to bench me." I shake my head, the memories like a bad weed that keeps growing inside me, refusing to stop. "After the first period, Coach pulled me aside and demanded to know what was going on. I told him..." I shake my head, but the memory of his pinched expression, worry heavy in his eyes, won't leave. "My anger changed to uneasiness, then worry. A nagging feeling that something was wrong took over. Unable to focus, I played like shit."

"We lost the game. I went to my locker and tried calling all three of their phones, but there was no answer. I sat on

159

the bench in front of my locker, my head in my hands, until I felt a hand on my shoulder. It was Alex." I blew out a breath. "It was all over the media. The pilot radioed, saying they were in distress from the storm." I audibly swallow, my stomach and chest burning from the grief. "I knew they were gone. I felt it. And I collapsed on the floor, crying like a lost child."

"Oh, Tristan. I'm so sorry." Her hands stroke me gently as she holds me.

I nod, squeezing her tightly. "When they found the plane, there wasn't much left. They crashed in a snowy forest, trees and rocks tearing at the plane. The initial impact killed the pilot and my parents." I swallow hard, imagining the horror they must have felt. "My sister was found in the woods. She'd been ejected from the plane."

"Oh, fuck, Tristan." Her tears drip onto the side of my neck. "I don't know what to say. What an awful tragedy."

"I know. I've thought so much about it, but I can't make sense of why it happened to three amazing people. The only conclusion I've come up with is me. I was the cause since I was horrible and selfish to them before the accident. Karma took what I loved most."

She pulls back, wiping the tears from her face. "You need to understand you had nothing to do with your parent's death. It was a tragic accident, not karma or punishment because their son loved them so much he wanted them with him during an important game." She cups my face, her eyes imploring. "You're *not* responsible for their deaths. And though I've never met them, I'm certain the guilt you're feeling would destroy them."

I study her, wanting so badly to believe her. After sinking beneath the weight of it for so long, it's hard to change my mindset.

Her words are on repeat inside my head, especially the last

thing she said. *"The guilt you're feeling would destroy them."* I hadn't thought of it from their perspective before.

Jordyn leans over, placing a kiss on the tip of my nose. "My opinion of you has changed."

Panic fills me as my eyes dart to hers, searching them for the disappointment and disgust I'm certain she's feeling.

"You're even more amazing than I previously thought. You've been through so much, yet somehow found the courage to not only get up and carry on but get back on the ice as well, playing like a hockey god."

My body sags into the mattress, relief filling me. "I'm glad you're not leaving me." I tighten my arms around her like a vice. "Not that I'd let you go anywhere. Not now. And not ever." I give her a smile, my finger tracing over her face as though I'm memorizing every inch of it. "It wasn't easy at all."

"I was so depressed that I couldn't get out of bed. My grandma came home for the funeral, staying in my parent's house. I was supposed to return to campus afterward, but I couldn't. I took the rest of the semester off and lived with my grandma in a house full of memories that were slowly killing me."

"Oh, Tristan. I'm sorry. Depression is natural when there's so much love between you and your loved ones. After my dad died, one of our neighbors told me I was fortunate to love someone so much to grieve so hard. I thought she was crazy until she said that some people have such shitty relationships with their families that when one of them dies, they grieve very little, if at all."

"You keep giving me new perspectives, kitten."

"That's what I'm here for." Her smile is so full of love, it leaves me breathless.

I shouldn't ask the next question, but I'm dying to know the answer. "Are you gonna stick with me, even though you're worried about Josh finding out about us?"

Her expression falls, and my heart drops into my stomach. Avoiding eye contact, long lashes rest on her cheeks as she traces slow circles over my chest. My anxiety is spiraling out of control as I watch her, a wave of dizziness washing over me. My thoughts spiral, imagining life without her and the way she makes me feel. How much easier it is to breathe around her. All the things she makes me feel that I've never felt before.

Her gaze lifts, locking with mine. A slow smile curls her lips, causing my heart to beat faster as hope fills my chest. "You're worth the risk, puck boy."

I'm so fucking happy that I roll with her so I'm on top of her, putting my ribs through agony and stealing my breath. She squeaks in surprise, and I grin before kissing her like I own every piece of her, relishing in the taste of her lips. "Or hockey god." My lips capture hers again. "Or sex god."

She slaps her hand against my chest, laughing. "Yeah, like I need to make your ego any bigger."

My voice is husky. "You're not denying I'm a sex god. I'll take the compliment." I wink at her before losing myself in her kiss.

For once, I don't feel guilty that the happiness she makes me feel takes away the loss and grief I've been living with.

"How about I reward you before we talk about your dad?"

"Is this the part where you ask me to get a book from my room?"

"No... I just ask you to pull up one of your books on your phone." *I'm so obsessed with her, she has no idea I've become a fucking stalker.*

Her brows draw in. "What? How do you know there are books on my phone?"

"You're a heavy sleeper. I snuck into your room and looked through your phone. Then I took a screenshot of the book page you'd been reading and skimmed through it. That book you're reading is hotter than hell. It took everything I had not to strip you naked and have my way with you."

"You're terrible. When did you do that?"

"I'm not telling."

She pouts before her brows draw together in anger. "Then I'm not sitting on your face."

"The hell you're not. You're gonna wear my jersey while you ride my face until your juices drip down my chin."

"Not until—"

I'm on my knees, pulling her up with me. Once I get her on her feet, I strip her, then pull my jersey over her head. She fights me, of course, which just makes it hotter.

Pulling her against me, I kiss the hell out of her, devouring her mouth, while my hand slides to her soaked pussy. "Mmmm... so fucking wet. Don't tell me you don't want to sit on my face, cause I'll call you a damn liar."

She blushes, her eyes full of desire as I shove two fingers inside her. "Fuck, Tristan."

I smirk at her, teasing her until she's a whimpering mess before I pull my fingers out of her and climb onto the bed. She's hesitant as she climbs on the bed. Grabbing her, I ignore how much the pain in my ribs makes me want to scream, dragging her so she's hovering over my face. "Sit."

She gingerly lowers herself. My hands grab her waist, and as I yank her onto my mouth, I growl, "I said sit. Let me feast on this sweet pussy, kitten."

CHAPTER 31

Jordyn

Two hours later, Tristan rolls me over. My limbs resemble wet noodles as I sag against his body, spent from the way he spanked me while eating my pussy like a starving man because I wore Gardner's jersey. Each time I got close, he denied me the orgasm. I begged and pleaded, but even hurt, Tristan was stronger and easily lifted me every time I was on the edge.

After edging me twice, the third time, I was punished for arguing with him about sitting on his face. His tongue teased me relentlessly until I was a sweaty, aching mess, whimpering and begging for release. Finally, he lifted me from his face, my juices shining on his lips, and told me to grab my phone and read to him, promising he'd make me come. I've never had such difficulties reading in my life. I barely read two paragraphs before he finally rewarded me, sucking hard on my clit. I detonated around him with such force that I was afraid I'd drown him from coming so hard.

Tristan gathered me in his arms. "Don't think I'm done with you yet, kitten. But I'll give you a break because I really wanna hear what happened to your dad." His finger strokes my cheek before he gently tucks a stray lock of hair behind my ear. I practically purr from the contentment that seeps through me, making my bones like jelly.

"Tell me about your dad, kitten." His lips lightly brush my temple.

I nod, tracing circles over his chest. "My dad was an amazing, hardworking man who loved his family. I have so many good memories of the three of us." The smile dies from my face as the day that changed my life hits me so hard in the chest that I'm back there, reliving it again.

"When dad became sick with a nasty cough, we weren't worried. He'd been working a lot of overtime to make extra money for Christmas. But the cough wouldn't go away and kept getting worse. Two days after Christmas, he was coughing up blood and wheezing." I take a deep breath and slowly exhale. "My mom drove him to the ER, and I sat in the back seat of the car, worried sick about my dad. I was afraid he was gonna die."

His arms tighten around me. "I'm sorry, kitten. That must've been so scary."

"They admitted him to the hospital and ran tests to figure out what was going on. He was diagnosed with a very aggressive form of lung cancer. Unfortunately, it had already spread to his bones."

"How old were you?"

"I was thirteen when he was diagnosed. He began treatments shortly after the New Year. It was rough." I pause, trying to rein in my emotions. "He died two days after my fifteenth birthday. The Strawberry Shortcake doll you held was my birthday present from him." Swallowing the lump in my throat, I lift my hand to wipe my tears, but Tristan stops me.

"It's okay to cry, my sweet kitten. Let it out."

I bite my lip and nod. "I know. It's just... I want to get this out before I break down."

Tristan nods and strokes my cheek. "Take your time. I'm not going anywhere."

Jesus. Warmth blooms inside my chest, making me flounder for words. My mind is blank as they repeat like a record player. *I'm not going anywhere.*

The sincerity on his face as he strokes my arm has my heart swelling for him. "What's the significance of the Strawberry Shortcake doll?"

An embarrassed grin covers my face. "When I was a kid, my favorite color was pink, and I loved strawberries. Santa brought me a Strawberry Shortcake doll for Christmas one year. It was my favorite toy. I was an only child, so that doll became my best friend. When I got older and stopped playing with dolls, she was the one I couldn't part with." The misery washes over me, making my breath stutter. Tristan strokes my back, his touch so comforting and supportive that it gives me the strength to continue. "Kids in school can be mean. They called me nerd girl because I spent more time reading than spending time hanging out and trying to be popular. The bullying and name-calling got worse, and I confided in my Strawberry Shortcake doll as if she were a friend."

Tristan's muscles tense and his nostrils flare. "Who are they? Give me names and I'll take care of them. I promise they'll never pick on you again."

I lay my palm flat over his rapidly pounding heart. Warmth curls through me as I walk my fingers up his chest and then place my index finger against his lip. "They don't matter, Tristan. I moved away after my dad started treatments and never saw them again."

He nibbles at my finger, and I giggle, pulling it away. The happiness dancing in his mossy irises fades, a serious look on his face. "If you do, I want you to point them out to me. If any of them are on this campus and they try shit with you—"

"I promise I'll tell you if I do." I give him a sweet, lingering kiss, before pulling back with a smirk. "Let me get this out." Taking a deep breath, I launch into the story of how the treatments made my dad sick and weak. My mom sold our house and we moved to a rental because of the expense of his treatments. During the move, my Strawberry Shortcake doll got lost and I was devastated. How lonely I was because I didn't have friends and I'd lost my doll.

"You didn't have any friends?" I hate the pity in Tristan's tone.

"I had acquaintances, not friends. I was so busy helping my mom care for my dad. Plus, it may sound silly, but I loved both my parents so much. I just wanted to be around them."

"It's not silly at all, kitten. I understand. I had a lot of acquaintances. Alex was my only real friend. I couldn't have done it without him."

"I met Chelsea in college. She was my roommate... And my first real friend."

Tristan squeezes me tighter. "And now you have Chelsea, Alex, and me." He presses his lips against mine. "So you moved to be closer because of his treatments, right?"

"Yes. My mom and I hoped they'd work, but it soon faded. He was so sick and sometimes, I still have doubts about encouraging him to undergo them. It seems they did more harm than good."

"Hindsight is always 20/20, kitten. When a loved one is sick, you'll do anything to save them."

I marvel at the truth in his words. "He went through hell for two years, battling every day. In my heart, I knew he was going to lose the war." My voice is flat, and time seems to slow down as I go back to that horrific day. "The day he died, he insisted I go to school. I didn't want to leave him, but I did."

My eyes stare vacantly at a spot on his comforter. "He looked bad, Tristan. So pale, skinny, and weak. I had this sick feeling inside, like I knew he wouldn't be alive when I came home from school. But after watching him slowly die for two years, I don't think I could've handled watching him take his last breath."

"Two hours after I arrived at school, I was called to the principal's office. It felt like I was walking through quicksand when I left the classroom. I walked inside and took one look at the sadness in the secretary's eyes, and I knew. I heard her say, 'I'm sorry, but your father—' before I fled. I ran as fast as I could toward home. My mom stopped and picked me up. She'd been on her way to get me...."

Tristan's breathing increases as he squeezes me tighter, offering his support. I cling to him, my heart aching, and my throat raw from swallowing so much, trying to prevent the tears from falling.

"Once inside the house, I held his hand and whispered how much I loved him, even though he was gone. I just felt like he could hear me, you know?"

"I know he did, Jordyn."

I collapse against him, tears flowing down my cheeks and onto his neck. His strong arms grip me, like a life raft in the worst storm. I'm confident he won't let me drown.

We stay like that for a few minutes, comfortable with the silence between us, words unnecessary. Once the sadness lifts, I finish my story.

"The coroners came and took away his body. All the days after that were dark and bleak. Mom and I were shells of the people we once were. We kept busy with arrangements, but after the funeral, day bled into night, and I had no idea what I did all day other than stare out my window and replay memories of better days."

The tears start again, coursing down my cheeks. "Things

never got better. Mom had to use money from the college fund she and dad created so that we could survive. We struggled so much that when I turned sixteen, I worked part-time at a bookstore to help mom pay bills."

"Sounds like the perfect job for you. Did you consider becoming a librarian then?"

"Not until Cornell. The librarians were so amazing there. They were my inspiration."

"What about family? Wasn't there anyone to help you and your mom?"

"My mom's parents died years ago, and my dad's parents had disowned him when he married my mom because they thought they were too young. They married while they were in college, and she had me when she was twenty-two. She wrote a few letters and called them, but they didn't respond. Nor did they come to my dad's funeral."

"Oh, God. How cruel."

"I know. Life can be cruel." My aqua eyes lock with his green eyes, my insides warming from the sea of devotion swimming in them. "Sometimes it rewards you by sending unexpected people into it that make you forget the pain and strife."

Tristan's lips part slightly. His voice is low and husky when he speaks. "Are you referring to me?"

"I am, captain." My hand cups his face before I plant my lips against his. "You ease my pain. Make me forget all the bad things in my life."

"Good." He pulls me so I'm lying on top of him. I begin protesting but he shuts me up with a kiss. "I want to know everything about you, but right now, I'm desperate to take advantage of the fact that neither Josh nor Chelsea are here."

"But your ribs...."

"Fuck my ribs." He cups my face. "I need you."

CHAPTER 32

Jordyn

Three days later, I'm heading into my office in the tutoring center, holding my phone slightly away from my ear as Chelsea nearly deafens me. "Oh my God. Tristan made you sit on his face and edged you? That's fucking amazing! This guy is so good for you."

"It didn't feel amazing at the time," I mutter, but a smile curls my lips. It was the most pleasurable pain I've ever felt, but I don't want to admit that to Chelsea.

"Uh-huh. Keep telling yourself that. Did he let you come?"

My face burns from embarrassment. "Yes. I had to read a scene from a book to him."

"Oh, fuck. I spit out my iced coffee." We laugh before she says, "Was it one of the smutty books we love?"

Unlocking the door, I hurry inside and shut it, my body overheating from the images rolling through my head. "Yes. It was a hockey smut book." I cringe, chagrined, as Chelsea howls with laughter.

"Oh, shit. Did he know it was a hockey book?"

"Yes. The bastard confessed he snuck into my room and

went through my kindle. He took a screenshot of the page I was on, then skimmed through the book, leaving it where I left off so I wouldn't know." Placing my bag on the table, I sit down at my desk. "He has a Kindle Unlimited subscription now."

"Wait, what? Did you go through it?"

"Yup. He handed me his phone, and I checked it out." I shiver at the memory of Tristan demanding I read a smutty scene out loud and then every part of it with me.

"Marry that man. Right now."

"Oh my God. Staappph." I giggle, my heart pounding vigorously at the thought of keeping him forever.

"So you worked everything out?"

"Yup. We had such a nice talk about our pasts while you were at the party with Alex." Shaking my head, I log into my laptop and pull up my tutoring schedule for the day. "I've changed my opinion of him. He's not a puck boy. He's lovable, not puckable. Well, wait... He's definitely puckable. Hence why I pucked him in the shower."

Chelsea giggles. "That's a lot of hockey wordplay in one statement. I'm glad Tristan isn't a fuck boy, or puck boy as you call him."

"I wanted to give you details on Sunday before you left, but Alex and Tristan wouldn't leave our side. Speaking of, I wanna hear everything about the party you went to with Alex." I frown as I look at my schedule. "But it'll have to wait. I have an appointment coming in any minute now."

"I've gotta go anyway. I'm meeting my group to work on a project."

"You're being careful, right?" I frown, worried about Erik getting his unhinged hands on my bestie again.

"I'm being very cautious. Don't worry." She makes kissing noises. "I gotta go. Love ya, girl."

"Love you, too." I hang up the phone, sipping my coffee

while reviewing my appointments. I choke on it when I see Bryce Gardner's name. Even worse, Tristan booked a session with me right after Bryce's.

As much as I'm irritated about Bryce booking an appointment with me, I don't have any good reason to cancel it.

I resign myself to the fact that I'll see Bryce in a few hours. Blowing out a breath, I lean back in my chair. I need to figure out how to end the session before Tristan arrives.

I'm sitting at the table, drumming my fingers against the wood, annoyance thrumming through me. Bryce is twenty minutes late. He hasn't canceled the appointment or emailed me to let me know he's running late.

Five minutes later, I snatch my laptop from the table, about to head to my office, when Bryce casually strolls in with a broad smile and a carefree attitude. I set my laptop down, scowling at him. His dark hair gleams beneath the fluorescent lights in my office as he pulls out the chair beside me, turns it around, and straddles it.

"You're late," I snap, glaring at him.

He shrugs. "Yeah. And?"

I gape at him, my mouth hanging open. "And?" I snarl, my brows drawing together. "I have another appointment after yours that I need to prepare for, which means this session ends in twenty minutes."

"Relax, Jordyn. The next person can wait."

There's no way in hell Tristan will wait, especially once he lays eyes on Bryce.

"Your attitude is disrespectful. Your time is no more precious than anyone else's."

He rolls his eyes and leans forward, a smug smile on his face. "You're even hotter when you're pissed." He smirks at me, and when I huff out a breath and turn to stomp away, he grabs my arm. "Sorry. Just speaking the truth. Let's get started."

I'm ready to bang my head against the table fifteen minutes later. Bryce keeps interrupting and looking at his phone, making excuses as to why he has to stop the session. I've told him at least six times to turn it off, but he refuses. I tried taking it from him at one point, but he snatched his arm away and grabbed my wrist, pulling me closer. I shoved him away, which only made him laugh. He wasn't getting it when he focused on the material. At all.

When he grabs his phone again, I snap, "Put that fucking thing away, or I'm throwing it through the window."

"Ohhh... Bossy and demanding. I can see why Harrington's banging you." His heated gaze lowers, stopping at my chest. "I mean, it's hard to hide tits like that."

I gasp, my palm itching to slap him. "Find another tutor, Bryce. We're done." Before I can stomp away, Bryce grabs my wrist, his hold on me like a vice. "What the hell are you doing?" I tug against his grip, trying to pull away.

Instead of letting me go, he yanks me closer. My balance teeters, and I grab his shoulder to prevent myself from falling.

"What's it look like? Do you really think you're anything more than a piece of ass to Harrington? Get real, Jordyn. Tristan doesn't do relationships." Emitting a vile chuckle, full of darkness, he hits on my biggest weakness. "Do you believe that shit he fed you about Janelle? The only reason he didn't finish fucking her on the couch is because you walked in, and he saw you as a bigger challenge."

Don't listen to him. I swallow hard, doubt swirling inside me.

"Didn't he ghost you the rest of the weekend? Where do you think he was?"

"Let go of me." I yank against his hold, trying to hide how his words affect me. My body is shaking, and I feel sick to my stomach. *What if he's right? Tristan said he was with Alex... But was he?*

173

"Josh told me he and Tristan have plans to fuck Janelle." He tugs on my wrist, pulling me closer. "Tristan plans to fuck her in the as—"

His words are cut off as I'm yanked back, and Bryce's hand is savagely ripped away from my wrist before I'm tugged against a familiar hard body. Tristan's woodsy scent makes my knees weak as he whispers in my ear, "I've got you, kitten."

"Well, well. I didn't expect to see you—"

Bryce doesn't get a chance to finish. Tristan yanks him out of the chair and shoves him over the table, his hand wrapped around the back of his neck.

"I should kill you for touching her." He pulls him back slightly and slams his head against the table again. "If I ever catch you touching her again, I'll fucking cut your hand off and shove it up your ass." The fury in Tristan's voice causes goosebumps to skate over my skin even as I shiver from the heat coiling in my stomach. "She's never tutoring you again, asshole. Understand?"

A vile laugh comes from Bryce. "The impossible has finally happened. You're in love with a girl, and it's Josh's stepsister. The off-limits one. I'll bet Josh will love hearing you're fucking her—" A pained hiss comes out of him as Tristan savagely twists his hand behind his back. I cringe, waiting for it to snap.

"But you're not going to tell, are you, Bryce? You won't say a fucking word. Wanna know why?" I've never heard such an evil laugh come from Tristan. Not gonna lie. It really turns me on. "I know all about you fucking Daddy's secretary on his desk. He wasn't happy about the two of you flirting, was he? And yet, two weeks later, you fucked her in his office." Tristan tsks, shaking his head. "Your mom will really be pissed and disappointed that you fucked her best friend."

Bryce's face is as pale as the white wall behind him. I blink in surprise, captivated by how Tristan seethes at Bryce, jaw clenching, veins running down his arm and popping against his skin, easily restraining him. The power he exudes makes me hot.

Defeat registers on Bryce's face. "I-I... I won't talk. I won't tell Josh."

"You shouldn't trust Josh. He's the one who shared the video with me." Tristan releases him, standing between me and Bryce. "If you ever book an appointment in the Learning Center, it will be with another tutor, or I'll fucking ruin your life and your hockey career. Got it?"

Bryce swallows hard, nodding at Tristan, before he turns and flees from the Learning Center.

All the adrenaline disappears as the fear takes over. My legs shake before giving out on me, but before I fall, Tristan's strong arms catch me, pulling me against his chest. "I'm so sorry." He peppers kisses over the top of my head, rubbing my back.

I melt against his body. "Thank God you showed up when you did." I pull back slightly, looking at his furious expression. His features soften when our eyes lock together, worry dancing in his irises. "He'll never bother you again. I promise." He cups my face, his thumb stroking the apple of my cheek. "If he ever looks at your tits again, I'll gouge his fucking eyes out."

A giggle bursts from my lips. "Eww. Don't give them to me if you do. I don't want them... Or any part of him." An involuntary shiver rolls through me.

Tristan chuckles. "I promise." His lips gently press against mine. "I'll always protect you, kitten."

"I know," I whisper softly. "Why did you schedule tutoring appointments? You don't need it."

A panty-melting grin spreads across his face. *R.I.P panties.*

"It's a brilliant plan. We'll tell Josh you're tutoring me so we can spend lots of time together." His head dips, kissing the shell of my ear. "I'll learn all the ways I can please you." He lifts me so I'm sitting on the edge of the table. I look around, but we're the only ones here.

Spreading my legs, he steps between them. "I just wanna touch..." His hands slide up my leggings, causing goosebumps over my skin. "Kiss." He lowers his head, kissing my lips until I'm breathless. His lips move over my jaw until they nip at the skin on my neck. "And suck..." I moan, tilting my head as he sucks on my neck, marking me. My hands slide to his back, fisting his shirt as he kisses over the spot he just marked, moving back up to my face. His eyes burn with intensity. "No part of your body will be left untouched. And then I'll stick my cock deep inside you and fuck you in every imaginable position."

Bryce's words run through my head, causing my spine to snap straight. Releasing his shirt, I pull back. "Tristan. We can't..." My voice sounds weak to my ears. I want to believe him.

His brow furrows. "What is it, Jordyn?"

I bite my lip. "Something Bryce said... It made me uneasy."

"Tell me."

I recite the horrible things he said to me, cringing and feeling ill by the time I'm finished.

"He's a fucking liar. I was with Alex, and Bryce knows that because he and Landin were there." His brows lower, and his expression tightens from anger. "I don't want to fuck Janelle. I don't care if she walks in here naked." His thumb pulls on my lip, freeing it from my teeth. "There's only one woman I want. You." Green eyes pierce mine, a promise burning in them. "You're all I see. All I think about. The only one I desire."

Licking his thumb, the groan from Tristan lights my nerves on fire.

"Let's go to your office, and I'll prove it to you."

With my eyes locked on his, I suck on his thumb,

watching his eyes heat and his lips part, raspy breaths feathering over my face. "How?"

He grabs my hand, placing it on his rock-hard cock. "Let me fuck you until you can barely walk."

Fuck. I moan, licking his thumb again before I suck it between my lips. "God, yes."

He lifts me, and I wrap my arms and legs around him. He carries me to my office, then shuts and locks the door behind him. Setting me on my feet, our lips crash together, hungry and desperate kisses. We tear at each other's clothing, only breaking apart long enough to pull the other's shirt over their head and their pants from their ankles.

He sets me on my desk and rubs the head of his cock against my clit as his lips find mine again. Then he slides inside, and I'm lost in his, moaning as he begins thrusting.

"Fuck. You're so damn wet and tight." His forehead falls against mine.

"Jesus. You're so big. You fill me up and stretch me so good."

He thrusts faster and harder. "Mmm. I could live inside your pussy. Night and day."

I grin at him. "Not possible."

"You sure about that?" He winks, pounding into me. "I love a challenge."

I groan, unable to speak. My head falls back as the pleasure overwhelms me. We fit together a missing puzzle piece.

My hooded lids fly open as he pulls out. He chuckles at the expression on my face before he grabs me, pulling me off the desk. "Don't worry." He bends me over, my cheek against the wood, his hand pressing into my spine, making me arch. As he slides inside me, he says, "I'm just gonna fuck you doggy style." Wrapping a fist around my hair, he pulls my head back and starts moving. "Then you'll ride me. But not before I have you grab your ankles as I fuck you from behind."

"Jesus, Tristan."

He chuckles and pulls out. My eyes snap open, frustration welling through me, making my hands clench into fists on the desk. "Stop edging me," I snap, hungry and desperate for him to fill me.

"Such a needy little bookworm." He slams inside me, and I whimper, the combination of pain and pleasure giving me goosebumps. "This pussy is choking my cock, not wanting me to leave. I like it." Leaning down, he sinks his teeth into my shoulder as he rams in and out of me, our skin slapping together.

"Oh, fuck, Tristan. Fuck me harder."

"Beg for it, kitten. Beg for me to fuck you until you scream."

"Oh, hell yes. Please fuck me harder." I arch as he slams in and out of me, the pleasure rapidly building.

"I'm gonna make you come so much. You'll be begging me to stop."

I look at him over my shoulder. "Do your worst, hockey boy."

My words drive him crazy. He fucks me so hard; I'm surprised we don't break my desk.

As he pounds me into oblivion, my moans and whimpers mixing with his grunts and groans filling my office, I'm capable of one thought. *Best tutoring session ever.*

CHAPTER 33
Tristan

Jordyn stands by the toaster, loading two pieces of bread into the slots. She's wearing a pair of leggings and a tank top that shows off every delicious curve. My gaze darts around, and when I don't spot Josh anywhere, I come up behind her, one hand on either side of her, pressing against her backside as I pin her hips against the counter.

"Tristan, what are you doing?" She hisses in a panic.

I lower my lips to the side of her neck, nuzzling her. "What does it feel like?"

"You can't do this." A moan slips from her lips as her body goes slack against mine. "What about Josh?"

"Fuck Josh. Hopefully, he's with Janelle. And if he doesn't wrap it, he'll end up with herpes."

Her giggle makes me smile. The sound is so beautifully perfect. I could listen to it every day for the rest of my life.

"Who cares if he does." Growing serious, she swats at my hand. "We're gonna get caught if we aren't careful," she whispers.

"Mmmm.... Sounds hot." My hand roams down the front of her leggings and cups her pussy.

"I'm serious," she breathlessly whispers.

"So I am." I breathe against her ear, feeling her shiver. My lips leave a trail of kisses down the side of her neck, her ponytail giving me access to her strawberry-scented skin. My hand slides beneath the waistband of her pants, moving down to her panty-clad pussy. She moans, her hand sliding around the back of my neck.

"Didn't you just have me a few hours ago? Aren't you bored of me yet?" A teasing smile is on her face.

I lower my mouth, covering hers. "Never," I whisper, meaning it with every fiber of my being. "I could never get tired of you."

Footsteps sound behind us, and I immediately pull my hand from her pants and step back. Jordyn jumps and whirls around, aqua eyes round. She looks at me, then over my shoulder to Josh.

"Hey, Jordyn. Tristan." There's an air of suspicion in his tone as his eyes skip back and forth between us.

I turn around, a friendly smile on my face. "Hey, Josh. What's up?" From the corner of my eye, Jordyn gives Josh a weak smile, her hand fluttering over her heart.

Way to be discreet, Jordyn. She looks like a deer caught in headlights.

His eyes narrow on Jordyn before they lock on mine. "The two of you look cozy."

I shrug my shoulders as Jordyn's body tenses beside me. "She thought the toast was stuck. I was checking to make sure it wasn't."

"I tried hitting the release, and nothing happened," she offered feebly. "Tristan saw me struggling and came over to check it out."

"Oh. Well, it's almost time for our morning workout. Wanna ride together, Tristan?"

"Sure. Lemme grab my gym bag. Want me to drive?"

"That's fine." His tone has softened, but his muscles are still tense.

I pat his shoulder as I walk over to him. "How's Janelle?"

He relaxes, a smug smile curling his lips. "An easy lay."

I chuckle as Jordyn snorts. "Gross." She grabs her toast, slathering butter on it. "I'm going upstairs to eat before I lose my appetite."

Rubbing my hand over my face to hide my amused smile, I glance at Jordyn as she scowls at me before heading up the stairs. To appease Josh, I give him a smug grin. "She isn't a fan of Janelle, huh?"

Josh chuckles, moving to the fridge. "Yeah, she's not a fan of anyone who's fun. Jordyn is as tightly wound as they come."

Rubbing my fingers over my lips so I don't inadvertently say something I'll regret, I murmur, "Mmm hmm. Lemme get my stuff. I'll be right back."

Josh waves his hand, heading to the fridge. "Take your time. I wanna make some eggs and a protein shake."

I can barely contain my whistle as I bound up the steps. Hurrying down the hallway, I head straight to Jordyn's room, closing the door behind me. She looks up from her desk, her half-eaten toast frozen in the air. "What are you doing here, Tristan?" The annoyance in her tone makes me chuckle.

I take slow steps toward her, a salacious smile on my face. Her breathing hitches before it rushes from her lungs. She drops her toast on her plate, her hands shaking slightly.

When I reach her, my hands press against the chair's armrests, caging her in. Inhaling her strawberry scent, my lips hover close to hers. "Explaining to you why I brought up Janelle." I brush my nose against hers. "I knew it would buy us some time. I successfully distracted Josh, who is no longer suspicious of us." I wink at her, lightly brushing my lips against hers. "Please don't be mad about it."

Her arms wrap around my neck. "I'm not." She kisses me. "Nice technique, captain."

"Kissing or distracting Josh?"

She smirks. "Both."

"Lemme prove how good my technique is. I bet I can give you an orgasm in five minutes."

She raises a brow. "You may be overestimating your abilities."

"Bet me." Tugging her to her feet, I yank her pants and thong down, then spin her around and push her so she's bending over her chair, her hands on the seat. Dropping to my knees, I don't give her a chance to say a word before I'm burying my tongue deep inside her.

"Holy shit," she gasps, spreading her legs wider. I smile against her wet pussy, eating her like a hungry man starving for breakfast. She buries her mouth against her arm, her legs shaking from being primed by the last orgasm I gave her.

Pulling back, I bite her ass cheek, making her gasp. I swat it, listening to the hiss of pain that turns into a strangled moan. Dragging my sweatpants to my ankles, I place one hand flat against her lower back, making her arch for me while the other guides the head of my cock against her tight pussy.

"Please, Tris—"

I thrust deep inside her, desperate to feel her again. She moans so loud that I reach around, my hand clamping over her mouth. "Shhh, kitten. Unless you want Josh to hear us."

Nipping at the shell of her ear, she shakes her head, flooding my hard cock with her wetness. "You sure about that? I can make you scream as you shatter around my cock." I thrust hard and fast, losing control as her pussy clenches around me.

She shakes her head, and I loosen my hand so she can speak. "No, he can't..." she moans as I thrust deep. "He can't hear us."

"Be quiet, kitten." I slide my hand lower, pinching her hard nipple through her tank top and bra. Her light whimper makes me smile. I thrust faster, my hand sliding to her clit, massaging it with light circles, at odds with my powerful thrusts. "You love the way my big cock stretches your tight pussy, don't you?"

She moans, turning her head to look over her shoulder at me. I smack her ass before my lips capture hers in a hungry kiss, my thrusts growing wilder as my control slips. Her legs tremble, so I rub her clit faster, knowing she's close.

"Come for me," I whisper against her lips, my hips bucking wildly as my composure snaps. Her entire body shakes as I kiss her wildly and hungrily, still thrusting as she soaks my dick. I lose my mind, pounding into her a couple more times before exploding inside her.

I collapse against her back, my gaze moving to the clock beside her laptop. "How's that for a five-minute quickie?"

She giggles, her body warm beneath mine. "You possess mad skills, captain."

CHAPTER 34

Jordyn

The Wolverines' next game is out of town, which makes it much easier for me to sneak out to dance at Sinful Sirens. So far, I've managed to do four shows without them knowing. The lies keep piling up, drowning me in guilt. Neither has questioned me, but the dishonesty made me break out in hives, causing me to take antihistamines. I don't mind lying to Josh, but I hate being dishonest with Tristan.

Chelsea is on her way to stay with me for the weekend, making me extremely excited and suspicious. Even though I know she's anxious to see Alex again, I suspect there's something more sinister going on. I intend to find out on the way to Sinful.

～

FOUR HOURS LATER, I'm on the highway, darting glances at Chelsea, who is smiling at her phone. Without lifting her gaze, she sighs. "I can feel your beady eyes boring into me. What's up, Jordyn?"

I don't say anything as my eyes move back to the road. Uneasiness swirls in my gut until I blurt out, "I'm worried about you, Chelsea. Something is wrong. I can tell."

She bites her glossy red lip, a tell-tale sign I'm right. "Don't freak out. It could be nothing."

My gaze leaves the road. "But...."

"I've had the sensation I'm being watched and followed. I don't have any proof, just the uncanny feeling of the hair standing on the back of my neck."

"Oh shit. Is Erik still committed?"

"I don't know. I've been trying to get information, but he's protected by HIPAA, and no one will release any information." She shudders in the seat, running a hand through her sleek, dark hair. "It's freaking me out that he may be on the loose. My nightmares have returned. Every time I close my eyes, I see the insanity in his black eyes, his dark hoodie slipping and revealing that evil grin...."

I wrap my fingers around hers and squeeze. "I'm sorry. What I witnessed was scary as hell. I can't imagine..." Shivers course down my spine.

"Thank God you heard the struggle. My vision was blackening... I really thought I was going to die."

I squeeze her fingers. "But you didn't. I was there, and the baseball bat was nearby. I swung for the fence when I cracked that thing over his back."

"Have I told you lately how grateful I am that you didn't hesitate to go after him? You were ready to kill him to save my life."

"No gratitude necessary. I love you, Chelsea. You're my best friend. Damned if I was gonna stand by and watch him kill you." We share a look, our bond stronger than ever. "Why do I feel like there's more you're not telling me?"

She sighs, averting her gaze. "I've received some creepy

185

texts from an unknown number. And I swear some of my clothing is missing."

I shiver as a chill runs down my spine. "Chelsea..." I choke out her name, fear slithering up my spine. "You need to get out of there. Can you go home?"

Chelsea shakes her head rapidly. "You know my parents...."

A sick feeling rises inside me. "Yeah, I do. Selfish bastards," I mutter. "What if you leave New York and stay here? At least temporarily."

Her phone beeps, and she smiles at the screen before turning her attention to me. I know immediately she's received a text from Alex by the look on her face. "I've debated doing that, but what if my parents figure it out?"

"Not to sound mean, but they likely won't figure it out until the end of the semester. That buys you time. Since they regularly deposit a lot of money in your account, you can take some courses at WHU. It's much cheaper than Cornell. Maybe Josh and Tristan will let you stay—"

"I don't wanna be a burden, Jordyn."

"And I don't want you dead, Chelsea," I snap without thinking. Her face pales, and the fear contorting her face before she turns away makes my heart ache. "I'm sorry. I shouldn't have said that."

She exhales before turning to me, a smile pasted on her face. "No, you're right, Jordyn. If it is Erik, I'm in serious trouble."

I'M GOING through the motions as I dance on the stage at Sinful Sirens, but my heart isn't in it. I'm distracted by everything Chelsea confessed. On the way inside the club, she told me the picture of her and her deceased brother, Shawn, disappeared on Monday. Erik would take it, especially since that photo sent him over the edge before.

The first time Erik had seen that picture, he didn't bother asking who it was. He just assumed Chelsea was "cheating" on him, even though she and Erik had only gone on a few dates. When he flew into a rage, Chelsea broke it off.

After he slammed out of our apartment, Chelsea curled up against me and told me Erik freaked her out. She said he was unstable, planning their future even though they barely knew one another. When she tried asking him to slow things down, he flipped out and started screaming she couldn't leave him. He told her he'd waited all his life to find her.

I completely supported her decision to cut all contact with him and stayed glued to her side as much as possible. We were shopping one day, and as we passed a thrift store that benefited the local animal shelter, a baseball bat caught my eye. I immediately tugged her inside and bought it, putting it in her room after we went home.

I'm glad I did. It saved her life.

Pulling myself from my thoughts, I realize the song is about to end. Chelsea gives me a grin and a thumbs-up. I relax, focusing all my energy on the routine. She's standing beside Gary, my favorite security guard, who has looked after her both times she's been here.

Once backstage, I change into my street clothes while Chelsea counts all the tips I made. "Holy crap, girl. I had no idea you could make so much money stripping to your bra and panties."

Raven Starling walks into the room to get ready. She wiggles her brows at Chelsea as she throws her duffle bag on the bench. "You earn more doing private shows. I don't recommend it for her. Those guys would go insane over the hot schoolgirl look Jordyn has going on."

Shaking my head, I slide onto the bench to remove my makeup. "It's not a look."

Chelsea giggles at Raven's stunned face. "That's her normal look, except for the makeup and stripping to her lingerie. Although she may do that for the hockey player obsessed with her."

"Chelsea." I slap her leg, a giggle coming out of me as I scrub my face with a wipe. "Stop it."

"A hockey player, huh?" Raven wiggles her brows at me.

"Stop." I stare at my reflection, not believing the words as I choke them out. "It's not that serious."

"What isn't? You and Tristan?" Chelsea gapes at me incredulously. "The hell it's not."

My cheeks are burning from the lie as I straighten my shoulders, trying to convince myself and them that Tristan is just a short-term thing. "It's not. He's going through a rough time, and I understand it. I've been there. Plus, the fact that we could get caught by Josh heightens everything, even as it causes anxiety."

Chelsea gapes at me as though I've lost my mind. "Are you kidding me? I've been around the two of you. Remember him ripping Bryce's jersey off you and replacing it with his own? He didn't give a fuck about the risks then. He claimed you, Jordyn." She laughs, her gaze meeting Raven's. "Thank God her stepbrother is as dumb as a box of rocks. I can't believe he didn't notice."

Raven laughs. "Oh, honey. if he's refusing to allow you to wear another man's jersey, he's staking his claim." She grabs a brush and begins applying powder to her face. "Better get your head outta your ass. This guy sounds as serious as a heart attack."

I bite my lip, worry coursing through me. *What happens when Josh finds out about us and kicks me out of the house?*

My dreams and Tristan will vanish, leaving me with nothing.

CHAPTER 35

Tristan

I have no idea what I've done wrong to make Jordyn avoid me like this. I understood her wanting to spend time with Chelsea but thought things would change Monday morning.

I waited in our usual seats with her favorite coffee in hand. She slid in it one minute before the Professor started class, giving me a quick, grateful smile as I handed her the coffee. Then, she proceeded to ignore me the entire class.

When class was over, she said she needed to talk to Jessica about tutoring schedules and being overbooked. I waited a few minutes until Alex pulled me away, asking me what was happening with her. I shrugged, looking over my shoulder before I said, "No idea, man. She's avoiding me, but I can't figure out why."

After practice, my phone beeped with a notification. She canceled my tutoring session with her with a note stating Jessica could assist if I needed help.

I marched home, but she wasn't there. I paced the floors, waiting for her to arrive. She finally did, but of course, Josh was there, and she headed straight to her room, claiming she'd had a long day and was tired. I tried to sneak into her room, but she locked the door. I could've gotten in but decided to leave her alone for the night.

I woke up the next day, determined to talk to her, but she was gone before I left for the gym. I texted her but didn't receive a response, which really pissed me off.

～

"WHAT'S UP WITH YOU? You look like you could kill anyone who glances at you." Alex falls in step with me in front of the rec center.

Opening the door, I gesture for him to go first, then step in behind him. "Jordyn's avoiding me."

Alex stops, his brows furrowing. "Why?"

"No idea. But it's pissing me off."

Alex opens the door and gestures for me to head inside. The front desk attendant opens the door to let us in, and as we head down the hallway, he asks, "How long has this been going on?"

"Since we returned from the away game. Chelsea was there, so I gave them some space. But you saw how late she was to class yesterday. Then, she made an excuse to talk to the other tutor, Jessica. She canceled my tutoring session with her last night with a note that said Jessica could help if I needed assistance and has ghosted me ever since."

"Are you tracking her phone?"

I stare at Alex in surprise. "What?"

"Oh, Jesus." He shakes his head. "The way you're so nuts over that girl, I figured you'd be tracking it."

"Sounds kinda obsessive."

Alex raises his brows. "Aren't you?"

"Yeah, maybe I'm obsessed. But tracking her seems out of line."

As we head up the steps, Alex says, "Does it feel out of line now that you have no idea where she is?"

"You're right. I'm tracking her phone as soon as our workout is done."

CHAPTER 36

Tristan

Once again, I could barely focus on practice, which cost me. Coach Jensen put me through the wringer, making me run through drills repeatedly. Alex smirked at me and whispered at me to get my head in the game and off pussy. I tried unsuccessfully to focus.

As I skate off the ice, anxiety courses through me. The fear of Jordyn being a distraction is coming true. I don't like it, but I can't walk away from her.

As soon as practice ends, I rush through my shower and change into sweatpants and a long-sleeved tee before racing out. Alex shakes his head but knows better than to say anything, especially with Josh suddenly paying attention to me. During practice, he commented about me being distracted and asked what was wrong. I lied and told him I was struggling because of the anniversary of my parents and sister's deaths, which was only a week away. Thankfully, he seemed to accept my response.

I stare at the dot on the app, which shows Jordyn's phone's location. I rush inside the rec center and head toward the room offering a group fitness class. Jordyn's blonde hair glistens beneath the fluorescent lighting as she heads toward the restrooms. I drag her into the first available room, which happens to be one of the supply closets.

"Jordyn, I need to know what the hell is going on." Running a hand through my hair, my breaths rasp from my lungs from sprinting over here. "Why are you avoiding me?"

Her eyes drop to my chest. Crossing her arms over her chest, she chews on her bottom lip, not saying a word.

"Did I do something wrong?"

Her gaze lifts to mine, and the sadness in her aqua eyes guts me. "No." She shakes her head, her blonde ponytail whipping back and forth. "It's just... I think we're moving too fast."

Too fast? Where the hell is this coming from?

"What brought this on?"

She heaves out a long sigh. "This is fun and all, Tristan. But we're opposites. Not to mention that my stepbrother can't know about us."

I open my mouth, almost blurting out what I've been holding inside, but then shut it. I don't want that to be a deciding factor for us. I need to know she really cares for me, and right now, I'm having too many doubts. "Why now?"

"Chelsea noticed and made a comment. It made me think...."

I scowl at her, irritation coursing through my veins. "So that's what you do, huh? When things get heavy, you run."

Her arms drop to her sides before they move to her hips. She glares at me, her body vibrating from anger. "You're a fine one to talk. Ironically, you're criticizing me for what you've already done."

My hand goes through my hair again, tugging at the roots. "Yeah, and I apologized and learned from it." I step closer to her. "I really care for you, Jordyn. This..." I gesture between us. "It's not a joke to me. We're both risking a lot. I thought we were on the same page and believed it was worth it."

She doesn't say a word.

"I guess I was wrong." Swallowing hard, my stomach hardens from the hurt welling inside. Shock and disbelief course through me as I stare at the only woman I've ever loved. The one that lights up the darkness, pulling me from it.

Without another word, I spin on my heel and exit the closet. My lungs constrict inside my chest, making it hard to breathe, as I exit the rec center.

Sucking in a breath of the cool September air, my thoughts are bleak. I clench my teeth as I stumble in the direction of my vehicle, my shoulders hunched from pain. I try to convince myself it's not as bad as it seems. That I won't always be alone.

Unlocking the door, I slide behind the steering wheel, letting the misery swallow me. My chest is as hollow as my sluggish heart.

Alone.

I'm destined to spend my life alone.

CHAPTER 37

Tristan

I avoid Jordyn the rest of the week, throwing myself into practice and my classes. She's obviously avoiding me, as she sat beside Jessica in class. She made eye contact with me when she walked into English Lit. When she thought I wasn't paying attention, I'd catch her staring at me.

Keeping my eyes averted, I pretended to ignore her. I was acutely aware of everything she did, the cracks she'd repaired fracturing and in danger of breaking into pieces.

"You okay?" The concern in Alex's blue eyes tightens my chest. I haven't seen that look on his face since my parents and sister died.

I squared my shoulders, blowing out a breath. "I'm fine. It's for the best. My focus needs to be on the upcoming draft."

"I wish she'd pull her head outta her ass. Quite frankly, I expected better from her."

"It's for the best," I say between gritted teeth.

I wish my heart would agree.

It's Friday night, and although it's the last thing I want to do, my teammates are going to a club named Sinful Sirens to celebrate Landin Walker's twenty-first birthday. Things have been tense between Bryce and me since the scene in Jordyn's office in the learning center, with Landin taking Bryce's side and Alex taking mine. As captain, I am responsible for bringing my team together, not pulling them apart.

I feel like a jackass for fighting with my teammate over a woman who doesn't want anything to do with me. The awkwardness between us this week has sent us into hiding in our respective rooms.

The only good thing about Jordyn and I avoiding one another is Josh no longer seems suspicious.

"You may wanna stop brooding and sighing if you don't want the other guys to ask questions," Alex whispers in my ear as he slides into his chair beside me. We sit around a table while a woman dances on stage, slowly peeling her skimpy dress off.

Spinning my glass on the table, I look up at him, bored with the atmosphere already.

"Another round of drinks will be here soon," Landin says as he returns to our table. I smile at the right winger on the team, pretending to be having a good time. Bryce cheers, giving Landin a high five.

The tension is palpable at the table, although Josh, Travis Holt, the left winger, and Bryant Lawson, left defender, don't seem to notice.

Travis takes a drink of his soda, his eyes on Alex. When he sets it down, he leans back in his chair. "Hey, Alex. What's up with you lately? You usually have puck bunnies hanging all over you, but you were pushing them away last I saw. You interested in a girl?"

Alex visibly tenses beside me. He hasn't stopped talking about Chelsea since the party they attended. I know they text often. "Nah, just focused on my game since I'm entering the draft. Taking lessons from my boy, Tristan. Women are a distraction."

His words strike a nerve. My jaw clenches as I visibly tense but wisely keep my mouth shut.

"Well, that leaves more pussy for me and Bryce." Landin releases a boisterous laugh before raising his glass, and Bryce lifts his, clinking their glasses together. He smirks at me but doesn't say a word.

Landin stops laughing and nudges Josh's shoulder, his eyes on the door. "I believe you have a stalker."

I look over, inwardly cursing when my eyes briefly meet Janelle's. Her smug smile, all the makeup caked on her face, and the provocative way she's dressed makes me recoil, a sickening feeling in my gut that I fucked her.

"Excuse me, guys." Josh is on his feet, staring at Janelle. "Duty calls."

Landin snorts before drinking his beer. "And by talk, he means he's gonna convince her to blow and fuck him in the bathroom."

I nearly choke on my drink at Landin's accurate assessment. "You're not wrong." The first genuine smile is on both our faces, a temporary truce between us, as I tap my glass against his before I drink.

"Are you sure she's not here to audition to be on the stage?" Alex's brows furrow as he looks her over. "I've seen lingerie less revealing than her dress."

I snort, nearly choking on my drink. "It leaves little to the imagination, that's for sure."

My eyes glaze over as I pretend to watch the girl dancing on stage, but my thoughts are on Jordyn. I overheard her telling Josh she planned to stay with Chelsea in New York this weekend.

Running away from me yet again.

Josh bounds over, his arm around Janelle. "You guys won't be pissed if I bail, right?" His pleading gaze skims over us, locking with Landin's since it's his birthday celebration.

"Nah. Go have fun." Landin winks at him, holding his drink up. "Don't do anything I wouldn't do."

As they walk away, Alex leans over. "I hope this girl finishes soon. She reminds me too much of Natasha." He shudders, a look of disgust contorting his normally jovial face.

I nod, sympathy rolling through me. *Poor Alex.* He dated Natasha our freshman year of college until she fell for her professor and dumped him. Alex was a fucking wreck, bouncing from depression to irrational anger. It took him a while to recover, and when he did, he vowed he was done with relationships. *I wonder if he told Chelsea that.*

The dancer on stage seductively concludes her dance, then beams at the audience before walking offstage, her hips swaying from side to side.

The announcer's voice booms into the mic, drawing my attention to the stage. "And for our next performer... Please give a round of applause for Aqua Spice."

Aqua Spice. What the hell kinda name is that?

I politely clap when the next stripper saunters onto the stage, her hips sashaying with confidence beneath the tight maroon dress she's wearing. Her blonde hair glimmers beneath the stage lights, resembling spun gold.

My heart pounds faster as the blonde gets closer.

No. There's no way. It can't be her.

My world ends as Jordyn stops in the center of the stage, her eyes locking with mine so wide I can see the whites around them.

A low, feral growl rumbles in my chest as I stare in disbelief at the woman I've fallen head over heels for, standing on the stage, about to dance.

What the puck is she doing?

CHAPTER 38

Jordyn

Oh my God. What the hell is Tristan and the Wolverines hockey team doing at Sinful Sirens?

Swallowing nervously, my eyes dart around the table of hockey players before searching the club. I breathe out a sigh of relief when I don't spot Josh anywhere.

Maybe he's in the bathroom. Once he comes out and sees me, it's all over.

Tugging at the hem of my maroon dress, my attention snaps back to reality when I hear a group of guys whistling at me. I dare a glance at Tristan, who is throwing murderous looks at his teammates. Despite the fear coursing through my spine that my world is about to implode, I can't help the thrill of pleasure from his jealousy.

As I move to my position in front of the pole, I can't help but sneak another peak at Tristan. His jaw and fists are clenched on the table, throwing looks that could kill at the table of men yelling beside him.

Alex leans over, his hand on Tristan's shoulder as he whispers something in his ear. Tristan's Adam's Apple bobs as he swallows hard, his green eyes flashing with betrayal and hurt when they lock with mine.

Even though I've been avoiding Tristan all week, I've missed him. Now that he's here, I'm irresistibly drawn to the intensity in his gaze, his presence so close yet far away.

One of the waitresses walks over to the table Tristan is sitting at, her scantily clad body drawing the attention of his teammates. He ignores her, his full attention focused solely on me. She bends down in front of him, trying to give him an eyeful of her cleavage, but he shifts his body, his attention never wavering from me.

The music begins to play, and a flirty smile blooms across my lips as I roll my hips, then lower myself, the pole at my back, spreading my legs. Even though his nostrils flare and his face is red from anger, the heat in his eyes warms me from the inside out. I forget about everyone inside the club and begin seductively dancing for him.

His jaw clenches when I grab the hem of my dress and slowly glide it up my thighs. I wink at him before dragging it up my body and over my head, revealing the lacy maroon bra and panties. His mouth drops open, and he pushes his chair back, but Alex grabs his arm.

His teammates are too distracted by my performance to notice his reaction. But he's throwing them deathly glares as they yell and scream as I perform. If Tristan had his hockey stick in his hands, he'd knock out every damn one of them with it.

When his eyes return to mine, I wink before my hand glides up the pole. I lift my weight, flipping upside down to do a split. I hear men hoot and holler as I wrap my left leg around it, extending my right leg and arms, arching my back.

Bringing my hands back to the pole, I bend my right leg so my left ankle rests on my knee, sliding down the pole before I release my legs and lower them to the floor. I whirl around, my hips moving to the beat, a smile blooming over my face at the impressed look on Tristan's face. His eyes roam over my body, burning into my skin, setting me on fire.

I'm no longer performing for the men in the club. I'm dancing for *him*.

As I dance for him, I've never felt more alive. Realizing that I've fallen so hard for him hits me like a shot in the chest. I've acted like a damn fool for avoiding him all week. I'm desperate for this performance to end so I can talk to him.

When the song ends, I bow, a fake smile plastered on my face. My gaze moves back to Tristan's seat, but it's empty.

Frowning, my gaze locks with Alex. He shakes his head, disappointment all over his face.

Oh, God. What have I done?

My gaze roams around the club, but I don't see him anywhere. I'm relieved I can't find Josh, especially since I forgot about him while I danced for Tristan.

With a wave, I grab my dress and money before hurrying from the stage, tugging it over me as I walk. A sickly feeling is in my stomach as I exit the stage through the door, nodding at Gary as I make my way to the dressing room. Not bothering to change or remove my makeup, I shove the bills into my duffle bag, then grab the leather jacket I wore here, putting it on over my skimpy dress.

A commotion in the hallway causes me to still. My heart beats frantically inside my chest as I grab my duffle bag, then run to the dressing room door and whip it open. A furious Tristan stands in the hallway, arguing with Gary.

"Stop." I rush over to the men, my heels clicking against the linoleum. Turning my pleading eyes to Gary, I say, "I know him. And I really need to talk to him."

Tristan's furious gaze bores mine as Gary sighs. "There's nowhere the two of you can talk in here. You'll need to take it outside." He gestures for us to follow him, and I glance at

Tristan as we move. The muscles in his jaw move, and his face is red from anger. I try to grab his hand, but he jerks it away, gesturing for me to go through the door first.

A lump is in my throat as I step outside into the cold night air. Grabbing the railing, I descend the steps until I stand on the pavement.

I whip around, facing Tristan's wrath. "I'm sorry. I know this was a terrible way to find out I've been dancing—"

His bitter laugh causes the words to die in my throat. "Terrible way? Are you kidding me with this shit, Jordyn?" He runs a hand through his hair, glaring at me, disgust contorting his face. "I can't fucking believe you. You ghost me for a week. Then I come here tonight to celebrate my teammate's birthday and get the fucking shock of my life when I see you on stage stripping."

Humiliation burns my cheeks. Crossing my arms over my chest, I shiver from the coldness in his eyes that chills me to my bones. A light wind blows, but I'm numb to it. "Please, Tristan. Hear me out."

"Hear you out? Oh, you mean like you did this week?" His voice drips with sarcasm. "I tried talking to you, but you froze me out." The venom in his voice paralyzes me. "You downplayed what we had."

His words cause agony to swell inside me like a wave. One word swirls inside my chaotic thoughts that spin around like water circling a drain. *Had.* Past tense.

"I'm sorry." Tightening my arms over my chest as though they can miraculously keep the pieces of my heart from splintering, I stare at the guy I've been too scared to love, fearing I've ruined everything. I used Josh as an excuse to keep Tristan at a distance, but the truth is, I've been too scared to love since my dad passed away. I saw what his loss did to my mom. His death nearly destroyed her.

"Sorry, huh?" He shakes his head, his tone like acid. "I'm

the one who is sorry. You played me for a fool, making me believe you were different. You drew me in, understanding my loss because of what you experienced. Although I promised myself I'd focus solely on my goals, I let you in. In the short time we've known one another, you crept beneath my skin and became a part of me."

A tear slides down my cheek as his words pierce my heart like arrows.

"But it wasn't reciprocated. You kept yourself at a distance, not allowing me in." His voice cracks, a tear rolling down his cheek. "I fell in love with you, and you couldn't even be honest with me."

I fell in love... Agony swells inside my chest. *He loved me, and I ruined it.*

I try to find the words to make things better. "That's not entirely true, Tristan. I let you in more than I've let any man in since..." I choke on the words, unable to finish them.

His stony stare bores into me before he folds his arms over his chest. "How long have you been dancing here?"

My breaths rasp in and out of my chest, knowing I can't lie to him, but once I say the words, he'll slip completely through my fingers. My hold on him is tenuous at best.

"A few weeks."

"You lied about your whereabouts. Instead, you came here, stripping and showing what I thought was mine to other men."

A sob bursts free from my shaking lips. "I need the money."

"For what? You aren't paying rent. You have a graduate assistant position." He glowers at me. "You confessed that your mom gave you money." He turns his head, his narrowed gaze locking on Sinful Sirens as though he wished he could burn it to the ground with a single look. "So why the fuck are you dancing here?"

The tears continue rolling down my face as I silently stare at him, knowing there's nothing I can say that will make things right between us. I can't tell him I've been saving money in case Josh finds out about us and kicks me out. It's pointless now since there is no us.

A bitter laugh escapes him as he looks up at the darkened sky. "Lemme guess. You worried Josh would kick you out?" His head slowly lowers, waiting for my confirmation.

When I nod, he shakes his head. "You never trusted me at all, did you?" His hands clench into fists. "Here's a secret I kept from you—I'm the only name on the rental agreement. That's why Josh asked me if you could move in. He wasn't being a polite roommate. He's been paying me rent." Anger burns in his eyes as he leans closer. "He doesn't have the authority to kick you out. I do."

I gasp, my hands flying to my cheeks. Shock has my mouth hanging open as I struggle to comprehend his words.

"If Josh found out about us, he could have threatened to kick you out, but he wouldn't have been able to do it." His breaths rasp from his lungs, passion burning in his eyes. "I fucking loved you, Jordyn. I would've tossed his ass out long before I asked you to move out."

"W-What?" I squeak, my body numb from shock and pain.

"I didn't tell you. I knew you'd feel obligated to pay rent I didn't want or need. And once we became involved, a part of me needed the assurance that you cared about *me*. I needed to know I wasn't a place to stay while you fulfilled your dreams." Angrily wiping the tears from his eyes, his voice is like gravel when he mutters, "How fucking stupid am I to think you cared about me?"

I open my mouth, but he holds up a hand. "Save it, Jordyn. I don't wanna hear it. I've been foolish enough." The deeply pained look in his mossy irises guts me. "I thought you were special. Instead, you played me for a damn fool." He whirls around, his large strides carrying him away.

I sink to my knees, trying to force his name through my dry mouth and lips, but the only thing that comes out is heart-wrenching sobs. The cold, hard blacktop cuts the skin on my knees, but I'm barely cognizant of it over the breaking of my heart.

I'm not sure how long I sob, my hands planted on the parking lot, my grief over losing him dulling my senses, making me oblivious to everything except the soul-deep agony that drowns me.

A large hand wraps around my arm. Alex's soothing voice whispers in my ear. "Come on, Jordyn. I'm taking you home."

As he lifts me to my feet, I shake my head, drowning in misery. "I don't have a home. I don't have anything."

Alex squeezes me against his chest. "Yes, you do. Tristan is upset and hurt. Rightfully so." He pulls out some napkins from his pocket, handing them to me. "Clean up your face. Where are your keys?"

I blankly look around, spotting my duffle bag on the ground. I have no idea when I dropped it. I think it was when Tristan and I began arguing, but I'm unsure.

Pointing to it, I hoarsely whisper, "Outside pocket."

Alex nods, carrying me to my bag. He easily scoops it up before he heads to my car. My head falls against his shoulder, the tears overwhelming me yet again.

As he opens the passenger door and sets me on the seat, I lift the napkins he'd given me to my eyes, wiping the tears from my face. "Where are you taking me?"

"To my house. It'll give Tristan time to cool down."

My chin quivers. "He h-hates me, A-Alex. He'll k-kick me out, and I don't b-blame him. B-But I don't c-care about t-that."

My throat closes, but I force the words out anyway. "I've lost him. Forever."

CHAPTER 39

Jordyn

Peeling my dry eyes open, I blink, groaning at the bright night filtering through the window. Closing my eyes, I throw my arm over my pounding head. I wince from the pain shooting through the palm of my hand.

Lifting my arm, I crack open my eyes, examining my skinned-up palm. Memories of last night whirl through my head so fast it makes the room spin. Groaning, I close my eyes again, despair making my chest cave in.

A knock on the door makes me jolt, then whimper as pain slices through my skull. The door opens before I can utter a word, and Alex's cheerful voice rings through the room. "Oh, good. You're awake."

I open my eyes, turn my head, and scowl at him. "I wish I were dead."

He chuckles as he crosses the room, lowering himself onto the edge of the mattress. "That's not true, Jordyn. You feel like shit from hurting so bad. But you don't wanna die."

"How do you know?"

"Because you're in love with Tristan. If there's a chance

you can make things right with him, you'll take it. That's reason enough for you to keep living."

"There's no chance I can ever do that, Alex. I might as well be dead. At least I wouldn't have to feel so fucking miserable." My scraped-up palm slides to my chest, fisting the shirt I'm wearing. Frowning, my confused gaze drops to it.

"Don't worry. You undressed yourself after I gave you one of my shirts." He leans closer, his eyes dancing with humor. "Don't tell Tristan you wore anything of mine. He'll go ballistic."

"Yeah, right. Like he'd care." A mournful sigh slips through my slightly parted lips. "He hates me, Alex. And I don't blame him. I lied to him. I betrayed him. And—"

Alex squeezes my arm. "Stop with the pity party. You're forgetting one very important thing."

My brows furrow as I blink at him through my tears. "What's that?"

"He'll forgive you because he loves you."

I snort in disbelief, hope surging through the broken pieces of my heart. "Yeah, right. Not anymore. I ruined that."

Alex's laugh grates on my nerves like nails on a chalkboard. "The good news is, once Tristan loves you, he doesn't fall out of love. He may get pissed as hell, but he never stops loving you." The goofy grin on his face would be endearing if I weren't so brokenhearted. "Trust me. I've pissed him off many times over the years. He still loves me." He winks at me.

"You're his best friend. Not a woman who lied and betrayed him."

He waves his hand dismissively. "He loves you in a way I've never seen him love. He's not gonna walk away that easily." The smile on his face is so reassuring that hope flares inside my chest. "You're lucky I'm here to help straighten things between you two."

"How are you going to help?"

"First, you're gonna get in the shower and clean up. Then I'll take you home so you can change into something that won't piss him off." He winks at me.

I eye him skeptically. "Do you think he'll let me through the door of his house?"

Alex grins. "Yes, he will. He's not home."

"How do you know that?"

"It's the anniversary of his parents and sister's deaths. He's at the cemetery, where you're going once you've changed. That will show him effort." His expression softens as he whispers, "He needs you, Jordyn. You understand what it's like to lose a parent better than anyone. That's one of the reasons he fell so damn hard for you. You're so damn strong. You understand what he's going through."

Although I'm touched by Alex's words and my heart clenches inside my chest for what Tristan is experiencing, I frantically shake my head. "I'm the last person he'll want to see."

"You're wrong. You're the only one he wants to see right now."

Alex lets his words sink in. "Tristan is the one who told me how strong you are. How much he admired you for all you did to support your mom after your dad died, including giving up your college fund and working to help pay the bills. All while you were grieving." Alex reaches over, pushing a strand of hair away that's fallen over my eye. "He cares about and respects you so damn much, Jordyn. Don't let him down again. You hurt him by what you did, but you can fix this. The first step is going to the cemetery and being there for him."

Swallowing hard, my hands shake as I nervously twist them together. "What if he tells me to leave?"

"He won't. He'll be too stunned and happy that you're there." Alex stands, holding his hand out. "Come on. Let's clean you up so you can show him how much you love him, too."

Although I never thought I'd be able to smile today, Alex has proven me wrong. Taking his hand, I swing my legs over the side of the bed and stand. "You know, I thought you were a big goofball. I never imagined this side of you."

"What? Gorgeously intelligent?" He runs a hand through his hair, flipping his head back. "Don't hate me for being pretty *and* smart."

I giggle, shaking my head. "Not to discount your looks or intelligence, that's not what I thought. You're level-headed and care about your friend. Loyal to a fault."

"We're kindred spirits, Jordyn. Gorgeous, intelligent, level-headed, and loyal describe you perfectly. You're all those things and more." He looks at me over his shoulder, pulling me from the bedroom. "Trust me. Tristan needs you."

The sadness lifts, replaced by hope. I squeeze Alex's hand, digging my nails into his skin. "Do you really think he'll forgive me? Let alone..." I can't say the word. *Love.*

"Yes, he will. And he loves you so much, Jordyn. I haven't seen him open his heart like this since his parents were alive."

We step into the bathroom, but I can't tear my eyes from Alex. Raising onto my tiptoes, I kiss his cheek. "Thanks, Alex. You're the best."

"I won't tell Tristan you kissed me or said that. He'll kick my ass, and I won't get drafted into the NHL." He winks at me and then points to a closet. "Towels are in there. And here's how you work the shower." He gives me a quick demo before heading to the door. "Hurry up. Your man is hurting like hell, and you're the only one who can ease his pain."

CHAPTER 40

Tristan

Running my hand over my parent's tombstones, tears flow freely down my cheeks. My throat and chest ache from the grief running rampant inside me. "Hey, Mom and Dad. I can't believe it's been a year since I lost you." My gaze moves to my sister's gravesite. "Elaine. I miss the way we teased each other more than I can say. Life is so unfair sometimes."

Bowing my head, my shaky hands lift to my Wolverines sweatshirt, fisting the material over my broken heart. Squatting down in front of their graves, my legs shake from the weakness permeating my body. My eyes are dry and achy from the tears I shed last night and this morning. Between Jordyn and the anniversary of my parent's death, I'm not doing well.

"You'd be so disappointed in me." My voice cracks, and I swallow multiple times, my throat constricting before I can go on. "I vowed to chase my goals and focus on hockey. Then I fell for a girl." I heave out a sigh, bowing my head.

"I tried to resist her, but I failed. It wasn't until I talked with Coach Jensen that I got my head straight and realized I could have both." I lift my head, my eyes moving to each of their tombstones. "Things were going great until they weren't. I was so hurt... So fucking betrayed by her actions, and now, I don't know what to do." I fall to my knees, the sobs taking over me. "I need your help. I don't have a fucking clue what to do. My life is a train wreck." I fall forward, my hands sinking into the cool ground.

I'm not sure how long I remain like that, sobbing my heart out while on my hands and knees in front of their graves, feeling more alone than ever. "I know I can't have you back." I sit back on my heels, wiping my face with my dirty hands. "But Jordyn... She made me feel things I've never felt. I could breathe around her. Her presence and love replaced the vast emptiness that lives inside me since I lost the three of you."

My breaths rasp in and out of my chest. My head tilts to the sky. "I've lost her, too."

A warm hand squeezes my shoulder. It feels like a dream when a soft voice on my right whispers, "No, you didn't."

The mental fog clouding my head makes me think I'm hallucinating Jordyn's sweet voice in my ear, her hand on my shoulder.

Turning my head, I see a pair of aqua eyes filled with tears. Sunlight cracks through the clouds, filtering around her and giving her an angelic aura.

I'm dumbfounded, blinking repeatedly, unable to trust what I see. "J-Jordyn?"

She nods, squatting beside me. "I'm here, Tristan." Blowing out a breath, her earnest eyes shine with sympathy and concern. "I'm so sorry."

I'm so pissed at her... but I need her. The weight on my chest has lessened by her mere presence. Her strawberry scent fills my nostrils every time I inhale, lifting my spirits. I know last night was shitty, but right now, I don't care.

I reach for her, dragging her against my chest. Burying my face in her hair, my arms cling to her like a lifeline. When she hugs me back with the same intensity, I close my eyes and let go, unleashing the crippling grief inside me.

When I have no more tears left to cry, I pull back. She pulls tissues from the pocket of her hoodie and begins cleaning my face.

My hand wraps around her wrist, drawing her eyes to mine. "Thank you."

She nods, sadness lingering in her eyes. "You're welcome. I'm here as long as you need me..." Her head bows, golden hair shielding her face like curtains. "Then I'll go...."

Fear and panic rise inside me. I remember all the terrible things I said to her last night, but in the harsh light of day, I realize I didn't mean any of them. She hurt me when she lied to me, but I withheld information from her, too. She was making decisions based on fear and necessity, but I was the one who put her in that position, blindingly expecting her to trust me. "Please, don't go."

Aqua eyes dart up to mine, hope flashing in them. My hands push her silky locks away from her face. "I'm so fucking sorry for what I said last night, Jordyn. Although I don't like you stripping, I understand why. It's partially my fault for not revealing the truth sooner."

"I'm at fault for lying to you." Shaky fingers fidget with the string on my hoodie. "But when Robert revoked my funding, he pulled the rug from beneath me, taking my dreams with it. I swore I'd never put myself in that position again."

Leaning forward, I press my lips to her forehead. "He's such an ass. It's no wonder you don't trust men." My hands cup her face, lifting it to mine. "I want to take care of you, Jordyn. I want to support you, helping you obtain your dreams." My finger presses against her lips when she opens her mouth, effectively shutting her up. "I want to work through this because you mean so damn much to me."

Her sigh as my thumbs skate over her cheeks causes my

heart to flutter. "We have a lot to talk about, but I wanna work this out, Jordyn. I can't live without you."

She blinks, and tears course down her cheeks. "I don't wanna live without you. I was absolutely miserable last night." A bitter laugh escapes her lips. "I'm to blame for pulling away from you. Even though it was my fault, I missed you so much. Although I was shocked to see you at Sinful, I was glad to see your face."

"I didn't like seeing you on stage, taking off your dress. That fucking bra and panties should have been for my eyes only," I growl, irritation drawing my brows in. "But, damn, you're sexy as fuck when you dance around a pole."

Her giggle makes my heart soar. Her smile fills me with warmth and repairs the broken shards of my heart. I know we have a long way to go, and serious conversations need to take place, but right now, having her by my side is everything.

She lifts her hand to touch my face, but I catch it, my eyes narrowing at her skinned palms. "What happened, kitten?"

"I fell on the pavement after you... left. It's just a little brush burn."

Sorrow fills me as I gently kiss her palms. "I'm sorry, kitten."

"I missed you calling me that." The serene smile on her face warms my heart. Her eyes are full of happiness as she waves a hand dismissively. "I skinned my knees, too. I cleaned them in the shower and put my ointment on them. It's fine." She nods at the three graves nearby. "Aren't you going to introduce me?"

"I'll kiss those wounds later." My ass plops on the ground, and I pull her so she's sitting between my legs. My arms wrap around her waist, and my chin rests on her shoulder. "Jordyn, this is my dad, Christian Harrington. My mother, Courtney, and my sister, Elaine." A light breeze blows through my short hair. "This is Jordyn... The woman I've fallen in love with."

She looks at me over her shoulder, her expression soft. Her hands cover mine as they rest against her stomach, our fingers curling and intertwining. "I've fallen in love with you, Tristan."

She nods in the direction of the three tombstones in front of us. "In front of your family, I'd like to apologize and promise you that if you give me another chance, there will be no more secrets or running away. If you want me to move out—"

"No. That's the last thing I want." A genuine smile blooms over my lips. "I'd rather kick Josh out if he can't deal. Fuck em. His daddy has money and would pay his rent somewhere else."

Jordyn's musical laughter rings over the hill, and my grief lessens. Although it still hurts, with her by my side, it's manageable. "I like that plan. But please don't think I'm with you because I need a place to—"

My lips are on hers before she can finish that statement. She moans against my lips, twisting in my embrace. She pushes me onto my back and rolls on top of me, kissing me until I'm drunk on her essence.

I pull back when my lungs begin to burn, needing oxygen. "You're under my skin, Jordyn. I can't and won't let you go." I rub my nose against hers. "You're stuck with me, kitten."

Her smile brightens my dreary life, lessening my grief. "Good. Because you're stuck with me, captain."

CHAPTER 41

Tristan

We remained at the cemetery for quite a while before I took her hand and led her to my vehicle. Once I started the engine, I cranked the heat, the cool fall air casting a chill. Guilt washes over me when I see her shivering in the passenger seat.

Leaning over, I fasten her seatbelt, then wrap my arms around her. "I'm sorry I kept you out in the cold."

She cups my face, a content smile curling her lips. "You're worth it."

Pressing kisses over her forehead, cheeks, and then lips, I whisper, "How about some breakfast? I know a diner out of town that serves it all day. We can talk."

She reaches up, fingers stroking the stubble on my chin. "I like that idea a lot."

Capturing her lips, I kiss her until we're breathless. "I can't get enough of you. But we should go." I settle behind the steering wheel, shaking off the fog of lust.

As we drive away from the cemetery, I wrap my fingers around hers. "How did you get here?"

"Alex."

My eyebrows shoot up, and I shake my head. "Now his texts make more sense. He said he had something of mine that he was holding hostage."

Jordyn laughs. "I don't think that can be classified as a hostage situation. More like a friend helping another friend."

"I'm sorry for hurting you, Jordyn. I shouldn't have left you at Sinful Sirens. I was so angry and hurt. I texted Alex to tell him you and I had gotten into a fight, and I was leaving. He must have searched for you right after I sent that text." Exhaling a shaky breath, guilt churns in my gut. "Thank God. If anyone else found you...."

"Don't think about the what-if scenario. Alex found me and worked his magic to get us to this point. I wouldn't have known where you were if not for him."

Gratitude for my best friend fills my chest. "I'll be sure to thank him later. First, let's get some food in that growling belly of yours."

She giggles, placing her hand on her belly. "I didn't think you noticed."

"Kitten, I notice everything about you."

She giggles. "You do not."

I smirk at her before my eyes move back to the road. "Whenever you eat bacon, you dip it in syrup. You do the same with scrambled eggs. Syrup is never involved when you eat eggs sunny side up. You rip the crust off your toast before you dip it in the eggs."

She raises her brows, her voice soft. "Wow. I'm impressed."

"Oh, I'm just getting started. You love chocolate chip pancakes. If you drink milk with them, it's never chocolate. But if you eat pancakes without chocolate chips, then you drink chocolate milk."

Jordyn stares at me in disbelief.

"You love bright pink but are not a fan of pastels. You love dogs, and you cry every time you see one hurt or abandoned.

You refuse to watch movies where the dog dies because it devastates you."

"Holy shit. You really do pay attention."

I lift our joined hands to my lips, kissing her knuckles. "You consume me, Jordyn."

Her breath hitches, and she squeezes my hand. "I'm sorry I ever doubted your feelings for me."

I glare at her before my face breaks into a grin. "Don't do it again. Also, the maroon dress and lingerie you wore last night. You're gonna wear that for me later." Turning into the parking lot of the diner, I find a parking space and cut the engine. Unbuckling her seatbelt, I pull her across the console so she's straddling me. "You're gonna give me a private lap dance, and I'm gonna fuck you until you have so many orgasms, you nearly black out."

Her lips part, and her tongue darts out, licking her bottom lip. I can't resist her anymore, capturing her mouth in a kiss that leaves me hard and breathless.

"If I wasn't so hungry, I'd say fuck breakfast," she whispers. A dazed look is in her eyes, and her puffy lips drive me insane.

"You need your energy for what I'm gonna do to you. Let's eat." My smile is salacious as I wiggle my brows at her. "You'll be my dessert."

CHAPTER 42

Jordyn

I sigh, staring into space, unable to concentrate on class. My thoughts are full of Tristan and all that has transpired since I sat with him at the cemetery.

Our conversation flowed easily, and we confessed all the secrets we'd kept from the other. After breakfast, he drove us to a nearby lake, where we talked about our goals and dreams.

As we were driving home, Tristan's phone rang. It was Josh, who said his father asked him to come home. He planned to spend the night and then drive back to campus tomorrow.

The second Tristan ended the call, he slammed his foot on the gas. We barely made it through the front door before we were both naked, and he proceeded to fuck me in almost every room of the house. We showered, and then he asked me to wear the lingerie and dress I wore last night on stage and give him a lap dance in his bedroom. Not only was that the hottest experience of my life, but Tristan ended up alternating between fucking and making love to me.

We spent the evening in bed, with Tristan leaving long enough to answer the door and grab the takeout he ordered for dinner. After we ate, I curled up in his arms and binged Netflix until we fell asleep.

The week has been passing in a blur. It's been extremely busy for both of us, but we always make time for each other. Now that I know Tristan's name is the only one on the lease, we've been slightly less discreet. Tristan is ready to confess our love to Josh, but I'm really worried about the effect it will have on the team.

"Hey, guys." Josh walked into the house, glassy eyes skimming over us as we worked on our group paper for English Lit. Alex ran to get us some ice cream, so Tristan and I took advantage and had been making out on the couch when we heard Josh's footsteps. "I won't be here long. Just grabbing a few things." He bounds up the steps without sparing us another glance.

I give Tristan a bewildered look. "What's going on with him? His eyes are bloodshot, and his hands are shaking."

"I need to make a phone call to Coach Jensen." Worried green eyes met mine. It darkened when Josh's loud music shook the walls. "I think he's using drugs."

"What?" My eyes lift to the stairs, worry knotting in my gut. "I never suspected... But the terrible way he's been playing combined with how distracted and oblivious he is... Well, it makes a weird kind of sense."

"Don't jump to conclusions yet. I'll have Coach test him and let him handle it."

I cup his face and give him a kiss. "Have I told you how amazing you are?"

He grins at me. "Every day. But I never tire of hearing you say it."

"Good. Because I'm not going to stop."

~

I FEEL ACCOMPLISHED after writing an outline and beginning the first of two large papers for the Composition and Writing class I'm taking. Standing, I stretch before gathering my materials and hitching my backpack over my shoulder.

Pushing through the library doors, the sky opens, rain soaking the campus. *Great.*

Pulling my phone from my pocket, I'm about to order an Uber when a horn blows. I look up, a smile stretching across my face as a familiar SUV pulls up in front of the library. I wave, racing around to the passenger seat of Tristan's vehicle, and climb inside.

"How are you here?" I launch myself at him before he can answer, grabbing his face and kissing him.

He chuckles when he pulls away. "Wow. That's a helluva greeting, kitten." Winking, he pushes my wet hair away from my face. "Coach let us out of practice early. I read your text and immediately rushed over, knowing you'd get soaked walking home."

"You are the sweetest boyfriend ever."

A slight growl leaves his lips. "Damn. Keep it up, and I'll fuck you right here." His expression softens, a smile on his lips. "You're the best girlfriend ever. And the love of my life."

I smile. "I love you."

"I love you with all my heart, kitten." His kiss is sweet and full of promises of forever.

As I settle into the passenger seat, he turns the heat up before reaching into the back of his vehicle and grabbing his sweatshirt. He puts it over my head before fastening the seat belt. His eyes meet mine. "What?"

I know I have the silliest smile on my face, but I can't help it. "I like the way you take care of me."

"Good. Cause I'm never gonna stop."

WE SIT in Tristan's SUV, the pouring rain pounding against the vehicle, puddles everywhere. "Ready, kitten?"

I nod, determination on my face.

He grins. "On three."

I have my hand on the handle, ready to open it and sprint through the rain. "One."

"Two."

"Three," I shriek as I slide out the door, slamming it shut. I make it around the front of his vehicle before Tristan scoops me in his arms, twirling me around in the rain. We are laughing, enjoying the feel of it on our skin, before our eyes lock and the passion takes over.

Holding me against him, his hands cup my ass as he claims me with the type of kiss that possesses me to my soul. My hands tangle in his hair, pulling him closer, no longer caring about getting soaked. Not caring about anything but losing ourselves in each other.

"What the hell?" Josh's angry voice breaks through my lustful fog.

We break the kiss, our heads turning to Josh, but Tristan doesn't put me down.

"You son of a bitch." Josh's fist swings, and Tristan immediately spins, protecting me. He stumbles from the hit as my feet touch the ground. Before Tristan can block his punches, Josh attacks with a fury. I scream, stepping back as Tristan hits the sidewalk, Josh on top of him.

"Oh my God. Stop it." I'm soaked, my hands slipping as I unsuccessfully grab Josh's arm. "Please, just stop."

Josh whips around, furious eyes burning into mine. I take a step back, and he advances. "You fucking bitch. How long have you been fucking him?" Before I can react, he shoves me, sending me flying against the porch. I slump against the steps, dazed.

"You motherfucker." Tristan tackles Josh, his fists flying. "You don't fucking touch her." The sickening crunch of bone beneath his fist is evident over the rain pounding against the porch roof. "You don't fucking call her a bitch." His face is twisted from rage as he pummels Josh.

I rub my aching head. "Tristan, please stop." Tears course down my cheeks. I don't want Tristan to end up getting into trouble. I've seen this too many times. Josh always wiggles out of whatever trouble he gets in.

Tristan fists Josh's shirt, lifting his head from the sidewalk. Dropping him, he snaps, "You're not fucking worth it." Releasing him, he backs up, his eyes on Josh. He lifts his arm, wiping his nose before he spins, his concerned eyes locking with mine. "Kitten."

Rushing over to me, he scoops me up. "Let's get you out of this rain, and I'll check you over."

"What about him?" I nod in Josh's direction as he rolls to his knees, puking onto the sidewalk.

He throws a glare over his shoulder as he heads to the door. "Let his father deal with him."

As he carries me to the door, the muscle twitches in his jaw as his eyes drop to mine. "If he hurt you, he'll never fucking skate again because I'll break both his fucking legs."

CHAPTER 43

Jordyn

Besides a bump on the head and brush-burnt backside from skidding across the concrete, I'm fine. Tristan isn't convinced, and even after helping me shower, cleaning my wounds, and dressing me in warm clothing, he's still hovering like a worried mother hen.

"Let me drive you to the wellness center. You need to get checked out."

"Only if you'll get your knuckles looked at." My gaze drops to them.

"Don't worry about them. They're fine," he growls.

"They're swollen and busted open."

"I said they're fine," he growls. He pulls me into his arms, regret filling his green eyes. "I'm sorry Josh pushed you. I shouldn't have—"

"Stop blaming yourself. It's not your fault."

"What can I get you, kitten? Anything at all."

"A snack. Something chocolate."

He grins. "You got it. Now get your ass in bed."

I blow out a breath, frustrated that he won't let me help. As my gaze circles his room, I spot his jersey thrown over the back of his desk chair. With a smile, I slip out of bed, shedding the sweatshirt and yoga pants and pulling his jersey overhead.

The frustration in his voice is evident as I hear him say, "Listen, Robert. You need to get your son. If he's doing drugs, he's not welcome here. He can return and pack his things later, but I want him out within the week."

Curses fly from his lips, and I hear his voice say, "Hey, Coach. I need to tell you something. You're gonna be pissed." He reveals the details of what happened, and then he's quiet for a bit. "I'm throwing Josh out. I'm not dealing with his shit."

Tristan is quiet for a while and then says, "I understand." I hear his footsteps move into the kitchen and begin heading toward me. He looks up, his surprise replaced by concern. "Why aren't you in bed?"

I hold up the picture, a small smile on my face. "I was going to ask you about this picture. Plus, I was bored and was coming to help you with my snack." I look at the tray filled with four different chocolate desserts in his hands. "Is that a snack or a buffet of desserts?"

He grins at me, heading up the stairs. "Come on. Let's get you back to bed..." His eyes heat as they travel over his jersey that I'm wearing, and he mutters some curses.

"Do you like?" I hold the hem of the jersey out, a seductive smile on my face.

"You know I do." He switches the tray to one hand, reaches around me, and swats my ass. "Get in bed."

"Yes, sir." I spin, putting an extra swagger in my hips as I head back to his bedroom.

"Swear to God, kitten, you're about to get it."

Stopping in the doorway, I wink. "Oh, I hope so."

I squeal as Tristan chases me into his room, deposits the tray on the nightstand, and grabs me, pulling me against his hard body. With a giggle, I melt against him, my arms around his neck. Our lips meet in a heated kiss.

"I can't fucking believe the two of you." We jerk back at the sound of Josh's furious voice. He stands in the doorway, soaking wet, bruises already lining his face. There's blood beneath his swollen nose and on his shirt. "I can't fucking believe you." He glares at Tristan. "I trusted you. You knew she was off limits."

Tristan shoves me behind him, facing Josh head-on. "What she and I do is none of your fucking business."

A bitter laugh comes from Josh as his eyes move to me. "Seriously. She's a fucking nerd. Look at her." He gestures a hand in my direction, and I move forward, grabbing Tristan's arm, who is clearly ready to attack Josh and beat the hell out of him. "Is it because she's a virgin?"

Tristan doesn't correct him. "No, it's not because she's a virgin. It's because I'm in love with her."

"Love?" His lips twist in disgust. "With her? Oh, come on—"

Tristan takes another step forward, pulling me with him because I'm still hanging onto his arm. "I suggest you keep your fucking mouth shut before I permanently ruin your hockey career." A smirk pulls up his lip. "Although, you may have taken care of that yourself."

"You motherfucker." Josh lunges at Tristan, and I take a step back, fearing I'll get assaulted by Josh again.

But there's no way Tristan is letting it happen again. In a flash, he grips Josh, slamming him against the wall. "Leave, motherfucker. *Now*," he seethes. "Before I break every bone in your fucking body."

"You're a traitor. You told Coach I was doing drugs." He shakes his head. "I fucking trusted you. I didn't think you'd end up telling on me like a little bitch."

My eyes widen, shocked by his words. *It's true. He is doing drugs.*

"Pack your stuff. Your father is coming to pick you up. We're done here." He releases him, his eyes never leaving Josh as he backs up, linking his hand with mine. "I don't want drugs in my house. I warned you once."

Josh smirks. "Yeah, I don't think that's the real reason. It's because of her." His eyes are disgusted as they flicker to mine, then back to Tristan. "You'll both pay for this. I fucking promise you that."

Spinning on his heel, he stomps away, his retreating footsteps striking fear in my heart.

Tristan gathers me in his arms. "It's okay, Jordyn. I won't let him hurt you."

I tremble in his arms, remaining silent. He pulls back slightly, his finger beneath my chin, tilting my face so he can look into my eyes. "I've got you, kitten. I won't let *anyone* hurt you, and I'll never let them come between us or ruin our dreams."

Doubt swirls through my veins as I tighten my arms around Tristan's waist. *I hope he's right.*

CHAPTER 44

Jordyn

A slight smile curls my lips as Tristan places one of my shirts on a hanger. He looks so boyishly cute as he takes in my expression, his brow wrinkling. "What?"

I giggle. "You look so domesticated. It's hard to believe the guy gingerly hanging up my shirt is the same vicious guy on the ice or throwing punches at my asshole stepbrother."

Tristan smirks. "What can I say, kitten? I'm a complicated man." He leans over, giving me a kiss. "I'm mean on the ice, a beast in the bedroom, but always sweet to you." Brushing a lock of hair from my face, his gravelly tone makes my stomach flutter. "I'll do anything for you." Cupping my face, the promise in his eyes makes me shiver. "I love you so damn much."

I lift onto my tiptoes, wrapping my arms around his neck. "I'm so damn lucky to have you in my life. I love you, Tristan." Rubbing my nose against his, a soft giggle leaves my lips. "Who would've thought the nerdy girl would fall for the hockey captain?"

He presses a soft kiss against my lips, stealing my breath away. "It was inevitable. We're meant to be."

I melt against him, every one of my nerves sparking from the euphoria coursing through me like lightning. "You have no idea how much you've healed me. I haven't felt like I belonged anywhere. But the first time you wrapped your arms around me, it felt like coming home." I tilt my head back, smiling at the love radiating from his eyes. "Wherever you are is home to me."

"You're my home." Loosening his hold, his hands slide to my ass, gently squeezing. "If I get drafted, I plan to finish my education before moving..." His forehead wrinkles with worry. "Would you go with me?"

His words cause my pulse to pound against my neck. I hadn't given much thought as to what would happen after he's drafted. But now, it hits me that he'll need to move, and he'll be traveling a lot.

Other than my mom and Chelsea, I have no other ties anywhere.

"There's plenty of online programs and schools." My gaze lifts to his. "As long as I can afford it..." I bite my lip, hating the fear and hopelessness that wells inside me.

Tristan squeezes my hands, his face darkening. "Money isn't an issue, kitten. I'm going to take care of you." His face darkens. "Did you quit working at Sinful Sirens yet?"

I bite my lip, knowing he's going to be angry. "I feel like I need to do it in person."

He rolls his eyes and runs a hand through his hair. "So fucking stubborn." I can practically see his mind whirling. "If you were offered a job at the rec center, would you take it?"

"Of course. But I already applied there. I applied for pretty much everything that was open, but I was too late. Jobs were filled in August."

He nods, his expression contemplative before his brows furrow. "I really don't like you working at Sinful Sirens."

"I know. I'm going to quit, okay? I promise." Standing on my tiptoes, I give him a kiss.

"Good." He squeezes my ass before turning back to the laundry, grabbing another shirt.

I shake my head as I watch him, a grin on my face. Reaching into the clothes basket, I'm astonished when I pull out a pair of small, navy reindeer socks. Turning to him, I hold them up, my brows raised.

Tristan blushes, a wry smile on his face as he scratches the back of his neck. "Those were my sister's lucky socks. We always got each other a silly gift for Christmas, and that was my gift two years ago. She wore those socks at every competition, calling them her lucky socks." He swallows hard, his eyes misty. "When I returned to the ice for the first time after my hiatus, I tucked those socks inside my pads for good luck."

I clutch the socks to my chest. "Oh my God. That's so sweet."

"They're my lucky socks now. I was so nervous when I played my first game, but I was on fire that night. We slaughtered the other team. Now, I keep them on me every game I play." He shrugs his shoulders. "What can I say? Hockey players are superstitious."

A broad smile spreads across my face. "I tuck my Strawberry Shortcake doll in my backpack whenever I have a test in a class, or any other time I need some luck."

Tristan's smile matches mine as he pulls me into his arms. "You're my lucky charm now." He nuzzles my neck, making me giggle. "Will you do me a favor?"

"Of course."

He chuckles, pulling back with sparkling eyes. "Wear those socks and my jersey to my game next weekend."

"I'd be honored."

CHAPTER 45

Tristan

"That was a helluva practice." Alex strips off his gloves and helmet as we exit the ice.

Sweat rolls down my body as I gratefully suck in a breath after removing my gloves and helmet. "You're not kidding. Coach Jensen and the new assistant coach, Riley Nelson, kicked our asses."

As we fall in step with one another, heading to the locker room, Alex nudges me. "What do you think of Coach Nelson?"

I shrug. "Since it's his first practice with us, it's hard to say. But he seemed decent when Coach introduced him. I like the things he said. And while he's tough, he seems fair." I smirk. "He earned bonus points when Josh showed up and melted down about his suspension from the team and Nelson said, 'So you're the rich, entitled druggie? Your behavior doesn't help your case much. Now get the hell outta the arena.' Then he followed him out to make sure he left."

"Damn, I missed it. I was too busy yelling at Bryce and Landin. Those two assholes are really getting on my nerves. I'm about ready to move out."

I raise my brows, studying him. "This isn't because of Jordyn wearing his jersey, is it?"

"Nah, but that didn't help. He's lazy and doesn't wanna do anything but play video games and drink in his downtime. That's why he's been sent for tutoring. He hasn't done a fucking thing in his classes from all I've seen. He blew off his classes yesterday. Wait til Jensen finds out."

"Fuck. He'll get benched as soon as Coach finds out. And if his GPA drops, he'll be off the team." I run a hand through my sweaty hair, my muscles tense from the stress of the shit going on with the team.

"Yeah, but we have some decent underclassmen who haven't gotten much game time. It may not be a big deal, especially if they play like they've been practicing."

"True. Maybe Coach will put Jasper Ryan in Josh's place. That guy has talent and he's a helluva lot better at playing left defenseman than Josh."

Alex raises his brows, a smirk on his lips. "Poor Jasper. That's not exactly a compliment since Josh has been distracted and playing so shitty lately."

I chuckle, punching his arm. "You know what I mean, jackass. Jasper has talent. He's hungry and focused." Frowning, I open my locker. "I overheard Coach chewing out Jasper for his grades in his Sociology class."

Alex shrugs. "Ask voyeur who can tutor him." A shit-eating grin is on his face. "Maybe he'll get a hot tutor. Then he can fuck a puck bunny and have the tutor—"

"Don't finish that sentence." Laughing, I pull off my jersey, throwing it at his head. "Fucking asshole. And why the hell are you always naked?"

He howls with laughter, grabs my jersey, and rubs it over his dick and balls. "Just giving you and the rest of the guys a show. Everyone in here knows I have the biggest balls since I'm the goalie. Now that they've seen my dick, they know I have a huge—"

"Stop." I'm laughing so hard I can't get dressed. "I don't know why I'm friends with you."

Alex tosses my jersey, which he just rubbed over his junk, at my face. I hurriedly catch it, trying to scowl but failing miserably. "Because you're a lucky mofo. Everyone dreams of having a best friend like me." He starts gyrating his hips.

His antics draw the attention of Bryce, Landin, Travis, and Jasper, who start laughing hysterically at the show he's putting on.

I point at him. "Anyone need a new best friend? This one's available."

ALEX and I exit the locker room, our bags thrown over our shoulders, heading toward our vehicles. "I have a meeting with Jensen and Nelson tomorrow. Jensen was bitching he hates paperwork and is so disorganized. He said he should hire a student to get him organized."

Alex gives me a knowing grin. "And you hate your girl stripping. Plus, she'd be perfect for the job. Her notes and outlines are fucking impressive. I've never seen anyone color code and organize shit like she does."

"I know. I thought I was organized until I saw that." My phone makes a series of beeps, indicating I have text messages. I glance down at my phone, smiling when I see Jordyn's name on my screen. I open her message and immediately begin cursing, turning my body away from Alex.

"Why are you... Oh, your kitten must have sent you something naughty."

I'm trying to shield my hard dick as my gaze drops back to her lying on my bed, wearing the sexy-as-hell maroon bra and panties she wore at Sinful. The last pose makes me sweat. She's on her stomach, her breasts nearly spilling out of the bra and her perky ass revealed in that thong.

Goddamn, that fucking ass of hers.

I change the subject so he doesn't notice my hard-on and break my balls over it. "Still talking to Chelsea?"

A huge grin lights up Alex's face. "Hell, yes. Remember when I asked you to video me stretching on the ice after practice a couple of days ago, and you thought I was insane? That was for her. My flexibility turns her on. She has a flex kink."

I snort, raising my brows. "A flex kink?"

"What can I say? The girl has class. She knows who the real MVP of the hockey team is." He smirks at me. "Flexible and a huge dick. What more can a girl want?"

"Someone with modesty, king kong dong," I joke as we part ways, heading to our respective vehicles. "Later man."

Alex's laughter follows me to my vehicle. "Later, stud."

CHAPTER 46

Tristan

A fter exiting my vehicle, I stealthily sneak around the house, slipping through the back door. Removing my shoes, I sneak through the kitchen and head up the stairs. Anticipation makes my hands shake from the need to kiss her. Touch her. Own her.

Light music trickles from my bedroom. She hums along as I creep closer. My fucking dick is so hard in my jeans I'm surprised it hasn't ripped through the fabric, sending the zipper and its teeth flying across the floor.

The clanking of her fingers against the keyboard directs me to my bedroom. I peer around the corner of the door frame, my insides vibrating from excitement and desire the second my eyes land on her. She's sitting cross-legged on the bed, the laptop balanced on her thighs, wearing my fucking jersey.

Jesus Christ.

All my senses heighten until all I see is her, in such vivid, sharp color that there's an aura of light surrounding her. Her breaths fill my ears, and her smooth, strawberry-scented skin beckons me.

My patience and resistance snap. I'm beside the bed in a flash, lifting her laptop from her thighs before tossing her over my shoulder. My hand slaps her bare ass as I carry her to the shower.

"Tristan! What the hell?" Her breathless voice ends in a moan when I smack her again.

Setting her on her feet, I admire my jersey hanging on her small frame for a few beats before I grab it, yanking it over her head so she's standing in the maroon bra and panty set. I bare my teeth at her, the predator about to devour his prey. Her pupils dilate, and her chest heaves from her accelerated breathing.

After turning on the water, I tear off her bra and panty set. She stands there in all her naked glory. Her lips part, and her tongue glides along her bottom lip as she watches me shed my clothing.

"Get in," I command. She swallows hard before she complies. My dick is so fucking hard it throbs as I step in behind her, watching the water bead over her perky breasts and trim stomach.

Backing her against the wall, I lean against her, pinning her with my size. "So you think you can send me sexy pictures of you in lingerie while I'm in practice, huh?"

"Yeah, so—?"

My lips crash against hers, the kiss hard and brutal yet full of need and desire. She kisses me back with just as much intensity. Her hands run through my hair, nails slicing my scalp, shredding my resistance.

Pulling back slightly, a satisfied smile spreads across my face from her puffy lips and the flames of desire burning in her aqua eyes. I adjust myself so my hard cock presses against her opening, a groan leaving my lips. She's fucking soaked.

"Tristan," she rasps, her voice breathy. "I need you."

My smile is full of malice as I fill her with one hard thrust.

Her loud gasp ends in a long moan. I pull out slightly, then slam inside her so hard she slides up the shower wall. "Do you know how hard those fucking pictures made me?" *Thrust.* "I've been throbbing, my dick like concrete, the whole way home." *Thrust.* "You're fucking lucky Alex didn't see what you sent. I'd hate to poke out my goalie's eyes."

"Oh, God." Her head falls back against the wall as I hammer into her.

"There's a God, alright. And it's me. Your hockey God." I pound into her, basking in the way her tight, wet pussy grips me. "You belong to me, and I'm claiming all of you." My gravelly voice is tinged with breathlessness, but I don't stop. Not until we both fucking explode.

"Is it cute now, kitten? Sending me those pictures?" I grab one of her wrists, pinning it above her head. Her thighs tighten around me, but other than that, she can't move. Not with my weight against her, my cock drilling her like a feral animal.

She moans but doesn't answer my question.

"Words, Jordyn. Use your words." I capture her lips with mine, biting her bottom lip, knowing how crazy it makes her. She floods my cock with her wetness, and it drips down my balls.

"Tell me, or I'll stop, kitten."

"No! Please... don't... stop." Her hot breath falls over my face, heating the outside of my skin so much it matches the fire inside. An animalistic satisfaction fills me from the way she pants for me, the desperation in her breathy voice, and the pleading in her aqua eyes.

"I won't stop," I pant out. "After I fuck you into oblivion here, I'll take you in every fucking room of this house."

A salacious smile curls her lips as she hisses, "I'll send you pictures every damn day if I'm gonna be punished like this."

I smirk at her. "Wrong answer, kitten." Sweat pours into my eyes as I piston my hips in and out of her, not letting her catch her breath or do anything but moan and take my cock.

"Keep sending me pictures, my love. I'll hunt you down and fuck you into oblivion. Every." *Thrust.* "Fucking." *Thrust.* "Time."

Her legs shake around me, eyes rolling back before she closes them.

"Eyes on me." My tone is deep and commanding, practically unrecognizable to my own ears.

She scowls at me as her eyes open. She's reaching her peak, but I will get what I want before she explodes.

"Tell me how cute it is now."

"Tris... tan," she whimpers, shaking her head.

"Speak up, kitten. Let me hear you say it before I make you scream my name." I slow my thrusts, my smile sadistic as a frustrated groan leaves her. Long nails dig into my scalp so hard she draws blood. I relish in the pain and the pleasure, loving this fucking woman so much I'd do *anything* for her.

Jordyn groans, her eyes locked with mine. Defiance shimmers in their depths as she smiles. "It was cuter than hell." She moans again, her legs shaking around me as my punishing thrusts do her in. "I'd do it again... and again."

"Defiant little kitten." My lips capture hers. "I should beat your ass until it's nice and red."

"Jesus Christ," I groan, slowing my thrusts. Jordyn arches, her body convulsing against mine. She screams my name until she's hoarse, her eyes squeezing shut. Her skin is flushed scarlet, water droplets coating her skin as her orgasm drags on.

Once she's finished, she goes limp in my arms. Her breathing is heavy as her long lashes open, revealing dazed eyes. She's always been so goddamn breathtaking, but after that performance, she's a fucking goddess.

A slow smile spreads across her face. "More."

I speed up, my thrusts hard and deep. Her nails dig into my back as I pound into her, praising her. "You take my fucking cock so well, kitten. Like you were fucking made for me."

She moans, her pussy dripping. But I don't stop thrusting or praising her, knowing how much she likes it. "That's it. Take my dick like the good fucking girl you are."

"Oh, God, captain. That feels so good."

My hand moves to her throat, applying gentle pressure. "Nuh-uh. What's my name?"

A sexy grin spreads across her face. "Hockey God," she murmurs. "I need your cum right now." She clenches around me like a vice, choking my cock, and I explode, spilling rope after rope of cum inside her.

Once I've finally finished, I collapse against her. My lips are against her thundering pulse, which matches mine.

After my heartbeat and breathing finally return to normal, I gently pull away from her soft, wet skin, breathing her in. Gently pushing her hair away from her face, my voice is full of love, shaking with reverence. "I love you with every fiber of my being. Don't ever leave me."

I bite my lip, trying to control my emotions, but she sees them all over my grief-stricken face. I know I'm asking the impossible. In the blink of an eye, death can reach out its bony hand and steal the lives of those you love and need the most.

Her hands cup my face, and her aqua eyes well with tears that spill over like a dam breaking. "I can only promise I will never willingly leave you, Tristan." Her voice trembles before she presses her lips against mine. All I can promise is to love you until my last breath."

A smile breaks across my face. "I know I'm asking the impossible. But your promise is enough." My lips press against hers, causing goosebumps to spread over her skin. "I'll cherish every minute until we take our last breath."

"I love you so damn much, Tristan." Her arms tighten around my neck, clinging to me. "Every minute until my last breath."

CHAPTER 47

Jordyn

S trolling into Sinful Sirens, guilt makes my chest tight. I bite my lip, anxiousness coiling in my belly as I head toward Ray's office.

My phone beeps, signaling an incoming text message, but I ignore it, knowing damn well it's Tristan. He'll be pissed when he finds out I'm here. But I'm doing this for him and for us.

More guilt consumes me when I appear in Ray's open doorway, and he looks up, a smile on his face. But it fades when he takes in my somber expression.

Gesturing me inside, he says, "Lemme guess. You're leaving?"

Straightening my spine, I nod. "Thanks for the opportunity. But I—"

Ray holds up a hand, and I snap my mouth closed. An understanding smile curls his lips. "It's okay, Jordyn. You're talented as hell, but quite frankly, you're destined for better things." A chuckle comes from his lips as his twinkling eyes search mine. "Also, Gary told me about a hot-headed young man who stormed backstage after your last performance."

A blush heats my cheeks, causing Ray to laugh harder. "Don't be embarrassed, Ms. Jordyn. From how Gary described it, that man is obviously in love with you. And that's worth a helluva lot more than this job."

A smile blooms across my face as I race toward him. He stands, giving me a fatherly hug. "You have goals, Jordyn. I know you'll accomplish them."

I squeeze him tighter. "Thanks, Ray. Although we haven't known each other long, I've always felt comfortable around you. Gary, too."

"I'm glad. Despite owning this place, I'm not a creepy perv. I've been married for forty-three years, and we have three sons." Pulling back, he gives me a wink. "If I had a daughter and she wanted to work here, I'd kick her ass."

I giggle, feeling lighter. "Do you mind if I say goodbye to Gary and anyone else in the dressing room?"

"I'd be upset if you didn't. Raven is here, as well as a few of the other girls. Gary is watching over them like a hawk, as usual."

I laugh. "Of course he is." I head toward the door, turning around one last time. "Thanks again for everything."

He shakes his head. "No thanks necessary. You work on your goals... And good luck with your guy. Remember, goals are important, but nothing is more important than love and family."

"Trust me, I won't forget." With a wave, I head out of his office to say my goodbyes to the others.

EXITING Sinful Sirens for the last time, I finally pull out my phone, reading text after text from Tristan. He's also called a few times.

My phone beeps again and I grin when I see his name.

Tristan: You should pay attention to your surroundings.

My head snaps up to see him leaning against the front of my car. His arms are folded across his chest, and his expression is indecipherable.

But I'm so happy to see him, I don't care if he's pissed.

I run to him, and he opens his arms seconds before I fling myself in them. He holds me as though he hasn't seen me in days instead of a few hours.

Tilting my head back, I whisper, "What are you doing here?"

"When you didn't respond to my calls or texts, I became worried. When I saw that you were here, I was pissed." His expression is soft as he stares down at me.

"You're tracking my phone? Then you followed me here?"

He stares at me from beneath lowered brows. "I'm not apologizing for it. Your safety is my top priority."

Before he can say another word, I shut him up with a long, deep kiss. I moan as his fingers tangle in my hair, and he kisses me harder.

When we part, we're breathing heavily. His lips curl into an infectious smile and his twinkling eyes make me feel like I'm floating on air. "Let's get outta here. You deserve a foot and back massage before I make love to you all night."

I squeeze his hand. "And they say the perfect man doesn't exist. They've obviously never met you."

CHAPTER 48

Tristan

I whistle as I head toward Coach Jensen's office, nodding at Assistant Coach Nelson before he steps into the small office with a shared copier and printer. A few seconds later, he curses, then grumbles, "these damn machines." He doesn't know it yet, but I have a solution to his problem.

Reaching Coach's door, I draw to a stop as loud, angry voices filter outside. I look at the nameplate beneath the door number when I hear a woman's voice floating out, her tone furious. "Your athlete needs to put in the work, Coach Jensen. I'm not coddling a student who refuses to make any effort."

My feet are rooted to the floor as a brunette woman jumps to her feet, her hands clenched into fists at her side. My eyes rake over long, chocolate brown hair, a black suit jacket, a pencil skirt, and black heels. Even with her spine snapped straight, Coach Jensen towers above her.

Coach is also on his feet, giving her his intimidating stare, looking at her from beneath lowered brows. I've seen that side of him often during games and practices and even been a victim a few times. No one on the team stands tall beneath his withering gaze and rage. Yet, this slim, firecracker of a woman stands her ground.

A flash of surprise flits across his face before his features harden again. "He is putting in the work. If it were a matter of sheer laziness, I wouldn't be defending Jasper." His jaw muscles work as he grits out, "He knows I don't tolerate laziness. I stress the importance of academics to my players. He left your office because he was frustrated and didn't believe you were helping him."

Jasper Ryan. He's the player I hope Coach replaces Josh with, even though he hasn't had much game time.

When Josh was playing shitty and clearly distracted during the last game, I practically begged Coach Jensen to bench him and let Jasper play instead. He refused but wouldn't tell me why.

But now I know. The petite firecracker standing in Coach's office, aggravating the shit out of him, is the reason. She must be the professor Jasper was complaining about in the weight room.

Coach runs a hand through his dark hair, clearly irritated. "Look, Professor Kennedy. Jasper has some stuff going on at home that's affecting him. I'm not at liberty to discuss his problems, but I feel it necessary to make you aware that outside factors influence his behavior. Despite his personal struggles, he's working hard in his other classes, turning things around. But he's complained to me that your class material is too difficult for an introductory—"

"Call me Morgan. And that sounds like Jasper's problem, not mine. My course material is *not* too difficult," she says through gritted teeth. "Yes, it's an introductory sociology class, but I do not find the material to be beyond the comprehension of a freshman, especially if you're willing to work."

Coach blows out a frustrated breath, his hands balling into fists as he struggles to contain his temper. He's so engrossed in their argument that he's not paying attention to my presence in his doorway. I'm afraid to move and draw his attention, knowing he'll turn his wrath on me, and any chance I have of trying to convince him to give Jordyn a chance will be shot to hell.

"Jasper is willing to work," Coach shouts, losing his cool. "What the hell do you think he's been doing? He has a tutor, he's doing all the assignments, he's studying daily for your class." Coach glares at her, folding his arms over his chest. He's our biggest defender when we're doing all the right things. When we aren't, he ruthlessly stays on our ass until we get ourselves in line.

Running a hand through his hair, he grits, "The problem lies with *you*, not him. I understand you are a new professor at Weston Heights and trying to secure your future here. But the material—"

"*How dare you?*" Morgan shouts back, her heels clicking as she stomps closer to Coach. I watch in wide-eyed horror as his face turns a deep shade of red. She plants her feet and stares him down, anger radiating from every pore. "You're a hockey coach, *not* a professor, so your opinion of my teaching is irrelevant."

Oh shit. Coach is gonna explode.

"The hell it is," he roars back. "I've been working at this university for fifteen years and know more about the inner workings than you do. WHU prides itself on the reputation of its hockey team, which recruits some of the top players and brings in funding. Overloading freshmen athletes with overly difficult material will not secure your future here. In fact, you're likely to end up a one-year professor who isn't invited back for a second year."

She gasps, shaking her head. "I'm glad you think you're the expert on education and this university, *Coach Jensen*. Maybe you should try teaching instead." Her voice drips with sarcasm, and I cringe, knowing her tone won't sit well with him.

His withering glare causes me to shrink back. I don't know how the hell she's standing there, her back straight, taking him on like a tiny warrior. He's seething at her, chest heaving beneath his shirt.

Lowering her voice, she defiantly says, "I'm not dumbing down the material I teach for a hockey player."

"And there it is—the real reason you won't make concessions. You don't like jocks."

Her mouth drops open. "I'll have you know I was married to a jock. He was extremely intelligent and didn't have his coach begging his faculty to dumb down the material."

Coach snorts. "And what happened? Did he leave you because of your holier-than-thou attitude?"

She gasps, her head snapping back like he slapped her. "How dare you?" Her entire body vibrates with anger as she stalks closer to him. "That's not what happened, you arrogant prick. I don't owe you an explanation. It's my personal life and none of your business."

"You brought it up." Coach shrugs his shoulders, in control again now that he's ruffled her feathers. "Since we're at an impasse, I have an idea. Why don't I schedule a meeting with your department chair? Let him review your syllabus, and we will state our case, then see what he thinks."

She huffs out a breath, crossing her arms over her chest. "Fine. *If* he finds the material too difficult, and I highly doubt he will, I'll be willing to change it. Otherwise, it will remain the same and be Jasper's problem. And *yours.*" She turns slightly, an arrogant smile on her profile.

Coach smirks at her, rocking on his heels. "You seem confident, Professor Kennedy. I can't wait until you have to 'dumb down' your syllabus and expectations. By the way, how are the other students doing?"

Her hands shake as she seethes, "We'll discuss this in Dr. Jacob's office." She whirls around, noticing me for the first time. Her brows furrow as her hazel eyes lock on me. "Sorry if I delayed your meeting with him. Hopefully, he doesn't waste your time like he did mine." She shoots Coach a scathing look over her shoulder before slipping past me, her heels echoing as she stomps down the hallway.

I slowly turn to Coach, swallowing hard. I feel bad for Jasper, but I'm also concerned about Coach's mood. "Wow. That was... surprising."

Coach shakes his head, running a hand through his dark brown messy hair. "Sorry you had to hear that. I didn't mean to allow her to delay our meeting." He takes a few breaths in and out, pacing behind his desk. The young, attractive professor clearly rattled him.

Leaning forward, I examine him more closely. The tension between them wasn't strictly professional. It was filled with sexual tension that even I could feel in the brief time they argued.

Blowing out a breath, he nods toward his chair. He gives me a distracted smile and plops into the chair behind his desk. "Enough of that." Waving a dismissive hand, he says, "What can I do for you?"

"I'd like to discuss hiring Jordyn to help you get organized."

He nods. "I'm listening."

I launch into the spiel I rehearsed for the past twelve hours, reviewing all her positive traits and organizational skills. When I pause to take a breath, a wide smile is on Coach's face as he leans back in his chair. "You really love this girl, don't you?"

Blinking a few times, I open my mouth and then close it, unsure what to say. I'm fucking head over heels in love with her, but I fear telling him that may ruin her chance of working for him.

"It's okay, Tristan. I don't need you to answer. I can tell you are." He steeples his fingers beneath his chin, analyzing me. "She sounds incredible. And the way you praised her skills, I'm almost convinced I should offer her the job right now. However, I'd like to meet her first." He holds up his hand when I open my mouth. "Just to have a conversation with her. If I hire her but don't 'interview' her, people will go nuts around here."

I blow out a breath, my muscles still tense. "Does she stand a chance? I mean, I know you haven't talked to her, but—"

"Tristan, please, stop stressing. The way you sang her praises... Well, she must be amazing for you to go to these lengths. I've never seen you do that for anyone except Alex when I nearly benched him for his temper. I will 'interview' Jordyn only as a formality so no one accuses me of being unfair." He gives me a wink, and I relax. "Give me her phone number, and I'll call her now and schedule a meeting."

I rattle off her number, hope filling my chest as he grabs his phone and calls her. From the brief conversation between them and the resulting look on his face, I feel confident he'll be impressed with her.

When he hangs up, he says, "I'll be meeting with your girl-friend. Anything else I can do for you?"

My smile is wide. "Nope. I'm good." Getting to my feet, I give him a smile before dashing out of his office, feeling hopeful.

CHAPTER 49

Jordyn

Chelsea grips my hand, her body vibrating with excitement as we sit in the seats reserved for family and friends of the players, courtesy of Tristan and Alex. My mom is on the other side of me, laughter in her eyes as they meet mine.

"I'm so excited. I can't wait until Alex comes out and stretches." She claps her hands, her eyes moving to the ice as the players skate onto it, warming up before the game.

"We would never have guessed," I respond dryly.

There's a bang on the glass in front of me. I jump, my hand on my heart, but the fear changes to excitement when I see Tristan's smiling face. "Excuse me, ladies." I jump to my feet, moving toward him. Not only am I wearing his jersey, but I also have the reindeer socks pulled up over my leggings. His eyes drink me in as I saunter to the glass, a flirty smile on my face. "Hey, captain."

"Hey, captain, my ass. Go over to that door. I need to kiss you before I fucking lose my mind."

I giggle and wink at him. "Bossy, aren't you?"

"Jordyn. Do not make me come and get you."

I grin, not at all scared of the punishments he dishes out. But when I see Alex skate up behind him, I agree, waving to the goalie. "Alright, captain. But only cause Alex wants to see Chelsea."

"Hey, bestie," Alex yells. Tristan turns, punching his shoulder. "She's not your bestie. She's mine."

"You can't hurt me through my padding, captain. And stop being jealous of my profound friendship with Jordyn. You're the one who left me to pick up the pieces. You're lucky she didn't fall for me." He strikes a pose like he's doing a shoot for an ad, and I burst into laughter.

Tristan glowers, looking positively murderous. "I swear to God, asshole. One of these days, I'm gonna knock your teeth down your throat."

Chelsea's arm wraps around my shoulder. With laughter in her voice, she levels Tristan and Alex with a look. "You're both wrong. She's my bestie."

"She's your female bestie." Alex immediately responds. "Everyone knows you need a male bestie."

"That's enough. She's mine." Tristan blows out an irritated breath. "Get that sexy ass to the door." He points in that direction.

I salute him, my smile salacious. "Yes, captain."

He growls as I turn and strut off, feeling powerful and sexy.

It seems like forever until I open the door, and he bursts through it like a bull charging at me, lifting me off my feet. "Coach is gonna give me and Alex shit for this, so make it worth my while." Then he plants his lips on mine.

I accept his challenge, my fingers running through his hair as I kiss him back just as hard and thoroughly as he's kissing me. We don't let up until we have to break apart, gasping for oxygen.

"My last name looks good on you. Jordyn Harrington has a nice ring to it, don't ya think?"

"I agree."

"Wow. I figured you'd freak out and run." He rubs his nose against mine.

"No way. I'm not going anywhere."

He winks at me. "Damn right, you're not. You can't escape me." His expression softens as he lowers me to my feet. "I like your socks."

Grinning, I lift my leg, giving him a better view. "Me, too. I hope they bring you comfort and luck today."

"They will... but my biggest lucky charm is you."

I'VE ALMOST MADE it to my seat when I hear footsteps thundering behind me. I whirl around, fear rolling down my spine as I look into Josh's bloodshot eyes, his expression furious.

"You fucking whore." He screams, grabbing my arms and pulling me closer. "This is all yer fault. Always tryin' ta ruin my life."

"Josh, let me go." I struggle against his tight grip, trying to break free. "What's wrong with you?"

"Nothin' wrong with me. But you and my former teammate fucking things up means big problems for the two of ya."

As he shakes me, I hear my mom's panicked voice, her long pink nails digging into Josh's forearms. "Let her go, Josh. What the hell are you doing here? You're suspended."

Bloodshot eyes turn to my mom, glaring at her. "Ahh. If it isn't my dad's whore of a wife, Mrs. Abigayle Fowler. What the hell are you doing here? My father's at home."

My mom gasps. "Joshua Fowler. You don't insult me like that."

Thundering footsteps fill the air, and the next thing I know, I'm being pulled away from Josh's grip. Tristan's furious green eyes meet mine before he shoves me behind him. He squares up, ready to fight, when a male voice yells Tristan's name before he steps between them. "He's not worth it. You have a game to play," he hisses. "You need to get back to the ice."

"But Coach Nelson—"

Coach Jensen grabs Tristan's arm. "To the ice. Now. We'll handle this."

Tristan gives me an apologetic look before Alex pats his back, ushering him toward the ice.

"Are you okay, baby girl?" My mom grips my arm, her concerned voice drawing my attention back to her.

"Yeah, I'm okay." My gaze slides to Josh, who is sandwiched on either side by the coaches heatedly screaming at him.

"I don't give a fuck," Josh screams. "I'll kick his ass and put that little bitch he's obsessed with in the hospital." He glares at my mom. "And that whore, too."

"That's enough." Coach Nelson grips his arm so hard that Josh winces. "Get the fuck out before we kick you off the team and ban you from stepping foot in the arena."

Security guards approach the group, grabbing Josh's arm. Coaches Jensen and Nelson follow behind, although Coach Nelson gives my mom a long, lingering look before he leaves.

"I better follow them. I'll need to call Robert." She squares her shoulders, heading toward the group. Coach Nelson immediately notices she's behind them and steps back, his eyes trailing over my mom as they head toward the exit.

Hmmm. I wonder what that's about?

CHAPTER 50

Jordyn

L eaping out of my seat, I throw my arms in the air, cheering as the puck flies into Ohio's net, giving the Wolverines the win. I look at the scoreboard as it buzzes. The final score is 2-4.

Chelsea, my mom, and I hug each other while jumping up and down. When I pull back, my gaze moves to the ice, searching for Tristan. I can't help but notice that Coach Nelson's eyes are on my mom—where they've been several times during the game before I find the mossy green eyes of the man I love.

Grabbing my mom and Chelsea's hands, I race toward the ice, intent on celebrating with the man I love. Our eyes lock as he skates to me, lifting me off my feet and swinging me around.

"Congrats on the win. What a goal," I yell in his ear, trying to be heard over the noise of the crowd.

"Thanks, kitten. Told ya you were my lucky charm."

My hands cup his face. "You make me melt, captain." My lips meet his in a sizzling kiss, and the entire boisterous celebration around us fades. "You're my forever," I murmur against his lips.

"You're my forever." He kisses me before lowering me to the ice. Holding me in his arms, we're lost in our own world. "If someone would have told me my roommate's stepsister would literally catch me with my pants down, and we'd still end up falling in love, I'd have told them they're insane."

"Ugh. I don't wanna think about you with your pants down around any other tramp." I scowl at him before looking around the rink, spying Janelle with her arm around Bryce. "She moved on quickly."

Tristan smirks. "Rumor has it she was fucking Josh, Bryce, and Landin." He shakes his head, his face twisted in disgust.

"Who cares what she does? You're mine and I'm yours. That's all that matters."

"You're right. Nothing else matters. Well, except those two."

I don't even have time to react before Chelsea flings herself at my back, and judging by the weight that slams me into Tristan, Alex is wrapped around her back.

"Congrats on the win! But more importantly, for getting the girl." Chelsea pulls back before planting a kiss on my cheek, her arm around me. Her smile fades and she glowers, pointing a finger at Tristan. "Don't hurt her or I'll run over your dick and balls with ice skates."

"Ouch." Alex puts his hands over his junk, wincing. He looks huge in all his goalie padding. "But I wouldn't turn down a blow job on the ice. Just sayin."

Chelsea laughs. "You deserve it for the way you played. But I'm not doing it with all these people around." She winks at him. "Maybe later."

"Oh my God, Chelsea." I move closer to Tristan, burying my face against his jersey, not caring that he's sweaty. "You're so bad."

"What? I like to have a good time." She looks up at Alex and winks. "Just so you know, I'm possessive and don't share. Goes along with being an only child. Jordyn and I have that in common."

Is it my imagination or does Alex look uncomfortable?

"Yeah, but technically, Jordyn has a stepbrother," Alex replies, his gaze moving to Tristan as he changes the subject. "Is Josh off the team?"

"I overheard Coach Nelson and Jensen talking. Josh must go to rehab and prove he's clean before he can play next semester. Personally, I hope Coach continues allowing Jasper to play. He's a helluva player. The breakaway was fucking genius."

"Yeah, but you bundled that player, giving him a clear shot." Alex raises his hand and he and Tristan high-five.

"But can we talk about Tristan's hat trick?" A dark-haired guy with an easy smile throws an arm around Tristan's shoulder. "Dude is my idol. And I wouldn't have had the breakaway if not for him, clearing the way."

Tristan gives him a broad smile, but the faint blush on his cheeks has my toes curling in my shoes as I lean into him, constantly needing to touch him. His humility and gratitude are two of my favorite traits, and they make me love him more.

"Jasper, this is my girlfriend, Jordyn. Jordyn, this is Jasper Ryan."

"Hi, Jasper." I stick out a hand. "It's nice meeting you."

"Don't get any ideas, Ryan. Jordyn's my bestie." Alex chirps, a wide grin on his face.

"I'm gonna knock your teeth down your throat." Tristan tightens his arm around me, glaring at Alex, as Chelsea and I burst into laughter.

Jasper puts his hands in the air. "I'm not getting in the middle of this." His warm gaze meets mine before he glances at Tristan. When he nods, Jasper clasps my hand, shaking it.

"Hey, Jordyn. Nice to meet you. Heard lots of things about you."

"All good things, I hope," I joke as I release his sweaty palm.

"Of course." His friendly grin makes me like him immediately. He stares at me for a few beats, a contemplative look on his face. "I know this may sound intrusive and bold, but I heard you're a tutor. Can you recommend someone who could tutor me in my Intro to Sociology class? Professor Kennedy is a hard ass." He runs a hand through his hair, looking distressed. "I went to Matt a few times. He's okay, but Sociology isn't his strongest subject. He's more a math and science guy."

"Oh, have you met Felicity Evans? She's double majoring in Sociology and Psychology. She's amazing."

"No, I haven't." Hope lights up his eyes.

Tristan grins. "I'll text you her name so you can set up tutoring appointments. Do you know how to do that?"

He shakes his head. "Not really. Matt was recommended to me by Coach for my biology class. He gave Matt my phone number and we texted, setting up our sessions that way." His brows draw in as he contemplates Tristan. "No offense, but why did you need tutoring?"

"I needed an excuse to be around her." Tristan squeezes me before giving me a kiss.

"Ahh. Well, damn. Maybe I can get a tutor and a girlfriend." He punches Tristan's arm, laughing.

Tristan smirks at him. "You never know." His eyes drop to mine. "Sometimes, unconventional meetings can lead to the best things."

CHAPTER 51

Tristan

The semester flew by, my days and nights packed with classes, hockey, and Jordyn. Having Jordyn close by while I practiced or worked out was sometimes distracting, but when I focused, I'd reward myself by fucking her in the jacuzzi. Or the weight room, steam room, and locker room.

We nearly got caught by Coach Nelson in the locker room. I'm almost positive he knew we just finished having sex, but since we heard his footsteps and she was wearing a skirt, we were able to cover ourselves and appear normal. Well, as normal as sweaty faces, disheveled hair, and heavy breathing can look.

Tonight, I'm taking Jordyn for an end-of-semester dinner at one of our favorite Italian restaurants. I smile at myself in the mirror, adjusting my tie. She has no idea I'm going to propose.

Jordyn comes up behind me, wrapping her arms around my waist. "Hey, captain. Has anyone told you that you're smokin' hot?"

"My girlfriend tells me every day. I'm taken, miss." Grinning, I turn around, whistling as I take in the little black dress and high heels she's wearing. "Oh, Jesus. Are those fishnets with gemstones on them?"

"Fake gemstones. And yes," she purrs, pressing herself against me.

"We may not make it to the restaurant." I press my lips to hers, swallowing her giggle. This woman makes me come undone in all the best ways.

"First, you have to feed me. Then you can fuck me." She's gotten bolder and more confident since we've been together. I love seeing how much she's blossomed from attention, love, and my endless devotion.

"We better get out of here. Because I can't wait to fuck you."

Grabbing her hand, I lead her from the bathroom. She grabs her clutch on the way out of our bedroom, and then we head down the stairs.

～

"I'm stuffed." Jordyn leans back in her chair, rubbing her stomach with a groan. "Why did I eat so much?"

I smirk at her over my glass of water. "You're carbing up before the big workout I'm gonna give you when we get home."

She giggles and leans over the table. The candlelight dances across her features and I swear, she's never looked more radiantly gorgeous than she does right now. "Did anyone ever tell you hockey players are insatiable lovers?"

"You just did." I wink at her, grabbing her hand. "Only for you, kitten. You're my world." Bringing her left hand to my lips, I kiss her fingertips, my eyes holding hers. "That's why..." I stand, still holding her hand. Walking around the table to her, she looks baffled, her questioning aqua eyes bouncing back and forth between mine.

When I drop to one knee, she sucks in a breath. I shift so I'm on both knees as I pull the box with the ring from my pocket. "Jordyn Isabella Reese. Will you do me the honor of spending the rest of your life with me?" I gaze into her misty eyes, my heart beating like a drum from anticipation and nervousness. "Will you marry me?"

The tears that fill her eyes spill over, running down her cheeks. "Hell, yes, captain," she says breathlessly.

My eyes shine with wetness as I slip the large diamond on her finger, two small sapphires on either side because blue is her favorite color.

She admires the ring for a couple of beats. "Oh my God. I love it, Tristan." Then she slips out of the chair, flinging herself into my arms. "But not as much as I love you."

With her arms still wrapped around me, I get to my feet, twirling her around. She laughs, throwing her head back before she plants her lips on mine.

Loud, boisterous cheers and clapping fill the room as Alex, Chelsea, and the rest of the hockey team, along with Jordyn's mom, the tutors she works with, and Coaches Jensen and Nelson surround us.

When I lower her to her feet, she wipes her eyes, a watery smile on her lips. "Oh my God. You all knew?"

"He may have given me a heads up, bestie. And I ran with it because I have a big mouth." Alex throws his arms around me and Jordyn, squeezing us tight.

"I'm gonna punch you in the nuts," I growl. "For the last fucking time, Jordyn is not your bestie."

Chelsea throws herself against Jordyn's back. "That's right. She's mine."

"I'm not doing this." I shake my head at our crazy friends. "Every piece of her is mine, so you can all kiss my ass."

Laughing, Chelsea and Alex pull away, allowing the rest of our family and friends to descend, offering their congratulations.

Jordyn's mom wraps her up in a huge hug, and my gaze automatically moves to Coach Nelson, who stares at Abigayle with a wistful expression on his face. He has it bad for her, even though she's married. Maybe she won't be for long. From what Jordyn has said, and as much time as we've spent with her mom lately, Abigayle and Robert's marriage is in trouble. Josh's drug problem and being sent to rehab have only strained things even more.

Jordyn steps back and grabs my hand. Her luminous aqua eyes sparkle up at me. "This is perfect, Tristan. I love you."

"I love you, kitten. You're everything I didn't know I needed but can't live without." My voice catches, my emotions overwhelming me. "You're the love of my life."

Her breath hitches. "You're my home. My forever. And I can't wait to marry you."

Leaning down, I rub my nose against hers. "I can't wait to marry you."

About the Author

Jennifer Rose writes dark romance and romantic suspense/thriller novels full of trauma and twists. She also writes lighter stuff, such as *Puck Right Off,* part of the Weston Heights Wolverines series. Writing is a passion she's dreamed of since she's been a little girl, and she's grateful for the love and support of her readers.

When she's not immersed in her writing, Jennifer Rose enjoys indulging in 80's horror movies, savoring frozen mocha coffee a bit too often, and taking leisurely walks. Her love for animals, especially dogs, is a significant part of her life.

She lives in Pennsylvania with her devoted husband, two dogs, and a rabbit.

She loves hearing from and interacting with her readers, so feel free to contact or follow her on social media.

Twisted Thorns & Roses: Jennifer Rose Reader's Group

Website: https://jenniferroseauthor.online/

Email: jenrose.author@gmail.com

Also by Jennifer Rose

Weston Heights Wolverines: College Hockey Interconnected Series

Puck Right Off

Pucking the Goalie - Coming Soon

King Morine: Masked Man Interconnected Series:

Devious Bastard

Buried Secrets

Deceived

A Standalone Stalker Novel:

Done Waiting

Divinity of the Chosen Ones: Dark Cult Interconnected Series

Bound in Darkness

Veiled in Darkness - Coming Soon

Shrouded in Darkness - Coming in 2025

Forged in Darkness - Coming in 2025

Printed in Great Britain
by Amazon

43666339R00149